A Light in the Darkness

A Wounded Warrior Legacy Novel

Nika Rhone

P9P PARK NINE PUBLISHING

With deepest gratitude to the military and first responders who keep us safe, and run toward danger when duty calls. Thank you for being on the wall.

And to those who raise and train guide, service, and therapy dogs, thank you for everything you do for the wounded warriors who sometimes return from that wall in need of support.

"There is a crack in everything, that's how the light gets in."

Leonard Cohen

Prologue

Today would have been her son's twenty-first birthday.

Carol Winchester flinched from the kitchen calendar and the gaily drawn star her daughter had put around the date in purple marker back at the beginning of the year.

No. Today *should* have been his twenty-first birthday. But Mikey would forever be only twenty years, seven months, and three days old. A baby. Her baby.

And he was gone.

Grief, the kind that still snuck in like a sword-wielding ninja when she least expected it, seared through her chest, a white-hot blade of pain and sorrow.

Oh, dear God, my baby is *gone*.

Hand pressed to her mouth to stifle the moan that rose from the deepest pit of her soul, she pivoted from the calendar to stare blindly out the window into the backyard.

None of it made any sense. The Earth still turned. The sun still shone. Flowers budded in the garden and birds sang gaily from the trees. By all appearances, it was a normal spring day like any other.

But it wasn't.

Because Mikey wasn't in it. And the unfairness of that permeated every immovable brick in a wall of rage and resentment so thick and high inside her she sometimes couldn't see past it. Not to her quietly grieving rock of a husband. Not even to her daughter Nicole, confused and shaken by the unexpected loss of her big brother. Hurting in a way never before experienced in her fifteen years of very sheltered life.

She'd tried. Lord knew she had.

But there were some days she just couldn't move past her own pain to deal with theirs, too. Days she couldn't even bear to speak his name out loud. Couldn't listen to stories that were meant to be comforting but weren't, about how wonderful he'd been. How caring and loving. How special.

Days like today. When her amazing, beautiful boy should have been celebrating a milestone into adulthood. Not lying cold in a grave.

A wet nose nudged her hand hanging fisted at her side. By reflex, her fingers unclenched and ran down the golden retriever's silky head in soothing strokes. "I know. You miss him too, don't you, girl?"

Sadie let out a soft whine, her body leaning more heavily against Carol's leg. She might have been the family dog, but it had been clear early on she'd chosen Mikey as her main human. Her husband David swore Sadie took his leaving for the Army harder than they had. Not a day went by since he headed off to bootcamp that Sadie didn't look expectantly at the front door around dinner time, as though waiting for him to walk in at any minute.

Something she'd caught herself doing as well. Especially these last few months.

Even knowing it wasn't going to happen.

Ever, ever again.

Her fingers tightened on Sadie's ruff as another wave of loss rolled over her. Not as sharp this time, or as long. More like the small, choppy whitecaps on the Long Island Sound hitting the shore near the end of a storm. Lapping. Ebbing. Diminishing.

But still enough to erode the sand out from beneath your feet if you weren't careful.

Taking a deep breath, she loosened her hold on the dog's fur and went to one knee to give her a hug. "He loved you so much, Sadie-girl. I hope you know how important you were to him. How much he missed you."

So much so he'd insisted they include her in the infrequent video calls he made home from whatever far-away place he was stationed despite the limited time they were allowed. A rare smile turned her lips at the memory of holding the laptop in front of Sadie so he could talk to her.

Each time, the dog would get super excited at the sound of his voice, furry butt wriggling with delight. But she'd never been able to grasp the concept he wasn't in the room with them, no matter how many times she ran behind the computer looking for him.

Sharp little puppy yaps drifted up from the basement family room they'd turned into a temporary whelping den, breaking the early morning quiet.

"Uh oh, looks like the minions realized you escaped." With a watery chuckle, she pressed a kiss to the dog's head and stood. "Let's go see what kind of trouble they're getting into, shall we?"

Because there was always trouble.

The cute, silly, can't-really-stay-mad-about-it kind only a litter of eight roly-poly golden retriever puppies could create. Which was a lot. Enough that she and David had already decided this third litter would be the last, even though Sadie wasn't even close to the top of the age range where it was safe for her to breed.

It had nothing at all to do with how Mikey had hated that they bred her for profit.

Lie to everyone else if you want, woman, but don't lie to yourself.

Okay, fine. That might have had something to do with it.

It felt wrong to keep doing something their son had been so vehemently opposed to. Even with the compromise they'd struck with him, donating half of the money they made from Sadie's litters to local animal shelters rather than it all going into the family vacation fund as originally planned.

Not that he hadn't loved the puppies. Mikey loved—*had loved,* an insidious voice corrected—all animals. So much so they'd had a makeshift wildlife hospital in their garage from the time he was ten. No, it was the idea of purposely bringing those puppies into the world just because they were purebreds that had frustrated him.

Infuriated him, actually.

"Coming with papers and a registration number doesn't make them better than any good old everyday mutt," he'd argued. "It's not fair. So many shelters are filled with dogs no one wants because they're not cute, or young, or perfect. They all need a loving home just as much as any of the puppies you want to sell. More, in fact. Some of those shelter animals have had horrible lives. They've been cold, hungry, abused, abandoned. I wish people would realize every one of them deserves to feel safe and happy, too. We owe it to them to know they're loved at least once in their lives."

That was her son. Compassionate to a fault.

At the bottom of the stairs, Sadie hopped over the low barricade across the doorway to the right. As soon as she stepped over it herself, she was instantly surrounded by a swirling mass of little pink tongues, sharp baby teeth, and, most of all, fur.

So much fur.

At ten weeks, they hadn't grown into their adult coloring yet. But since Sadie was a true gold and their sire was a dark gold with a heavy reddish tint, they could end up being anything in between by the time they matured into adulthood.

Something Mikey won't ever get to do.

Shoving that cruel voice aside once more, she lowered herself to the floor, back against the wall, and let the yappy hoard swarm over her. There was nothing more certain to banish the urge to cry than being covered in hyperenergetic puppy love.

"Okay, okay, I know. It's so horrible. Almost eight whole hours since anyone loved on you. How terrible of us. Hey, stop that!" With a laugh, she gently pushed an inquisitive cold nose out of her armpit.

The black nylon collar the pup wore marked it as the male the breeder had chosen instead of a stud fee. The alpha of the litter, he took the mild reprimand in stride and attacked her sneaker lace instead, challenging his sister in the purple collar with a mini-growl as she tugged on the other one.

The color system helped keep straight who was who without having to look at the name tags. Purple, yellow, and brown were heading to stringently vetted buyers next weekend. Green, who they'd named Ginger, was staying with them. And the ones with the red, white, and blue collars would leave today to start their new lives at a training facility to become future service dogs for veterans.

Nicole had suggested the idea after one of her meetings with the grief counselor they were all seeing. She'd pitched it to them at a family session as a way to blend Mikey's lifelong legacy of helping others with his love for Sadie. Giving some of her last puppies a role in aiding wounded soldiers, just like he had.

It was a bittersweet cause she'd been okay getting behind.

Until she heard the *other* part of her daughter's suggestion.

That they "honor" Mikey's sacrifice by naming the three pups after the men he'd given his life to save. As if she wanted that constant reminder under her own roof every day, even for a few months, of why he'd died. Of the fact all three men had lived to go home to their families. While Mikey, in his role as unit medic had gone under enemy fire to render aid, only to come home in a flag-draped box.

Talk about grinding salt into an open wound.

She'd adamantly opposed the idea. So had David.

At first.

But the counselor had pointed out in that irritatingly calm tone of hers how clinging to displaced anger about what happened wasn't helping the healing process. That to blame the men for surviving when that was the very outcome Mikey had sacrificed himself for actually diminished his actions. Devalued his selfless-ness.

She'd hated hearing that. *Hated* it.

Hated the counselor even more for being right.

Even so, she couldn't let go of her deep, burning rage. Hating those men sometimes seemed like the only thing that kept her from unraveling entirely. From curling into a screaming ball of pain and grief and never getting up again.

David had caved. He'd always been the more empathetic of the two of them. The one to more easily forgive and smooth the path to harmony. It was part of why she'd fallen in love with him almost thirty years ago.

The big softhearted jerk.

But when Nicole had looked at her with such pleading and hope in her eyes, eyes the exact same shade of blue as Mikey's, she'd ended up caving, too.

She'd agreed to the names.

The anger about them, however, she just couldn't let go of.

So, to get through the last few months, she'd basically ignored the three puppies. They weren't abused or neglected. She'd never do that. But she never called them by name. Never played with them. And she never, ever held them.

It had seemed like the best compromise she could make.

At least it had kept the peace.

Then Nicole took things a step further. Which had been one step too far.

She'd written a letter to each of the people who would eventu-ally get Samson, Bailey, and Cooper—God, how she hated those names—as their service animals. To tell them about Mikey was all she would say. She'd left them on the kitchen table to read for themselves.

David had. But Carol had tucked the envelopes in a drawer, out of sight. Until she was ready, was her excuse.

That was a week ago. She still wasn't ready.

Might never be ready.

Writing the letters may have been cathartic for Nicole, but she couldn't imagine letting strangers read things about her son. Her baby.

Why would they even care about a boy—no, a young man—they'd never met? How would they ever understand what a special person he'd been? The gentleness with which he'd dealt with both animals and people. The thought he'd put into crafting handmade presents on birthdays. The genuine joy he got from releasing an injured rabbit he'd nursed back to health into the woods behind their house.

None of them would ever comprehend the light that had been snuffed out of the world. The vast potential lost in the blink of a bullet, when Mikey had been so cruelly stolen from her. From them all.

How did you put any of that into mere words?

She only realized she was sobbing when one of the puppies crawled into her lap with a barrage of concerned whimpers. Cuddling the warm weight tight to her chest, the emotional dam holding back all the pain as it built and festered inside her let loose with a blast. Through the torrent, the puppy lay docile in her tight grasp, head tucked under her chin, the quiet comfort of its presence doing what all the talky-talk share-your-feelings grief counseling hadn't.

Pain. Grief. Anger. Frustration. Guilt. It all came spilling out along with the tears as she told the puppy about her precious boy. How she was so proud of him. And so angry. At the Army. At the people who'd shot him. At the men he'd saved.

At him.

For doing what was, for Mikey, the only thing he could have done.

Finally admitting the deep-seated anger she'd been holding onto was at least partly directed at her dead son was both shameful and freeing. Like an infected wound being lanced, that acknowledgment helped drain a little of the hurt. Of the guilt.

The anger remained. But maybe, just maybe, it could begin to ease now as well.

When the tears eventually slowed to a dribble, she loosened her hold and stroked the pup, who promptly wriggled around so it could lap at her wet cheeks. The unique scent of puppy breath filled her nose.

"Thank you, but eww." She pulled the puppy away and pressed a kiss to its snout, earning another swipe of its tongue. A small laugh somehow bubbled up from the remnants of her grief. "Okay, that's enough of that. Geez." As she shifted her head out of licking range, the flash of white from its collar caught the edge of her vision.

She froze.

"Bailey."

It came out a pained whisper, but the puppy squirmed excitedly at its name, bouncing in her grasp in another attempt to lick her face.

Damn it.

Why did it have to be one of *them* who'd given her comfort?

As if knowing she was seconds from rejection, Bailey whined and shimmied to snuggle against her again, tiny head resting right above where Carol's heart was tripping wildly in her chest. A small sigh of contentment escaped the pup before it promptly fell asleep.

Carol sat frozen, one hand supporting the puppy. The other hung helplessly in the air, as if it didn't know whether to pluck her away or cradle her closer.

As the moments ticked by, her body didn't care that her brain remained frozen by indecision. Her racing heart slowed. Her choppy breaths steadied. And the soft weight of the puppy in her arms became less burden and more comfort, like a weighted blanket during a thunderstorm.

Finally, a long breath escaped her, like a purge of the last air tainted by hate.

Displaced anger.

Okay, maybe the counselor knew what she was talking about, after all.

She settled back against the wall in a more comfortable position for them both, stroking Bailey's soft fur like a worry stone.

"Mikey would have adored you, you know. He loved animals so much. All animals, even ones who aren't as cute and cuddly as you." They still had the bat house in the yard he'd made for shop class instead of the assigned birdhouse, since 'bats need a place to live, too.'

"Raccoons with missing tails. Baby squirrels with broken legs. He wanted to help them all. And the ones he couldn't…well, those hit him hard. He was so like his father that way. A total emotional marshmallow." She grinned at the memory of the face both of them had made when she'd said that to them once. "But dogs? He loved them most of all. He would have brought home every stray he saw if we'd let him."

And in that instant, she knew they'd be finding some other way to generate extra income not just for the family vacation fund, but to keep donating to the shelters as well. Mikey would have wanted that.

She wanted that.

To carry on Mikey's passion for helping the neglected and forgotten.

When her arm started going numb, she deposited Bailey with her littermates and went back up the stairs. Her eyes ached, her throat was raw, but her heart sat a little lighter in her chest than it had before she'd gone down them.

While the coffeemaker saturated the room with its delicious aroma brewing her first cup of the day, she assembled the ingredients for breakfast. Again and again, as she measured, as she stirred, her gaze drifted to the end cabinet drawer.

The drawer.

And every time she pulled it away again, struggling to ignore the increasing need building inside her.

Pancake batter ready, coffee poured, table set, there was nothing left to distract herself with. Her gaze went once more to the drawer.

And stayed.

"What the hell. In for a penny, right?" she muttered as she walked over and yanked it open. The envelopes sat where she'd shoved them a week ago. Three copies of the same letter from her daughter to the eventual recipients of the three puppies downstairs destined to be their service dogs.

Sucking in an unsteady breath, she picked up the one on top and stared at it like it might explode in her hand. Which shook just a little as she drew out the single sheet and unfolded it. Her daughter's neat handwriting filled the page of purple stationery she'd gotten last Christmas.

"That girl and her purple fixation." She closed her eyes for a second, questioning once more what she was doing, then opened them and started reading.

Dear Serviceperson,

First, I want to thank you for your service. If you're reading this, it means that you were wounded in some way and are in need of a service dog, and for that, I'm truly sorry. But if you're reading this, it also means that you're getting one of the dogs that was born to my brother Mikey's dog, Sadie, and for that I'm glad. You see, Mikey was a medic in the Army, and he was killed trying to help some wounded soldiers just a few weeks before he was supposed to come home.

I'm sorry to say I was really angry with my brother when I first heard what he'd done. I guess it's selfish of me to think he should have cared more about keeping himself safe than risking his life for other people. But the more I thought about it, the more I realized there was no way he could have done anything else. Mikey was always the kind of guy everyone could rely on. He was smart, and funny, and the best big brother anyone could ever have. I loved him lots, and I'm going to miss him even more, every single day of my life.

I'm not telling you any of this to make you sad. I just wanted to explain about my brother, and why the dog you're getting is so special. My brother spent the short time he had on this Earth helping others. I can't wish him back to life, but I can wish this: that his generous spirit live on in the love and comfort you receive from your service dog. Take each day you have together as a gift, and maybe once in a while think about Mikey. I know when I do, I'll be picturing him smiling down on you, knowing that his legacy, and Bailey, are in good hands.

Wishing you a happy and fulfilling life,

Nicole

Dear lord.

Had she really thought Mikey couldn't be captured in mere words?

Clearly, she'd underestimated her daughter.

And done her a great disservice.

Seeing an admission of anger at her brother so like her own, anger that she, the adult, had only just been able to acknowledge, was a surprise. A painful one.

Because she hadn't known how she felt. Hadn't given Nicole the chance to *let* her know. Too caught up in her own pain for her daughter to feel she could come to her with those confusing, hurtful feelings. When she needed her mother most, she'd been left adrift to navigate her grief all by herself.

Guilt bit her, sharp and deep.

I'm so sorry, sweetheart. I'll do better. I swear.

One of her children was beyond her ability to help. She wouldn't continue to fail the one who wasn't.

As she refolded the letter and slipped it back into the envelope, the silent form of her husband in the kitchen doorway caught her attention. Like she'd been found with her hand in the secret stash of Milano cookies, she quickly tucked the letter in the drawer and closed it. "Good morning."

David walked to her with slow steps. The way you'd approach a skittish animal.

"You finally read it. I didn't think you would."

She picked at the speck of batter that had splashed onto her sleeve, not meeting his gaze.

"I didn't plan to. But...I'm glad I did. I was wrong." She glanced toward the stairs, where the sound of puppies demanding breakfast was getting louder. "About a lot of things. Especially about shutting everyone out."

Their daughter wasn't the only one she'd let suffer through their shared loss alone.

With a low sound of relief that seemed to come from somewhere deep inside him, David pulled her into an embrace that was almost too tight.

She wrapped her arms around him and held him even tighter. "I'm sorry."

"Don't be. Everyone has their own path through grief. I'm just glad you've found your way back to me. To us." His arms tightened to the point of stopping her breath for a second before he released her.

As he wiped at damp cheeks, he stepped back and looked over at the batter bowl as though searching for some sense of normalcy to retreat to. "So, what's for..." He stared. "Chocolate chip pancakes." His voice went husky. "Mikey's birthday breakfast."

"Well, it's his birthday, isn't it?"

"I didn't... Yes. It is."

There was so much in his eyes as he looked at her. Relief. Love. Understanding.

Gratitude.

In for a pound.

"I want to go with you today."

"You do?"

She nodded. "To drop off the puppies." She drew a deep breath. "And to the cemetery."

Because Nicole wanted to bring flowers and wish Mikey a happy birthday.

"Are you sure?"

"Yeah. I think it's time."

Time to step out of the shadows of grief and start moving forward again. To take all the pain and anger and turn it into something good. Something positive.

Something Mikey would be proud of.

And it all began with those three dogs who would become his legacy.

Chapter 1

SOMETHING WAS ABOUT TO go horribly wrong.

The knowledge was there in the itchy sensation that crawled up the back of Neil Crawford's neck like a troop of fire ants, setting his nerves ablaze and sending his body into hyper-vigilant mode. Sixth-sense, primal fear, soldier's intuition. Call it what you will, it was screaming at him shit was going to hit the fan in a spectacularly awful way, and he was about to get a face full of it.

His hand dropped instinctively to grab the weapon at his side, but fell instead on the camera bag slung there.

What the hell...

Panic and confusion clouded his thinking for precious seconds before he remembered.

Not a soldier anymore.

This time around, he was just a civilian. His job was to document the ongoing struggles of the people caught in the middle of a never-ending war for the documentary they were shooting, not to join in the fight.

His fingers twitched, still searching for the phantom rifle that had once been like another limb. Almost four years since he'd last set foot in this hellhole, and it was like both yesterday and another lifetime ago. Instincts that had kept him alive before demanded he protect himself now. But he had no weapon. The unit they were imbedded with was supposed to provide all the security they needed.

Which would have been fine if the LT spent a little more time with his head in the mission, and a little less trying to charm his way into Jessica Lynch's pants.

Not that he could really fault the man for his interest.

Jessie was a fine-looking woman, even dressed in dusty BDUs and combat boots and five days out from a shower. More to the point, though, she was a civilian American woman, something most of these grunts hadn't seen in the living flesh for far too long. He remembered the feeling well.

All the guys jockeyed for a chance to talk to her, be near her, take selfies with her. She was like a little piece of home caught in a bottle, and these kids hadn't been home in a very long time.

But there was a time and a place to try for a piece of ass. And neither was when they were out in the open the way they were right now, in the center of the tiny village at the ass-end of beyond they'd entered half an hour ago.

He looked to where the lieutenant was standing hip-cocked against the crumbling wall that surrounded the communal well, chatting up Jessie like he did every chance he got. As he watched, Jessie glanced idly around as though looking for something. When her gaze landed on Neil, he realized she'd been looking for him.

To ride to her rescue yet again, no doubt. Just like every other time she couldn't politely extricate herself from Lieutenant Henderson's presence.

She didn't want to alienate the man. He could easily sabotage the entire documentary, and they'd both agreed he was exactly the kind of asshole who'd do just that in a fit of petty revenge. So, Neil got to be the bad guy instead, always cock-blocking him by dragging Jess off on some flimsy excuse or another.

Leaving him currently front and center on the LT's shit list.

Sure enough, the look in Jessie's eyes was one of desperate pleading, despite the smile she wore as she listened to whatever Henderson was saying. He considered leaving her to work her way out of this one on her own, just to ruffle her pretty reporter feathers a little. Because he was sure the hell sick of playing her stooge instead of her cameraman.

But that itch on his neck was getting worse. And suddenly it seemed an excellent idea for both of them to get the hell out of the open.

He had taken one step from the meager shade he'd been savoring when half of Henderson's face disintegrated. A mist of pulverized bone and muscle and blood sprayed out onto Jessie in a wide arc. She gasped, hunching in like someone unexpectedly doused with ice water, clearly not yet understanding what had happened.

An indistinct roar of yelling and gunfire and screams filled his ears as the unit realized they were under attack and scrambled to find cover. But Neil remained frozen in place, foot still raised to take that next step that wouldn't come.

Bewilderment etched Jessie's expression as she stared at hands splattered with blood and other things, before raising horrified eyes to meet his.

Run!

He shouted it, but only in his head. He couldn't seem to say it out loud.

Run!

Jessie held out her hands towards him, the gesture pleading with him to help her.

To save her.

Run, damn it, run!

A bullet skipped off of the wall beside his head, sending sharp lances of fire into his face where the stone shrapnel bit into his skin.

Like a balloon had popped, all the muffled sounds suddenly came rushing in at him with full surround sound clarity, waking his body and unsticking his brain. Nearly overwhelming him with sensory memories. Of other villages, other firefights, other times the scent of blood and gunpowder had seared his nostrils and coated his throat with the acrid taste of death.

"Run!"

A weight like a small fist pressed into his side, again and again.

Ignoring it, he ran for her. But no matter how far he went, he never seemed to get any closer to the woman still standing beside the well, hands extended, an expression of absolute horror on her gore-speckled face.

Something warm and wet ran down his cheek.

"Jessie, get down! Get down!"

The wetness moved to his ear, and then his neck.

As he ran, a small hole dotted the center of her forehead. He saw the split-second of surprise on her face before she collapsed to the ground like a suddenly boneless doll. All of that life and vitality snuffed out in the merest instant. A wave of pain and grief crested over him even as he felt the push against his body, rocking him to the side.

"Nooo—"

Neil jerked awake with the hoarse cry on his lips. Disoriented, he stared at the ceiling above the bed, uncertain where he was. When he was.

Fuck, *who* he was.

A soft whine and a warm, wet swipe of a tongue against his neck immediately grounded him. He threw an arm around the furry body lying partially on top of him. As he sucked in lungful after lungful of air, the band of terror squeezing his chest loosened by small increments as he slowly came back to himself.

Knowing the drill, Bailey stayed wedged against him, her wet nose pressed tight to the spot under his ear. As she always did, she seemed to recognize the second he was truly back in the present again. Her tail thumped lightly against the mattress and she pulled off him enough to plant a sloppy kiss on his cheek.

"Good girl," he croaked, giving her an awkward pat, limbs still not quite in synch with his brain.

True to her training, Bailey had already pawed the light switch to turn on the bedside lamp before going into her waking and deep pressure therapy mode. It cast the bedroom in a soft glow, further pushing back the clingy hold of the dream by proving he was safe at home in Tennessee, not seven thousand miles away in some desert death trap.

Swinging his legs over the side of the bed, he grabbed the bottle of water from his nightstand and chugged half of it down. A futile attempt to wash away the acrid taste of sulfur and fear that always followed him out of the nightmares.

Damn it!

Wasn't he *ever* going to be free of the memories? The horror? The guilt?

He ground the heels of his hands into his eyes as he hunched over. "Fuck, fuck, *fuck*!"

Whining softly, Bailey belly-crawled to his side again and wriggled her way around so she could lay her snout on his thigh. When he dropped his hands from his face, her big brown eyes rolled up to look at him with quiet adoration and calm acceptance.

He wished to hell the people in his life would look at him with half as much understanding as the friggin' dog did when he fell into the hellhole of his mind.

Then again, he'd never given the people in his life much cause to.

A glance at the clock on the nightstand showed 2:19. Fucking wonderful. Not like it mattered, really. Sleep was still a tricky thing for him, even when it wasn't being haunted by ghosts of memories past.

"Fuck," he said once more with feeling. Scrubbing a hand through his short, sleep-ravaged hair, he looked down into the soulful eyes still watching him, waiting for the magic words.

"Ice cream?"

Like a shot, the golden retriever bounded from the bed and raced to the closed bedroom door, where she did a quick donut and came back to sit at his feet, entire body quivering with anticipation.

Bailey's excitement about their ritual post-nightmare treat dragged out a grin despite the residual terror that left his muscles aching from being clenched so tightly. A small scoop of ice cream was her reward for a job well done. For him, it helped cover the lingering tastes of war his mind managed to reproduce in such exacting detail.

Of course, a few shots of Jack Daniels would do it better.

But the thought was a fleeting one. He'd worked damn hard to get sober. One more fucking nightmare wasn't enough to tempt him to backslide now. Not when he had come this far. So much farther than he'd ever anticipated he could.

Especially since he had fully expected to be dead long before now.

Opening the bedroom door, Neil followed the now amped-up dog to the kitchen, where she sat at perfect attention beside the refrigerator. After scooping out a small ball of strawberry/vanilla swirl from the gallon container, he dropped it in the plastic bowl he used only for treats, not regular food, so she understood the difference.

With an affectionate stroke on her soft head, he gave the release command and she greedily attacked her reward while he scooped out a larger portion for himself. He leaned against the counter to eat while Bailey chased the dish around the faded linoleum floor, licking for every last drop.

My brother spent the short time he had on this Earth helping others. My wish is that his generous spirit live on in the love and comfort you receive from your service dog.

The words from the handwritten letter given to him after he "graduated" with Bailey from the service dog training course a year and a half ago had stuck with him.

Love and comfort?

Those were small words to describe the enormous impact Bailey made on his life.

It never ceased to amaze him how freaking lucky he'd been the day she'd been walked into his dorm room at the Another Step Forward campus and introduced as his. It wasn't overstating things an inch to say she had literally saved his life.

And kept on saving it, every single day since.

Of course, the fact a recovering alcoholic had ended up with a PTSD service dog named Bailey was an irony not lost on either Neil or his therapist.

After checking to make sure every door and window was still secure despite having done the same inspection right before going to bed, he headed to the small front bedroom. He'd converted the unused space into his darkroom-slash-office after moving into the house the previous year. If he wasn't getting any more sleep, he might as well do something productive with the long hours till dawn.

Alex wasn't expecting the project she'd commissioned from him to be finished for another few weeks yet. Still, it wouldn't hurt to have some early proofs to show her and make sure their vision about the final product meshed. The two of them were usually pretty like-minded on projects, but that was work. This was personal, and he wanted to make sure he got it absolutely right for her.

After closing the door, he settled into the office chair he'd picked up for a steal at a garage sale thanks to the puppy-chewed seat, patiently pressing down the silver tape he'd used to cover the damage. There were very few things in life duct tape couldn't fix.

Too bad he was one of them.

With a contented grunt, Bailey collapsed next to the desk. Within minutes, soft doggie snores filled the room.

"Show off," he muttered under his breath as he booted up his computer and brought up the files of the photos he'd shot the previous weekend. Digital photography might make it possible to take twice as many shots while he tried to get just the right one, but the purist in him still missed using film.

There was just something about it that was more...organic. More honest.

Or maybe, as had been accused more than once, he really was simply stuck in the past, unable to move on. He hoped that wasn't true, because his past wasn't a place he really wanted to stay.

One trip through hell had been more than enough for any lifetime.

"I look like a poodle!"

Squinting at the picture being waved in her face, Alexandra McKenna shook her head. "No, you don't." Personally, she thought the resemblance was closer to a Pomeranian, but voicing that opinion wouldn't be wise. She needed to talk Vanessa down from her high horse, not stick a burr under her saddle.

"A big, fat, *poofy* poodle!"

Well, yeah, okay, she kind of did.

Biting her cheek to keep from grinning, she said, "Really, Vanessa, you look fine."

"He did it on purpose, you know."

"Who, Neil?"

"He always makes sure to shoot me in the least attractive way possible." Vanessa brandished the picture again as proof. "That man is a hack."

Tired of the familiar refrain, Alex plucked the picture from Vanessa's fingers and placed it face down on her desk. "*That man* has won awards for his work. It's not his fault it was windy that day."

Or that Vanessa had chosen to get a perm the day before, which had taken on a life of its own. A subsequent trip to a salon in the city had resulted in a successful repair job, but not before the damage was already done, photographically speaking.

Vanessa sniffed, because she couldn't refute facts. But she wasn't about to be put off that easily.

"If someone had simply *told* me my hair was a mess, I could have done...something." She frowned, because really, nothing short of a net would have helped contain the poof and she had to know it. "In any case, we'll just have to reshoot them."

This time, Alex didn't even try to hold back her laugh. "These pictures were taken on Founders Day," she said, in case Vanessa had forgotten that tiny detail. "We can't 'just reshoot' everything."

"Not everything. Just the ones with me in them."

How very Vanessa.

"I really hope you're joking right now, Vanessa, because if not, then you're delusional." Sadly, Alex knew she wasn't joking. In Vanessa's world, anything that benefited her was what mattered most, and nothing would stand in the way of her getting it. It was what helped her rise so quickly from fledgling reporter to featured anchor at the station.

And made her the least-liked person in the WMKN family.

Forestalling Vanessa's reply, Alex leaned back in her chair, fingers steepled the way she'd seen her grandfather do a hundred times.

"Here's what I'm going to do. I'll ask Neil if he can fix the pictures you find the most objectionable. Maybe with Photoshop or something he can make your hair look a little less..." *Edward Sissorhands.* "...flyaway."

"Well, he'd better be able to do something, or—"

"*If* he can," Alex interrupted with a raised finger, another weapon from the Colin McKenna arsenal, "then we'll update the pictures currently on the station's website. If he can't..." She spread her hands in an "oh well" gesture.

"That's unacceptable," Vanessa sputtered. "You can't leave those pictures there with me looking like *that*. Not when..." Her glossy lips pressed together.

"Not when the other networks you've sent your resume to might see them?" She smiled thinly at Vanessa's surprised reaction. "Worst kept secret of the year, Nessa." She knew the other woman disliked the nickname, but she'd had just about enough of her prima donna crap for one morning. "If you're that worried about it, I can go ahead and take all the pictures you're in off the website entirely. Problem solved."

Vanity warred with professional practicality as Vanessa visibly struggled with her choices.

"Fine, then. Leave them up. But if your pet cameraman is as good as you keep insisting he is, then it should be a moot point, anyway. He shouldn't have any trouble at all making me look gorgeous again."

With a dramatic swirl that tossed her now beautifully curled blonde hair in a showy arc, she stormed out of Alex's cramped office, closing the door with enough force to rattle the frosted glass panel.

"Only on the outside." After waving away the residual cloud of Chanel Vanessa always left in her wake, she flipped over the picture printed from their website's events page and studied it again.

It showed Vanessa interviewing the mayor as he concluded his Grand Marshal duties at the Founders Day parade. Her over-permed hair, aided by the wind, was blowing up in a big blonde cloud around her head, making her look like a dandelion about to burst into seed.

Despite her confidence in Neil's photographic abilities, even she had her doubts he'd be able to make Vanessa appear any less ridiculous.

Shoving the picture aside, she got back to the tedious station work Vanessa's visit had interrupted. The myriad reports and contracts were her least favorite part of the executive producer's job, but they still needed to get done. She was slogging through the week's sponsor sheets when there was a knock on the door.

Welcoming the interruption, she called out, "Come in."

The door opened quickly, pushed all the way open in a smooth arc. From that motion alone, she knew who it was. Neil Crawford rarely entered a room without visually clearing it first. It was one of his many quirks and tics which had long since stopped being odd and were instead just a part of who he was.

Neil tipped his head towards the computer screen once he'd completed his inspection and settled his gaze on Alex. "Hope I'm not interrupting."

"Yes, you are, and *thank you* for that." She closed the current file and put the computer into hibernation, saying again, "Come in."

It was difficult to tamp down the little frisson of sexual awareness that always accompanied being in Neil's presence. He wasn't good-looking in the slick, manscaped male model mold like some of the men who worked on-air for the network. Rather, he had a more earthy appeal with his square jaw and broad shoulders, tapering down to a nice, lean torso and long, well-defined legs that would have done any cowboy proud.

Alex had always had a secret weakness for cowboys.

Dragging her mind from thoughts that would embarrass them both if Neil ever realized she lusted after him with all the wistful longing of a horny teenager, she waited for him to close the door and take a seat.

As always, he chose the one which put his back closest to the wall.

Bailey, wearing her little blue service vest, stood with her feathery tail waving, but she didn't leave his side until Neil gave her a soft "shake" command. Only then did the dog approach and offer her paw in exchange for a petting and one of the dog treats Alex kept in a jar in her desk drawer.

It had been an adjustment for her when Neil and Bailey first started at the network. Animals were her kryptonite. Show her any dog or cat, and Alex wanted to get right down on the floor and love on them.

But she'd done some research on service dogs when they hired Neil, which he'd reinforced on his first day at the station when she asked. And the simple act of petting or even talking to a service dog without permission was not only rude, it could distract it from its job. Sometimes with dire consequences.

So, she'd learned to wait until Neil gave Bailey permission before getting in her small doggie-love fixes.

After a final pat, Bailey settled on the floor at Neil's feet, leaving Alex free to concentrate her attention on the far-too distracting man now seated across from her.

"So, what's up?"

Neil fished in his pocket and drew out a silver flash drive.

"I put together some preliminary layouts for the birthday album you wanted." He slid the drive across the desk to her. "I thought you might want to take a look before I go any further. See if there are any changes you want or if there's anything I left out that you want me to add."

She took the drive, more than a little surprised.

"I wasn't expecting to see any proofs for another week, at least." The shrug she got in answer told her nothing, but the dark smudges beneath Neil's eyes did. The long-lashed eyes were a light blue, almost the color of well-washed denim, and one of his most arresting features as far as she was concerned. But right now, they looked tired.

And a bit guarded.

She couldn't claim to know Neil well—she didn't think anyone at the station could—but she knew enough to not ask questions when he wore that closed-off look.

"This is great," she said instead. Gesturing toward her computer, she added, "Do you mind if I...?"

Another shrug.

A man of few words was their Neil.

She woke up the computer and snapped the drive into place, all the while hyper-conscious of the man watching her with the quiet intensity that never failed to make her feel clumsy and gauche. Neil Crawford had worked for her grandfather's news network for a little over a year now. And she knew practically nothing more about him than she had the first day he'd shown up for work.

Other than he was an *outstanding* photographer.

As she watched the pictures both old and new Neil had assembled fill the screen, her already high opinion of his work skyrocketed. He'd turned the simple digital album she'd asked him to assemble as a surprise for her grandfather's eightieth birthday into an artistic slideshow telling the story of Colin McKenna's life and family. There were some photos she'd never even seen before.

"These are...amazing."

"I can change anything you don't like."

"Are you kidding?" she asked, disengaging the drive. "I love it all. Don't change a thing."

"It's just the mock-up. I'm not done yet."

He sounded slightly defensive about it. Probably because he was such a perfectionist. That she understood. She was one herself.

"Then I can't wait to see the finished product. Colin is going to love it."

It was always *Colin* around the station. Never Grandfather or Gramps, even when no one else was around to hear. Colin had always been very clear about keeping personal and business relationships distinctly separate.

Alex might bear the same last name, but she'd earned her place in the executive producer's office *despite* it, rather than *because* of it. Colin McKenna suffered no fool lightly. And when it came to the running of his beloved network, everyone who worked for him had to prove they were worthy of the honor. Even family.

Especially family, unfortunately for her poor cousin Richard.

As Neil reached for the flash drive she held out, his hand stopped as it passed over the picture of Vanessa and the mayor laying on the desk. He looked at Alex with a question in his gorgeous eyes.

She blew out an unhappy sigh.

"Yeah, I wanted to talk to you about that. Is there any chance you can, I don't know, *fix* it a little? Vanessa's hair, I mean," she added quickly, not wanting it to sound like she found fault in the actual photography, which was just fine. "It's a little..." She waved her hands around her own head. "Big."

There was a long pause as Neil studied the picture. Thinking about ways to fix it? Or how to tell her it wasn't his job to Photoshop out bad life choices? He ran a hand through his short-cropped hair as he thought, disrupting the silver-shot brown locks into a sexy mess.

And unknowingly giving her a tiny thrill as his biceps flexed beneath the edge of his dark blue tee. She swallowed and looked away.

Drooling wasn't polite.

Finally, he tipped his head to the side in a partial nod. "Yeah, I can probably do something with it."

"Great." One diva crisis averted. "Thank you."

"But there's nothing I can do about the interview segments we filmed," he added, totally deflating her premature relief. "Stills are one thing, but video..."

Alex swallowed a groan. She'd forgotten about the slew of interviews conducted during the Founders Day celebrations to be run as part of the station's Hometown Heritage weekend show over the next month. Vanessa must have forgotten them, too.

For now.

Alex didn't look forward to when she remembered.

"No chance you can work a little CGI magic, I suppose?" she half-joked.

"Spielberg and Lucas *combined* don't have that much magic."

His wry comment surprised a laugh out of her. Neil rarely made jokes, but she could see from the slight twitch of his lips he was more amused about Vanessa's situation than he had let on. It was no secret he wasn't Vanessa's favorite person. Alex just hadn't realized the feeling was mutual.

If she didn't know how much of a professional Neil was, she might suspect there was actually something to Vanessa's accusation of photographic sabotage.

"Well, then, it is what it is."

Not that Vanessa would agree. But really, what else could they do other than scrap the interviews altogether? And there was no way *that* was happening. Founders Day was a huge deal to the people of Shelby, and since WMKN's studios were based there, that made it a big deal for the network as well.

She held out the flash drive to Neil again. As his slightly calloused fingers grazed hers to take it, she had to bite her lip to repress the shiver of awareness that tingled up her arm.

Her stupid body seemed to have a mind of its own where Neil was concerned. It didn't matter how many times she reminded herself the man had shown zero interest in her beyond their working relationship. She couldn't convince her hormones to stop doing the mating dance whenever he was around.

She could only pray he remained as oblivious to his effect on her as he always seemed.

As Neil closed his fist over the drive, Bailey rose to her haunches, looking up at him as she pressed against his leg. He used his free hand to stroke her head in an almost absent fashion for a few seconds before standing, shoving the drive into his pocket as he did.

"I won't be able to work on fixing Vanessa's shots until later." A small hand gesture had Bailey moving to stand in front of the closed door, waiting. "I'll be out most of the day with Penny."

A ridiculous spurt of jealousy hit her gut before she realized he meant he'd be on a location shoot with the attractive young reporter. Working.

She should know. She'd scheduled the piece herself two days ago. *And* been the one to assign Neil as Penney's cameraman since she was still learning the ropes and Neil was, well, Neil. Smart. Talented. Dependable.

Hot.

Oh, this was so bad.

"Okay, sure," she said, reopening the sponsor file on the computer to make herself look busy. It was rude, but anything was better than trying to meet his eyes when she could feel a blush starting to heat her cheeks. "Let me know when you have something to show Vanessa so she can climb down off the ledge."

"Will do."

The urge to glance over as he left was strong. So strong.

She stared at the computer screen for all she was worth instead, despite not seeing a thing on it. Only after the door closed behind him did she drop her head with a low groan.

Lusting after one of her employees was *so* not smart.

In fact, it was dumb, reckless, and completely unprofessional.

Although...*technically*, Neil was her grandfather's employee as Colin was sole owner and CEO of the network. And would be until he deigned her ready to take over the reins and finally stepped down into what some thought was a long overdue retirement. Still, she was Neil's direct supervisor, which should have been enough to keep her rowdy hormones in check.

Sadly, it wasn't.

So, it was a good thing she had a date with Steve Prentiss that evening.

He was another of her mother's many attempts to match her up with "someone of the right caliber" to marry into the McKenna clan. Of course, Helen McKenna's idea of right and hers didn't usually mesh. Like, at all.

But every once in a while, her mom wore her down enough to agree to a blind date with another of her meticulously chosen candidates. This one happened to be the youngest son of one of her mother's "dearest" friends.

God help me.

Still, he'd seemed nice enough from the brief phone conversation they had to decide on a place for dinner. And after how she'd practically been salivating all over poor unsuspecting Neil just now, maybe going out with another guy was exactly what she needed. Despite her reservations about someone her mother thought was "right," she could at least manufacture a little enthusiasm for the evening.

Because really, even if she and Steve didn't click, how terrible could it really be?

Chapter 2

"OH, MY GOD, IT was *awful.*"

With a laughing groan, Alex collapsed back onto her best friend's sofa, careful not to spill the extremely full glass of wine she had just poured for herself. After saying goodnight to Steve at the restaurant, she'd stopped and bought the bottle before heading over to Dionne's cozy little apartment for the blow-by-blow postmortem of her evening.

With a lot more grace, Dionne Jackson settled on the opposite end of the sofa. She picked up the remote and turned off the reality show she'd been watching, then curled her legs up as though getting ready for an even juicier bit of entertainment. Her dark eyes sparkled in anticipation. "How awful?"

Alex almost laughed at Dionne's expectant expression.

"I was ready to stab myself in the eye with my shrimp fork before the entrée came."

"Let me guess. All he did was talk about himself."

"No, not really."

"Seriously? He never brought up his family's money? Or the fancy school he went to? Or the super-sexy sports car he drives that probably cost more than a normal person makes in a lifetime?"

"He never mentioned his family other than to apologize about his mother conspiring with mine to arrange the date in the first place. And he only brought up his school when I asked him about where he'd gone. Harvard," she added reluctantly in response to Dionne's questioning look.

"Let me guess. He's a lawyer."

A rueful smile twisted her lips. "Orthopedic surgeon."

"Of course, he is," Dionne laughed. "Helen McKenna wouldn't settle for any kind of *regular* doctor for her only daughter. It would have to be a specialist."

Much as she wanted to share her friend's amusement, the comment struck too close to the bone. Her mother really was a colossal snob.

She could only be glad her friends didn't hold it against her.

"And the car?"

"A Prius." Which had looked a lot less out of place being brought around by the valet at the restaurant than her RAV4 hybrid SUV had.

"Hmph." Dionne took a sip of wine, looking vaguely disappointed. "So, let me see if I have this right. He was nice, smart, didn't try to impress you with his or his family's wealth, and has the same practical-but-boring taste in cars as you. Maybe I'm slow, but this guy isn't sounding all that awful to me. Did he smell bad or pick his teeth or something?"

She snorted. "No. It was the *date* that was awful, not Steve. Steve was...perfectly nice." And there was the problem in a nutshell. He'd been perfectly everything: perfectly charming, perfectly well-mannered, perfectly polite. His dinner conversation had been perfectly entertaining.

And after the first twenty minutes, she'd been perfectly bored out of her ever-loving mind.

It didn't make sense. And from the puzzled look on Dionne's face, her friend didn't understand her reasoning any better than she did herself. Logically, she should have had an absolutely wonderful time tonight. Maybe even agreed to a second date for the upcoming weekend when Steve hinted around the possibility.

Instead, she'd thanked him for a nice evening and driven back to Shelby to ease her disappointment in all of that bland perfection with a bottle of mid-priced Riesling and a sympathetic ear.

What was wrong with her?

When had nice manners and pleasant conversation become *boring*?

It was all Neil Crawford's fault. She swallowed a large gulp of the crisp white wine. The man had scrambled her hormones so much, they'd short-circuited her brain or something. It was the only explanation.

All she had to do was have her fingers touch his by accident, and her body went bananas. When Steve had put his hand on the small of her back as they walked to their table, always a serious erogenous zone for her, she'd felt nothing. Zip. Zilch. Nada.

Not a single hormone had so much as even cared to notice.

Fickle hormones.

"There just wasn't any...spark."

"Sparkage is important," Dionne agreed with a solemn nod. "Doesn't always happen right away, though."

It did when the man in question was Neil.

"It's because of that guy," Dionne said suddenly, shaking an accusing finger in Alex's direction. "Isn't it?"

"What guy?"

"The one you told me about months ago, from work. You know, the one with the nice, tight ass and the big...*camera* that made you tingly in all the right places." Dionne wiggled her eyebrows.

She sucked in a hard breath and choked, horrified at how close her friend had come to hitting the nail on the head. Was she freaking psychic or something?

"It *is* about him!" Dionne crowed triumphantly while Alex coughed and sputtered.

"This has nothing to do with Neil," she finally managed to wheeze out. "Nothing at all."

"Then why are you turning all red and splotchy?"

Damn her fair complexion! Not for the first time, she envied Dionne's dark skin tone. *She* never lit up like a neon sign every time she got embarrassed.

Hoping snark would cover her discomfort, she replied, "Maybe because I just nearly choked to death?"

"Oh, please. Don't even try to give me that innocent act. You suck at it."

"Do not." She totally did.

"Girl, I have students who could win an Oscar playing innocent. *You*, on the other hand, wouldn't make it past first auditions."

So true. Alex had never been able to lie convincingly, not even as a child. Every time she tried, she broke out in great big hives.

Her older brother, Lyle, didn't have that problem. Neither did her cousin, Robert. Which she found extremely unfair, since he was one of the biggest liars she knew. Talk about Oscar-worthy performances.

"It might have something to do with Neil," she admitted with a sigh, "but it *shouldn't*. That's the problem."

"Why? You like the guy, right?"

"I'm attracted to him. It's not the same thing."

"It's a start. And it's more than you had with perfect Steve," Dionne pointed out when she started to protest. "I think you like this Neil guy more than you're admitting. Why is that, I wonder?" She took a sip of wine, watching over the rim of her glass as Alex squirmed.

"Oh, I don't know, maybe because he's never given any indication *at all* he might think of me as anything other than his boss?"

"*Pfft.*"

"Don't *pfft* me. I'm serious. Just because I like him doesn't mean he feels the same way about me."

"So, you *do* like him!"

She considered denying it again, then groaned instead. "Yes, okay, I like him. He's quiet, and kind of withdrawn, but he's got this, I don't know, this *aura* of strength and trustworthiness and...and...dependability about him. That doesn't mean anything's ever going to come of it."

"Is it because of his thing?"

Alex could only stare. "Excuse me?"

Dionne huffed and rolled her eyes. "Not his *thing* thing, dirty bird. His other thing. The post traumatic thing."

Oops.

The heat in her face flared hotter.

"No, that has nothing to do with it."

She'd done a lot of research on Post Traumatic Stress Disorder when Neil was first hired. It could be debilitating, certainly, but not a reason she would ever dismiss his potential as a romantic interest. Not that she ever thought of him with any kind of interest, of course. Romantic or otherwise.

Geez, she even sucked at lying to herself.

"Then it's because you're chicken."

"Am not!"

"Really? So, you wouldn't turn him down if he asked you out?"

Would she? She considered it.

"Probably not," she said finally. "But he won't." That was pretty much a given, seeing how he barely spoke to her other than about work-related subjects. Which was really too bad, because it was a crying shame to let all of that sexual sizzle go to waste.

"You don't know that."

"I *do* know that. Especially not after the way my mother talked to him at the Founders Day celebration, when he asked about getting access to some of the old family photo albums for the project he's doing for me." She cringed at the memory. "You'd think he'd asked to go through her underwear drawer by the way she reacted."

"Somehow I don't see the big, bad Marine—"

"Soldier," she corrected. "He was in the Army, not the Marines."

"Who cares?"

"Trust me, they care." That she knew for a fact. She'd made the same mistake once.

And only once.

Dionne did another eye roll, which was amusing because it was something she was constantly on her students about doing. "Whatever the hell he is, I don't see him being scared off by Helen McKenna and her snooty attitude."

"Scared, no. Frostbitten, yes."

Not that Neil had shown any reaction to the snub. He'd simply stared her mother down until she'd blinked first, which was a pretty impressive feat. Afterward, he'd blown it off as no big deal, but she had still been mortified by her mother's obnoxious attitude.

"I seriously don't know what got into her," Alex said, echoing her words to Neil when she'd apologized after the incident. It was truly perplexing. "My mother can do snooty with the best of them. But it usually only gets to that level of rude when she thinks someone is 'getting above themselves,' whatever the hell that means."

"Hmm." Dionne drummed her fingernails lightly against her glass.

"Hmm, what?"

"Nothing. Stray thought." Before Alex could press, she turned the subject. "You never did say why you went out with another of your mother's Stepford dates. Didn't you swear after the last one never again?"

"I don't think I said *never*." Wow, was she being a big, fat liar tonight or what? She was surprised her pants hadn't already started smoking.

"Never. *Ever*. Again. Your words exactly." Dionne's gaze dared her to deny it.

"Okay fine, maybe I did say that, but only because the last one was so—"

"Awful?"

She thunked her head back against the cushion with a huff. "You know, you really suck right now."

"I'm just trying to understand."

That made two of them.

"I guess I figured it was...time."

"Hmm."

"Again with the hmm."

Dionne pursed her lips in thought before tilting her head to the side. "What does that mean, it was time? Did your biological clock suddenly start ticking or something?"

"Very funny."

"It's a legitimate question."

"What, just because I went on a *date*, suddenly I'm hormonal?"

"Because you went on a date *now*," Dionne corrected. "With a man your mother picked out. That practically screams of desperation."

"I am not desperate."

Dionne shot her a *cut the crap* look.

"Okay, fine. I'm not desperate, but maybe I am the tiniest bit...jealous." She gulped down the rest of her wine before reaching for the half empty bottle sitting on the coffee table in front of them. This discussion was clearly going to require more alcohol.

A lot more.

Dionne touched her ear. "I'm sorry, what was that, now?"

"I'm. Jealous." She enunciated the words with exaggerated care, knowing Dionne had heard her just fine the first time. Her gaze flicked to the gorgeous cushion-cut diamond on her friend's left hand and away again, the now familiar burn of happy-tinged-with-sad swirling inside her chest. "You're engaged. My brother's married. Heck, even Richard is talking about finally 'putting a ring on it,' as he so eloquently announced to the family last week."

"Your cousin's an idiot."

He really was.

"Franny could do so much better than him."

"I happen to agree, but she says she loves him." Alex shrugged. She didn't get it either. But Franny had been pretty clear she was going into her relationship with Richard eyes wide open to his many, *many* faults. "I think she believes once she gets Richard away from his parents' influence, he might stop being such an egomaniacal jerk."

"Eh, maybe, but I wouldn't want to put money on it." Dionne held her glass out for Alex to refill. "So…tiny bit jealous. Go on."

Alex shot her friend a dirty look, but it had no real animosity behind it.

"So," she mimicked as she poured. "With all the connubial bliss I'm surrounded by, I started thinking it could be time to maybe, possibly find someone I could, you know, be happy with, too."

Dionne shot forward in her seat. "Shut up! Are you telling me that after all these years toiling away as Grampy Colin's underpaid workhorse, you're actually thinking about getting yourself a *life*? Well, hallelujah and hold the presses!"

"Hold the presses is for print," she replied peevishly to her friend's over-exaggerated excitement. "We're broadcast. It would be 'breaking news.' If it was, which it's *not*. I have a life, and a very nice one, thanks very much."

"Oh, please. You've been busting your skinny Scottish butt trying to make that old man proud since the day you got back from college. You spend more hours a day at his damn studio than he does."

Alex's back stiffened at the familiar rebuke. "I have responsibilities."

"You're thirty-one and you haven't had a steady relationship with a man since Todd, and that was what, almost two years ago? Screw responsibilities. You need a *life*."

The fact Todd had said something very similar the day he'd dumped her rubbed Alex on the raw, making her response sharper than intended.

"I can have both, you know. A life and a career. They're not mutually exclusive."

"They are the way you've been doing it. Okay, okay." Dionne relented, waving her glass like a white flag. "Whatever you were doing before, we'll agree to disagree on. The important thing is that *now* you're going to start living for *you*. I approve wholeheartedly with the plan, and I'm behind you one hundred percent in whatever way you need me to help. So, tell me. What can I do?"

Alex's annoyance slid away at her friend's earnest words.

They didn't always see eye-to-eye on everything, *especially* anything to do with Colin. Dionne insisted her grandfather had taken advantage of Alex's adoration of him to turn her into a clone of himself after his sons both chose other careers. Ones outside the news network he'd built from the ground up, rather than following in his impossible-to-fill footsteps.

Alex didn't see it that way. She saw herself as her grandfather's last chance to keep his beloved network in the family once he finally retired.

But despite their disagreement, she knew Dionne truly had her best interests at heart whenever she spoke her mind.

"Well, since my Stepford date"—she pulled a face at the too-accurate description of perfect Steve—"didn't pan out, maybe you can help me figure out where I'm supposed to find this someone who will make me happy, since I really don't have a clue where to start looking."

Dionne sent her a pitying look.

"Oh, sweetie, truer words were never spoken. You seriously *are* clueless. And if you can't see the answer that's right in front of your face, then your cousin isn't the only idiot in your family."

"Check."

The raspy voice pulled Neil's attention back from his turmoil of thoughts to the chessboard in front of him. Damned if the old man hadn't already managed to endanger his king. Without putting much thought into his move, he captured the threatening piece with his queen and sat back.

And realized too late he'd done just what his opponent wanted him to.

Fingers bent and gnarled with arthritis shifted the black knight to take Neil's white queen as Gus cackled with glee. "Mate in two."

Studying the board, he was disgusted to see Gus was right. He'd totally lost any way to protect his king, even to a stalemate. Bowing to the inevitable, he tipped the piece and resigned even though it rankled. It wasn't the losing he minded. It was losing because he couldn't keep his mind on the game.

And off the distracting woman slowly driving him insane.

"Good game," he said.

"No, it wasn't. You played like shit." Gus started to reset the board. "Rematch? If you think you can keep your head out of your ass this time, that is."

Neil grunted his reply. He couldn't take offense. Gus called things as he saw them. And sometimes he saw them too damn clear. It was one of the reasons he enjoyed spending time with the crusty old vet.

Most people danced around him and his PTSD like he was a live grenade that could go off unexpectedly if they didn't treat him with kid gloves. Gus was the only one who just treated him like a regular person.

Well, him and Alex.

Shit.

He didn't want to think about Alexandra freaking McKenna anymore tonight. The damn woman had been invading his thoughts all day, ever since he'd accidentally brushed her hand when she returned the flash drive earlier. Just a quick split-second, and it had felt like he'd grazed a damn live wire, sending tingles zinging up his arm and straight down to his cock. It was a ridiculous reaction to such a brief, innocent touch.

And yet here he was, more than eight hours later, still mooning over her like a fucking schoolboy with a crush.

And a hard-on.

Disgusted with his lack of self-control, he shifted uncomfortably in his chair and forced himself to focus on the game and push his green-eyed tormenter out of his head.

But she just wouldn't go.

"Damn, son," Gus said as he took Neil's last pawn, leaving only three of Neil's pieces facing off against ten of his own. "If I didn't know you could play better than this, I'd swear you were a rank amateur. What the hell's wrong with you tonight?" His gaze turned suddenly sharp despite the cataracts clouding both eyes. "You didn't say much at the meeting tonight. Anything you need to get off your chest?"

If only it were that easy.

He moved his knight to protect his vulnerable king. It was futile, but he'd play the game out to its inevitable conclusion. Gus made the expected response, maneuvering his rook into position for the final attack. "Nothing that will make me lose my chip."

His hand went to his pocket in an unconsciously protective gesture. He carried his AA two-year chip as a talisman against the temptations of falling off the wagon. Not that he hadn't come close a few times.

But the memory of how hard he'd worked to get where he was, and how bad it had been at its very worst, inevitably gave him the strength to deal with his problems in other, less self-destructive ways.

So far, anyway.

After moving his own rook to block, he watched in resignation as Gus took the piece, setting himself up for another mate. With a grimace, Neil tipped his king.

"Your game."

"Not even worth gloating over," Gus grumbled, leaving it to Neil to reset the board this time. "Not when you're playing like a pussy."

"I guess that means you don't want another game, then?"

"Fuck, yeah, I want another game." Gus slapped the tabletop with his gnarled hand, making the plastic pieces dance on the board. "Even playing like you are tonight, you're still more of a challenge than most of the old fucks in this place. Plus, you don't take twenty minutes to make a move. I'm seventy-three fucking years old. I don't have that kind of time to waste dicking around."

"Doesn't that make you one of the 'old fucks,' too, then?" He couldn't resist needling the old bastard, even as he felt a pang at the reminder Gus was, as he often put it, closing in on his expiration date.

"Course it does, but at least I don't act like it. It's barely nine o'clock, f'chrissake." Gus swept a hand around the large room which held half a dozen tables for gaming, and several sofas and cushy chairs around a large screen television currently dark. Aside from the two of them, the community room was empty. "Pussies. All of 'em."

It was a familiar rant, but there was a new hint of frustration underlying the words that caught Neil's attention. Gus had moved into the Manor Hills assisted living facility about six months ago, after Neil had talked him into it. He'd just lost his driver's license due to his worsening eyesight. And rightly so.

But Neil had worried being stranded in his dingy little apartment, sitting around waiting to die, might be what sent Gus back to the bottle again. Though he held a five-year chip at the moment, he'd been on and off the wagon many times over the years. Moving into Manor Hills had seemed like a good way to make sure Gus made it to year six.

Now he wondered if he'd made a mistake.

Sticking his nose into other people's business wasn't his thing. But Gus didn't have any family. Or, at least, any that cared enough to check up on him. The crotchety old bastard didn't have any friends, either, besides Neil. No one else would put up with him.

But Neil understood him. Unlike the most recent returning veterans, Gus had served in an unpopular war and come home to an ungrateful nation. Neil had gotten handshakes and strangers saying "thanks for your service," while Gus had gotten shunned and spit on. Yet both of them had simply done what their country had asked of them.

It was enough to make any man bitter.

They'd naturally gravitated together at Neil's first local AA meeting, two loners in a roomful of people you were expected to share your private demons with. He'd learned at some of his first meetings back in Tiptonville there were limits to how far he could willingly bare himself to people who had no concept of the hell he'd seen. That he'd lived and then relived for years, locked inside the privacy of his nightmares.

But Gus...Gus had the same demons. What neither could bear to open up about with the group at a meeting, they talked out between themselves in private. It might not be exactly the same, but at least it was something.

"You know, maybe if you stopped calling everyone a pussy, you might have a few more takers when you wanted someone to play," he said dryly. Then chuckled when Gus flipped him off.

"Wouldn't matter. They'd still be pussies." Gus made his opening move. "A rose by any other name, and all that shit."

"Wow, Gus. Your fucking eloquence moves me."

He did his best to really give his attention to the game this time. In the end, though, it was more likely Gus's flagging energy level than his own skill that gave him the win. A glance at the clock told him why.

It was late, well past visiting hours, but as usual he'd been given some leeway. None of the staff ever wanted to interrupt them when Gus was being what, for him, passed as content. They were all just a little bit intimidated by the crusty old tunnel rat.

He was pretty sure Gus considered all of them pussies, too.

"'bout time you proved you were worth putting up with," Gus grumbled as Neil took his king.

"Yeah, well, maybe I just didn't want to let you keep thinking you're the shit when all you were was lucky," Neil shot back, resetting the board. This time he got the double bird in reply. "Rematch tomorrow?"

"Cutting out on me already?"

"Still have some editing to get done for work."

He brushed away the pinch of guilt that he hadn't even started on the photo retouching Alex asked him to do. He'd meant to get to it before he picked Gus up for dinner and their AA meeting, but found one excuse after another to keep putting it off. Until finally it had been too late to bother starting.

Now, he'd have to get it all done before he could crawl into bed. It was going to be another long night with little sleep.

Of course, the less time for sleep, the less chance there was to dream.

Gus grumbled under his breath as he banged his chair back from the table, but Neil could tell it was mostly for show. The old coot was practically dragging his bony ass.

Knowing better than to offer help unless asked—or the stubborn bastard started to tip over, which had happened just last week—his muscles tensed to act as Gus got up. Using both the table and his cane to push to his feet, he wobbled there for a few seconds before finding his balance.

"Tomorrow's bingo night." Gus said the words like they tasted bad. "So, hell yeah, come and save my sorry ass if you can."

Bingo. Christ.

"Roger that."

He watched his friend shuffle away, gait uneven and slow as he maneuvered through the vacant tables and out of the room that always smelled faintly of lemon-scented cleanser. It seemed like he was leaning a lot more heavily on his cane than in the past. Neil recognized pain overcome by sheer stubborn determination when he saw it.

Gus took the bare minimum of the pain pills the doctors prescribed. He'd said more than once he'd rather spend his last years feeling the pain, knowing he was still alive, then in a medicated stupor.

Spent too many years like that already, he'd stated with a self-loathing grimace. *Figure I should at least try to be clear-headed for what few I've got left.*

At his feet, Bailey stirred and sat up to place her chin on his leg.

Running a hand over the dog's silky head, the anxiety he hadn't even been aware was building ebbed at the contact. The retriever wasn't just an early warning signal, she was also a relief valve.

He dared anyone who scoffed at the studies that found the mere act of petting an animal lowered your blood pressure to try it and not be mellowed by the action.

Of course, Bailey wasn't infallible.

Something proven just this morning in Alex's office. The dog's training included watching for the small tics that could signal growing anxiety or discomfort. For Neil, his tell was small. The mere tapping of his little finger.

He hadn't even realized he did it until the trainers at the service dog foundation had pointed it out to him. But Bailey knew to watch for it, and any time that finger started to quiver and tap, she knew it might indicate an oncoming anxiety attack. Or, worse, a full-blown flashback, which thankfully hadn't happened in almost eight months.

Unfortunately, what the dog *wasn't* trained for was being able to tell the difference between anxiety brought on by one of his PTS triggers, or by another, more basic physiological reaction. Like arousal.

Which was why she'd alerted on him in Alex's office after their fingers brushed.

The reminder of how he'd reacted like a smitten schoolboy was humiliating. It was just a damn touch. Alexandra McKenna's skin was just like every other woman's. No different, and definitely not special.

Oh, hell, who was he kidding? Alex's skin was special because it belonged to *Alex*. So much about her drew his interest. The woman had a quick mind, a will of steel, and a long, lean body that was built to be wrapped around a man.

Around *him*.

Aw, fuck no.

He rejected the idea as quickly as it sprang in vivid high-def 4k into his brain. The last thing he needed in his screwed-up life was another woman.

And the *very* last thing he needed was to get involved with someone like Alexandra, reigning princess of Clan McKenna, no matter how intriguing he found her. He couldn't think of a worse mistake he could possibly make.

No.

He'd made a good life here in Shelby. He had a job he could actually handle. A home that gave him the quiet and privacy he needed. And people who didn't look at him like he was some kind of monster, just waiting for him to storm the village and terrorize small children on a dark and stormy night. After what had happened back in Tiptonville, it was almost more than he could have hoped for.

He'd already picked up the shattered pieces of his life to start over again once. He wasn't about to risk having to do it all over again.

Not even for Alexandra freaking McKenna.

Chapter 3

"Thanks for coming."

All Alex got from Neil in reply was a grunt. Huh. It was a good thing the man had mad visual arts skills, because his verbal ones were severely lacking.

"I'm really sorry for the short notice," she tried again.

"Don't worry about it."

An actual response.

Woohoo.

But as Neil removed the camera equipment from the back of his battered black Ford Expedition, the stiff set of his shoulders said the opposite of his words.

"No, really. Answering your phone on a Saturday morning when you're not on call is above and beyond. Thank you."

"No problem."

Okay, gratitude didn't help. Maybe she could joke him into a better mood.

"That's not a 'no problem' face," she said with a teasing grin. "That's a 'woke a hibernating grizzly' face."

"It's a 'haven't had enough coffee yet' face." Neil slammed the tailgate closed with a little more force than necessary.

Ah. Well, that at least she could fix.

"Then I guess it's a good thing I planned ahead." She lifted the large thermos she'd filled before leaving her house in a rush.

She hadn't expected to be working this morning, either.

Neil eyed the silver cylinder like it was the Holy Grail, then frowned. "It's not one of those weird frou-frou flavors, is it?"

"Nope. Just good old Columbian dark roast."

He grunted again. "Good deal."

"I hope I didn't ruin any plans you had for the weekend."

"Not really."

Which wasn't a no. Damn. She already felt guilty about asking him to come to work on his weekend off. It would be even worse if she was keeping him from something.

Or someone.

Stop that.

Squashing the little voice of jealousy that seemed to pipe up all too often lately, she grabbed the bag with the video camera and slung the strap over her shoulder. Neil looked like he was going to protest, then just grabbed up the rest of his equipment and walked with her down the path from the park's rapidly filling parking lot to the softball fields. Bailey plodded patiently at his side in her little blue vest.

She should have let it go. But her mouth couldn't seem to leave well enough alone.

"Seriously, I wouldn't have bothered you if Evan didn't call last minute to tell me he was stuck in Gatlinburg with car trouble and wouldn't get here in time for the assignment. And then Jasper didn't answer his dang phone even though he's on call—"

"I said it wasn't a problem."

Except his tone and body language still said it was.

Not that there was anything she could do about it. They needed live footage of the charity softball game being played today between county law enforcement and fire rescue for the morning broadcast. And a longer taped piece for the Home-town Heritage segment. With her other two cameramen currently missing in action, Neil was it, day off or not.

The game was a big annual event, drawing hundreds of people and raising thousands of much-needed dollars for several worthy organizations. The media coverage the station provided always ensured additional donations found their way into the charities' coffers. If ruining Neil's Saturday was the only way to make that happen, then that was just the price of being in the news business.

It wasn't like she hadn't had other plans, too. Of course, it wasn't any great sacrifice to call Steve and beg off of their lunch date. One she'd only just agreed to the day before in a moment of weakness. And desperation.

Damn Dionne for putting that word into her head.

"Well, still. Thank you."

She got another grunt in reply. Fine, then. If Neil was going to be surly, let him. He wasn't the only one cranky without their morning coffee fix.

They stopped at the edge of the crowd milling in between the backstop and bleachers while the teams warmed up on the field. Food trucks had set up shop around the perimeter, filling the air with the scents of sizzling bacon, sausage, and other delicious, artery-clogging delights.

Her stomach rumbled. The banana she'd grabbed on her way out the door was a sad substitute for a hearty breakfast burrito. "Where would you like to set up?"

Ideally, they would have gotten there before the crowd arrived to stake out a spot with the right sight-lines for filming. But nothing about this morning was ideal, so they'd just have to do the best they could.

Hands full of equipment, Neil jerked his chin down the third base line, past the infield and away from the crush of people still funneling into the park. "There." He pushed ahead, his long legs quickly eating up distance and leaving her to follow in his wake.

By the time she caught up with him, he'd already unpacked the big Canon digital still camera and was taking some test shots towards home plate with the telephoto lens to find the range.

She placed the video bag by his feet. "Can I help with anything?"

"No." Neil put the camera down and reached for the bag, then paused before adding grudgingly, "Thanks."

The belated show of manners soothed her growing annoyance.

Until he opened his mouth again.

"Why are you even here, anyway?"

"I'm starting to ask myself the very same question."

At least he had the good grace to look embarrassed. "I meant, are you here because your reporter bugged out on you, too?"

"No, no early morning calls from Penny, thank God." She glanced at her watch. "She is running late, though. She should have been here by now."

It was unlikely Penny would be a no-show. Still under a trial contract with the network, she couldn't risk blowing off an assignment, no matter how mundane. But if she didn't get there soon, Alex might have to step in and do the live shot for the morning show herself.

It wouldn't be the first time. Like every other job at the station on her way up to the executive producer's office, she'd done her time in front of the camera. She'd hated it, really, *really* hated it, but she'd done it. And, in a pinch, she could do it again.

And still hate it just as much.

"So then, why are you here?" Neil repeated.

"Misery loves company?" she replied with a shrug. "I don't know. I guess I kind of felt like if I was screwing your weekend up, then I should have to suffer, too. Lead by example and all that."

It was such a thin excuse you could have read a book through it. But it was the one she'd given herself when she decided to spend the day with surly Neil rather than with perfect Steve, so she was sticking with it.

She glanced at her watch again. "Penny's really cutting it close."

"Maybe she just can't find us," Neil said as he set up the tripod for the video camera. "She's kinda short."

It was totally wrong to take pleasure from that less-than-flattering observation about the petite but well-endowed reporter, of which Alex was neither. Still, she found herself holding back a smile as she pulled out her phone. "I'll check on her and see what the problem is."

A few quick texts later, she'd lost any urge to smile.

"She's on her way, but she says the traffic all around the park is horrible, so she's not sure when she'll get here." Yet another reason getting to a shoot site early was wise. Time was money in their business. She and Neil at least had the excuse of being last-minute replacements for their late start. Penny didn't.

Something they'd be discussing after the assignment.

"Better put your on-air face on, then," Neil said, not even glancing up from his equipment.

She grimaced. She hated the heavy makeup required to keep from looking like a corpse.

"Didn't bring it. I can just do my commentary from off-camera." She glanced down at her navy capris and blue and white striped tank top. "I'm not exactly dressed for being on-air, anyway."

This time, Neil did glance up. His gaze ran the length of her body as he did a quick visual inventory. "Nah, you look cute." His eyes caught hers for a second before he dropped his head and went back to fiddling with his camera. "You just don't want to do it because you hate being on-camera."

"Guilty as charged." Her tummy did a little flutter, first from his words, and then from the glimpse of hot male appreciation she'd spied in his eyes.

No, no, no. This was exactly why she had accepted Steve's lunch invitation.

Neil wasn't the guy for her. One hot look meant nothing. He had zero interest in her, and she refused to make a fool of herself over a guy ever again. College had taught her self-respect was worth a hell of a lot more than the attention of a man.

No matter how tempting he might be.

Dragging her thoughts back to work, she used her phone's note feature to jot down some things to say on the live they'd be doing in—she checked her watch again—less than thirty minutes. Lucky for her, they covered the event every year, so the segments were pretty much the same every time. But knowing Colin would no doubt critique her performance as stand-in reporter, she'd love to come up with some slightly fresh angle on an otherwise rinse-and-repeat story.

"Hey, lady, you can't have your dog here."

It took a second for her to register that the words were directed at her.

She blinked away her focus on her notes and looked up. There was a tall, dark-haired man probably about Neil's age in his late thirties, dressed in baggy gym shorts and a ribbed white tank top, glaring at her. She actually looked behind herself to make sure he was talking to her. "I beg your pardon?"

The man jabbed a finger in Bailey's direction. "No dogs allowed in the park. There are signs all over the place. Can't you read?"

Alex looked at Bailey in surprise. She'd almost forgotten the dog was there.

"Oh, well, I guess you didn't see the vest she's wearing." Which was bright blue with the words "Service Dog" emblazoned on it. Kind of hard to miss. But she'd give him the benefit of the doubt since Bailey was lying down, which may have made it harder to read.

"So what? Just because you put clothes on your dog doesn't mean you get to break the rules."

She couldn't hold back a short huff of incredulous laughter at the ridiculous remark.

"It's not clothes, it's a working vest. To show she's working." Duh. "And it's not breaking the rules. It's the law. Service dogs are allowed in places other dogs aren't."

"Bullshit. There's no such law."

Was this guy for real?

"The Americans with Disabilities Act," she said, carefully enunciating each word so he wouldn't miss it. "The one that says service animals are allowed in all public places and are exempt from any 'no pets' rules." She hadn't thought she needed to spell that out. Did the man live in a cave?

"Yeah," Mr. Caveman snorted, "you really look like you're disabled."

Before she could grind out a reply, Neil spoke up.

"It's not her dog." He stood from where he'd been kneeling down working on the sound equipment a few feet away, and Bailey rose with him to press against his leg. "It's mine."

Alex saw the quick reevaluation that went through the guy's mind as his target changed from a mere woman to a man who matched him in height and weight. Neil was solidly built, but his muscles were hidden beneath his black tee, while Caveman's were on full display. She was pretty sure he even flexed a little.

It was only then she realized there were more than a few eyes on them.

Oh, damn, damn, damn. If Caveman was playing to an audience, there was no way he'd back down quietly.

"Yeah, and you look even less disabled than her, pal. I think this is some bullshit scam so you can get away with breaking the rules the rest of us have to follow." Caveman looked around as though asking for support. "Am I right?"

Alex was appalled when there were actually a few murmurs of agreement from the onlookers.

"No, you're dead wrong," she shot back, feeling her temper start to slip the leash she usually kept it on.

She might have inherited no more than the hint of red hair of her Scottish ancestors that highlighted her plain brown locks, but she'd certainly gotten all of the temper that went along with it.

"You don't know anything about him, or his situation, and you have no right to judge what you don't understand. Bailey wasn't bothering anybody. In fact, most people probably didn't even realize she was here until you started going off about it."

Unlike the loudmouthed jerk causing all the trouble, she didn't look for agreement from the people around them. But she got it anyway.

Caveman was not pleased at her stealing his thunder.

"Listen here, lady—"

"If you've got a problem with my dog, then talk to me, not her," Neil interrupted.

"Yeah, I got a problem," Caveman snapped, biceps flexing again. "I think you're full of shit, and I think you need to leave."

"He has every right to be here."

"Alex..." Neil warned softly, but her Scottish temper was running fully off-leash.

"Don't you 'Alex' me," she retorted, hands going to her hips as she swiveled from him to Caveman, who was now eyeing her a little warily.

Too late now, jerkface. You've just pissed off my inner Highlander and I'm about to go Outlander on your sorry ass. "And *you*—"

"Is there a problem here, folks?"

She turned sharply toward the new arrival, ready to give him a piece of her mind, too, if he was there to give her grief. Luckily, she reined her tongue in just in time when she saw he was a member of the sheriff's department softball team, all kitted out in catcher's gear.

And looking none too happy with any of them.

She couldn't blame him. They were disrupting what was supposed to be a fun day for him and his fellow officers and their families.

"Yes, sir, there is," she said, but Caveman started speaking right over her before she could explain.

"They've got a dog here, Frank," he charged, stabbing a finger at Bailey again, as though they were somehow trying to hide the sixty-pound retriever behind Neil's leg. "Park rules are no dogs. Period. That's what the sign says. Can't get much plainer than that. But these two seem to think they're special and the law doesn't apply to them."

As much as she wanted to go right back at the moron and explain, *again*, that they didn't need to leave because the law *did* apply to them, or to Neil, at least, Alex bit her tongue and waited. For one thing, it seemed the officer and the jerk knew each other, which could present a problem. And second, she knew they were in the right. No need to point out to the idiot that he was an idiot and make things worse than they already were.

It only took a quick look for the officer to figure out the situation.

"That's a service dog, Chuck," he said, sounding aggrieved. "It's allowed to be here."

"That's bullshit!"

"Watch your mouth," Frank the cop snapped. "There are kids here."

Chuck mumbled out what might have been an apology. Alex had her doubts. The dip of Frank the cop's eyebrows said he did as well.

"And it's not bull," Frank continued, "it's the law."

Caveman Chuck wasn't buying it.

"Oh, so I have to follow the rules and can't bring my dogs with me when I come watch my kid's Little League game, but this guy can get away with this sh...crap because he claims he's disabled? I mean, come on! Look at him. There's nothing wrong with him. He's as fit as you or me."

The first thought that flashed through Alex's mind was, *This guy procreated? Society is doomed.* The second that followed closely on its heels was, *This is a personal grudge for him, and he's never going to let it go.*

Frank the cop looked torn. Clearly, he knew the law said they could stay. But he just as clearly wanted the problem to simply go away so he could get back to his friends, who had already taken the field in preparation of starting the game.

"Do you have any proof that you need the dog?" Frank asked Neil finally.

Again, Alex was appalled. She'd researched the nuances of the ADA laws when they'd first hired Neil to make sure the network was in full compliance. So, she knew there were only two questions the law allowed to be asked of anyone with a service dog in their company. Neither of which was to demand proof.

She waited for Neil to set Frank straight, but he said nothing.

That was when she took her first really good look at her too-silent cameraman.

His expression was pinched. Sweat dotted his upper lip despite the mild temperature, and Bailey was practically sitting on his foot, whining softly as she alternately pawed and nose-nudged his leg.

Not good.

Kicking herself for not paying closer attention, she said more quietly to Frank, "You know you can't ask him that."

Frank's expression got even more frustrated. "Look, lady..."

"You can ask if Bailey is required because of a disability. The answer is yes. And you can ask what tasks Bailey has been trained to perform. Among other things, she's been trained to aid returning war veterans and ease their integration back into civilian life."

She hoped Frank the cop was intelligent enough to read between the lines, because Neil's PTSD was nobody's business but his own unless he chose to bring it up first.

Although, as she glanced at Neil again, if she didn't get this situation diffused in the next few minutes, that particular kitty might be out of the bag whether he wanted it to be or not.

When Frank said nothing, she played her last card.

"We're just here to do our job." She glanced meaningfully at the camera equipment, which was stamped with the network's logo. "We'll leave if we have to, but..."

As she'd hoped, pointing out that asking them to leave would mean losing the local media coverage the event relied on for donations was the tipping point. Not to mention the potential fall-out of any hint the sheriff's department had ignored ADA compliance and kicked them out of a county park illegally.

Frank looked like he wanted to utter one of the words he'd warned Caveman Chuck about using before giving a quick nod.

"Okay, fine. You can stay. But if anyone complains about the dog..."

Alex smiled, knowing it was an empty threat. "Bailey won't be any trouble. I promise."

"What?" Chuck seemed stunned. "Frank, what the fu—"

"Let's go find your seat, Chuck," Frank said, grabbing his arm and leading him back toward the bleachers. "I'll explain it to you on the way."

"Better use small words," she muttered under her breath. She was so angry she was practically vibrating with contained fury. As the crowd swallowed both men, the spectators melted away as well, now that the possibility of a fight was over.

Vultures, she thought with disgust as she turned back to Neil.

Despite the end of the argument and the dispersing of the crowd, he still looked like he was on the edge of some very steep internal cliff. Bailey now stood at his side, her mouth gently surrounding his hand as she tugged, as though to try and lead him away.

"Neil," Alex said softly, then repeated his name twice more before he finally looked at her. His eyes were a little wild, but at least he seemed to recognize her. "Neil, why don't you go out to the parking lot and wait for Penny at the head of the path? I'll text and tell her to meet you there, so she doesn't get lost."

His throat worked as he swallowed hard a few times.

"Neil?"

"Right."

He grabbed up Bailey's leash before sort of lurching away in the general direction of the parking lot. Luckily, with the game about to start, the crowd was now concentrated around the bleachers, leaving the rest of the area deserted aside from a few late arrivals.

Alex watched him go, anger and frustration swirling inside her, along with a healthy dose of helplessness. She'd never witnessed that kind of negative reaction to Bailey before. Everyone back in Shelby loved her. Or at least accepted her.

But now she had to wonder.

Had Neil encountered situations like this before they'd both finally been accepted by the people in town? How often had he been asked to leave somewhere, or been denied entry at all, because of his service dog? How many times had people accused him of trying to scam the system because he didn't look "disabled enough" to them?

Probably more than he'd ever admit to.

From her experience, Neil's default to disagreements always seemed to be to deflect and disengage whenever possible. It was undoubtedly one of the ways he coped with his condition, avoiding confrontation.

She grimaced.

She'd done the exact opposite, pushing back against Caveman Chuck and his Neanderthal thinking. Because damn it, she hated to let narrow-minded bullies get away with that kind of crap.

People needed to be willing to speak up and shut them down whenever they started spewing their toxic bull.

But in this case, maybe she should have taken Neil's feelings about how best to handle things into consideration before she'd opened her big, fat mouth. Because she had a bad feeling she'd only made things worse for him, not better.

She shot a worried look in the direction he'd gone. Darn her temper! All she'd thought about was protecting his rights, and instead she'd escalated the situation into what had looked like the start of a mini-panic attack.

Stupid, stupid, stupid!

"Great job, McKenna," she growled, as she sent a quick text to Penny about meeting Neil. "Superlative people skills." She shoved the phone into her pocket. "Moron."

The urge to go check on Neil was almost impossible to ignore, but she couldn't just abandon the station's expensive equipment. Plus, they had a live coming up in less than fifteen minutes she needed to get ready for.

Personal feelings aside, she was the boss, which meant she had a job to get done.

And currently no reporter *or* cameraman to do it.

Frustrated, worried, and thoroughly pissed at the world in general, she switched on the video camera Neil had already anchored to its tripod and started getting some taped shots of the game that had finally begun.

It really was a good thing she was trained in all the jobs at the station. Because she wasn't entirely certain that it was a question of *when* Neil was coming back, but of *if* he was coming back.

And after the way he'd just been treated, by Chuck, Frank, *and* her, she wouldn't blame him the least if he didn't.

Chapter 4

WHAT AN UTTERLY FUCKING miserable clusterfuck of a fucking day.

Neil avoided the sparks that flew into the growing darkness as he dropped another log into his backyard fire pit. The flames immediately licked at the dry wood with a hungry crackle and snap, releasing the clean scent of pine into the cooling evening air.

Satisfied it wouldn't roll off, he sank back into one of the old Adirondack chairs the previous owner had left behind and took a long swallow of Coke, which had grown lukewarm and flat. Didn't matter. He'd gotten used to drinking it that way when he was overseas, where a cold drink in the desert was about as likely as a soft bed or clean sheets.

Hell, they'd all been happy just to get their hands on some of the real stuff, and not the local knock-off crap that tasted like camel piss, warm *or* cold. Anything from back home had been a treasured treat.

Sometimes it was the only thing that reminded them there was more out there than just sand and flies and people who wanted them dead.

As he was about to take another swallow, a loud pop exploded from the fire.

Instantly, his body clicked over to survival mode, screaming at him to *get down, get down, get down!*

But other than a violent full-body flinch, he held off the impulse to hit the ground and stayed seated. With the help of the breathing exercises his therapist taught him, he even managed to suppress the roil of nausea that usually accompanied one of his triggers.

He'd laughed his ass off the first time Isaac demonstrated, saying there was no way in hell he'd be huffing and puffing like he was about to give birth.

But desperation was a great motivator.

The next time he had a panic attack, he'd given in and tried it. And damned if it hadn't helped. It wasn't perfect, of course. He'd still felt like absolute crap afterwards. But at least he hadn't lost his shit or puked his guts up in the bank parking lot.

Releasing the last deep breath, he ran a hand over Bailey's head where she'd laid it on his knee. Grateful for her presence, but guilty that she'd had to work harder than normal today. He usually spent his days off at home, where they both just chilled and relaxed. Maybe went for a walk through the woods behind his house or played chase-the-frisbee.

Normal, non-triggering stuff.

Alex's early morning SOS call and the subsequent shit-show at the park had pretty much screwed that plan to hell and back.

"I'm sorry, sweetheart," he crooned as he rubbed the retriever's ear, laughing softly as she groaned in ecstasy and attempted to climb into his lap. Only the front half fit. "I know, you worked your furry butt off for me today. I promise we'll relax tomorrow. Maybe I'll even take you for a swim at the lake. You'd like that, wouldn't you?"

Bailey's tail thumped furiously against his leg.

"Yeah, you know what I'm saying, don't you? You're a damn smart girl. Smarter than half the people I know." He laughed again as her tongue took several swipes at his face, making him twist his head out of the way. "Cut it out. Christ, you have dog food breath." He sputtered as another wet swipe got him right across his open mouth. "*Ugh.*"

"I hope I'm not interrupting anything...private." Alexandra's amused voice came out of the twilight.

He hadn't even heard her approach. Which should have made him jump as bad as the sap-filled log popping in the fire had. Instead, it barely caused a twitch.

As though he'd known she was there on some cellular level. Which was ridiculous.

While he tried to form a reply that sounded better than "what the hell are you doing here?" Alex came closer, stepping into the ring of light thrown by the flames.

"I, ah, knocked at the front door, but there was no answer. I could smell the fire, so I figured you might be back here and couldn't hear me." When he still didn't answer, she shifted uncomfortably. "I'm sorry, that was... I can just go." She turned.

"No. Stay."

He hadn't meant to say that. But evidently his mouth had gone rogue.

"If you're sure." Before he could withdraw the invitation, she added, "I brought sustenance." She lifted both hands. One held a six-pack of Coke, red cans glistening with the promise of icy-cold goodness. In the other was a brown paper sack with the bold red and black logo of Babe's Best BBQ.

His mouth watered at the sight.

The frozen dinner he'd nuked for himself earlier had been more about fuel than food. What was inside that grease-stained bag...*that* was gastronomic Nirvana.

And he wanted it.

He waved to the other Adirondack chair.

At least, he was pretty sure it was just the food he wanted. It couldn't possibly be to spend time with Alex. Not after today.

Ignoring the little voice calling him a liar, he scooted Bailey off his lap so he could accept a soda and one of the foil-wrapped pulled-pork sandwiches from Alex.

Careful to *not* touch her hand in the process.

Having Bailey alert on him again for that would be one humiliation too many for the day.

Nature's soundtrack filled the silence that fell between them as they dug into their food. The cicadas were a background hum with their weird rhythmic, high-pitched song, joined by a serenade of frogs. Somewhere in the woods behind where his yard ended, an owl hooted, likely out on the prowl for dinner. Another answered from farther away.

It was nice.

Especially when the angle of the chairs in the dim ring of firelight allowed him to look at Alex without being obvious about it. The golden glow highlighted the feminine line of her jaw. Limned her hair as it slid over bare shoulders every time she leaned in for a bite. Caressed her throat, stretched long and smooth as she tilted her head back for a swallow of Coke.

Watching her was both pleasure and agony.

Because he could look, but never touch.

And as peaceful as the silence was, he had a feeling it wouldn't last much longer. He'd avoided any discussion earlier at the ball field about his incipient panic attack after wrangling it into submission and returning to work. Thankfully, before Penny had finally shown up. But it looked like that reprieve was about to expire.

Why else would Alex have driven all the way over to Babe's in Pigeon Forge, then all the way back through Shelby to his side of town? Just for the pleasure of his sparkling company on a Saturday night?

Hardly.

In fact, he was amazed she even knew where he lived. He'd never invited her over. Hell, he didn't invite anyone over. Wasn't the whole point of having a house out in the boondocks total privacy?

As if she had a newsfeed straight into his brain, Alex said, "This is really nice back here, Neil. Quiet and secluded. I can see why you like living here."

She had no idea why he lived there.

Once the bubble of silence was broken, it seemed there was no going back. Alex continued to chatter on about random things, seemingly as they popped into her head. The next episode of their Hometown Heritage series. Community causes she wanted the station to get more involved with. The status of her grandfather's upcoming birthday bash, and the big surprise they'd cooked up for him in addition to the photo album.

Finally, both the food and the one-sided conversation ran out. As they sat in quiet contemplation of the flames, the breeze and fragrant smoke helped keep the bugs at bay. And as the minutes ticked by, he felt something completely unexpected.

Peace.

The firepit was where he came to unwind, to clear his head and find his balance. Isaac called it communing with nature. Neil called it escaping the four walls of his house before he went totally batshit crazy.

It felt strange sharing this personal ritual with anyone besides Bailey. Intimate, almost. Like he was baring an intensely private part of himself.

It was weird but...he kind of liked it, too. The sharing. He'd been so alone for so long he'd forgotten what simple human companionship could be like. Isaac had warned him his intense isolation wasn't healthy. Neil had been willing to take that trade-off to avoid something far worse.

He could live with being lonely.

He couldn't live with knowing he'd hurt someone close to him.

Not again.

And just like that, the peace of the evening shattered.

He dropped his hand over the side of the low-slung chair and stroked Bailey's head. He did *not* want to think about the past, damn it.

So, of course, that was exactly what Alex brought up.

"I want to apologize for what happened earlier today at the park," she said, her voice loud in the night's stillness despite her soft tone. Thankfully, she was looking into the fire rather than at him and didn't see him flinch.

"Don't." Hearing how harsh he sounded, he added, "Don't apologize for other people's actions. That's not your responsibility. You're not the boss of everyone, you know."

Alex harrumphed.

"No, but I am the boss of you, and I'm the reason you were put in that position in the first place. If I hadn't asked you to cover the game..."

"I could have said no," he reminded her. But he hadn't. He couldn't think of a single time he'd ever said no to Alex.

Even when he probably should have.

"True. But what I was actually apologizing for was my own actions. I never should have engaged with that jerk, and I definitely shouldn't have kept jumping into the argument as though you couldn't handle the situation just fine yourself." She cleared her throat, a tiny little rumble that inexplicably made his dick twitch. "I sometimes have trouble parking my Type A attitude in neutral."

He affected a shocked look. "No? You? Really?"

As hoped, that earned him a small laugh.

"Shut up." The amusement drained, though, as she said, "I'm truly, truly sorry for making you uncomfortable today. I could have, no, I *should* have handled things better. And I promise in the future I'll take my cues from you on how to proceed instead of jumping in on my own and, well, screwing things up."

It took a few long seconds of silence for him to realize she was finished.

"Okay."

"That's it?" She looked caught between surprise and annoyance. "Just...okay?"

He shrugged. "Yeah. I mean, if you feel you need to apologize for something that wasn't your fault in order to feel better about it, then...okay."

"That's not..." She blew out a frustrated breath. "Why are you being so difficult?"

"Difficult?" Would he ever understand women? "How am I being difficult?"

"Because you...you're...you just are." Looking thoroughly disgruntled, she drank down the last of her soda, refusing to look at him.

Freaking hell.

This was why being alone was better. He hated trying to figure out emotional crap. He sucked at it.

Why couldn't women be more like men? They just tossed whatever issue had crawled up their ass out there for everyone to see, dealt with it, and moved on rather than making you try to figure out what was bothering them on your own.

"Look." He cudgeled his brain for the right words. "I appreciate the apology, even though it's not necessary. You standing up to that loudmouth was a brave thing to do."

Stupid, but brave. If the muscle-bound jackass had lifted a finger in her direction, he would have ended him. "Could I have handled the situation better than you on my own? Who's to say? Differently, sure, but better...who knows. But you did just fine, too, so stop beating yourself up over it."

"But my arguing made you...upset."

And there was the crux of everything. His fucking panic attack.

"*You* didn't make me anything." He forced his clenched jaw to relax and took a drink, hoping the sweetness would settle the sudden lurch his stomach made.

The hell of it was, he really couldn't blame her for wanting to talk about it. He'd walked off and left her there, holding the bag. Literally. Yes, he'd gone back. But that didn't change the fact he'd been damn close to losing his shit right there, on the job, in front of God and country.

And Alex.

Which was the worst part.

He'd been so careful around her all these months. She knew about his PTSD issues, sure, but she'd never seen them before. Never had them shoved in her face like today. And as long as that had held true, he could at least pretend he was normal with her. Now...

Now she'd gotten a glimpse of his damage, and nothing would ever be the same between them. And until that moment, he hadn't realized how much he'd come to value the almost-normal relationship they had.

Well, fuck. He'd known it wouldn't last forever.

Nothing good ever did.

He sighed and stared into the fire the same way she had to avoid eye contact. "You didn't cause my panic attack. It was the crowd, mostly, more than the argument." Only a partial lie. The argument certainly hadn't helped.

"The way everyone was starting to close in on us, circle us, pinning us down. It was too much. Sometimes I'm okay with crowds, but sometimes it can feel like I can't catch my breath. Like if I don't get away, I'm going to be crushed to death."

"But you didn't go," Alex pointed out softly.

"Yeah, well, I couldn't just leave you there by yourself with those two chuckleheads, now, could I?" After she'd put her chin up and been prepared to throw down in his defense? No way. Not unless he'd felt himself start to seriously slide over the edge.

And even then, he'd have insisted she leave with him.

Probably.

If he'd still been able to speak.

Or think.

Before she could find some way to assume guilt for his staying, because that's what Alex did, take responsibility for *everything*, he said, "I didn't thank you before. For sticking up for Bailey the way you did. That was pretty awesome."

"I was sticking up for *you*."

The fierceness in her tone made him look from the fire toward her. Her eyes were deep, dark wells in her too-serious face.

"I know you and Bailey are a team, and I love that she makes life easier for you to deal with in ways I probably can't even comprehend. But this was about you and your right to live your life to the fullest possible, and to hell with the idiots too stupid to understand the law. You're a hero, for pity's sake. You fought to protect this country. You damn well deserve to be protected, too."

Emotions bubbled up. Gratitude swirled with darker strokes of inadequacy and shame.

He wasn't anybody's fucking hero.

If she only knew how little he'd been able to protect anyone. The people he'd let down over there, the blood on his hands... She certainly wouldn't be looking at him with such warmth and understanding.

She'd be disgusted.

And having her learn his biggest failing was a thousand times worse than having her witness his panic attack. One just exposed the damage to his psyche.

The other bared the stain on his soul.

Shifting uncomfortably in his chair, he slammed back the rest of his soda, wishing he had a chaser of Jack to back it up.

Stop being such a pussy. Gus's raspy voice in his head followed on the heels of that dangerous thought, helping stomp it out before it took hold.

As he reached for the remaining soda cans by their feet, manners ingrained by his mother at an early age kicked in. "Want another?"

Damnation.

The offer was as good as an invitation to stay. And that was the last thing he should want right now.

"No, I'm good, thanks."

"You sure? I have sun tea inside if you'd prefer. Or water."

What was he *doing*? Didn't he want her to go?

His brain said yes.

His dick, which had been semi-hard since Alex first showed up, said no.

It seemed his mouth was siding with his dick.

"Water would be good, if it's not too much trouble."

Fuck.

Well, he'd offered. Putting his unopened soda aside, he pushed to his feet and left the comforting cocoon of light thrown by the fire to tramp the well-worn path back to his kitchen door, Bailey at his side.

Lights attached to motion sensors blinked on, illuminating the patio and entire back of the house. He yanked the screen door open, all the while hyperaware of the woman sitting in his yard, invading his space. And his peace.

He needed her gone.

And he didn't want her to go.

Contrary bastard.

After filling a small glass with water—how's that for mixed signals—he turned from the sink, only to be surprised to find Alex standing right outside the screen door. As he stared, she quickly opened it and stepped inside, a sheepish expression on her face.

"Sorry to let myself in like this. But the mosquitos…" She scratched at her left arm, where the welt from a bite was already erupting on her fair skin. "I was kind of getting eaten alive out there."

Of course she was. He should have realized the blood-suckers would find Alex a much tastier treat than him.

"Let me get some lotion for it. Stop scratching." He put the glass down, then strode down the hall and grabbed the pink bottle and some cotton balls from under the bathroom sink. When he got back to the kitchen, Alex was scratching the bite again with desperate vigor.

"You're only making it worse, you know."

"I know, but it *itches*."

The small whine in her voice when he was used to her always sounding sure and in charge brought a grin to his lips. He gave the bottle a shake and saturated a cotton ball. "This will help. Give me your arm."

She complied. Her body twitched like she had ants crawling on her as he gripped her wrist and dabbed at the welt. After a few seconds, she stopped jerking and sagged against the counter with a sigh of relief.

"Better?"

Alex nodded. "Definitely better. Thanks."

Dabbing a little more of the pink stuff on, he noticed the welt seemed larger than a normal bite should. Either a monster skeeter had bitten her, or…

"Are you allergic to mosquito bites?"

"A little," she admitted. Her right hand went to her neck and gave a quick scratch. "I'm usually okay as long as I put repellant on, but, well, I didn't know we'd be outside when I came over, so I didn't." She gave another scratch. "Dam—darn it, that itches!"

"Let me see."

Taking her chin between his fingers, he tipped her head to the side to inspect her neck. Sure enough, there was another welt erupting there. While Alex held her hair back, he dabbed the cotton ball on the bite, hating that she'd suffered silently for no good reason.

"Next time, say something." Annoyed the ugly welts had marred her perfect skin, he didn't realize he'd practically growled the words until she turned her head slightly and smiled sweetly at him.

"I will." Her voice was soft and far too filled with something he didn't want to acknowledge.

Too close.

Their faces were only inches apart. He could feel the warm puff of her breath, slightly sweet and tangy from the barbeque sauce, and every bit of self-preservation he had screamed *back away!*

But he was caught, looking down into eyes that had always reminded him of the deep green of the moss-covered stones dotting the riverbank he liked to hike along. Vibrant and alive, just like she was.

As he stared, her pupils dilated, and he knew it had nothing at all to do with the dim light in the room. Her breath caught, then puffed against his skin in a rush, allowing him to breathe her in more deeply.

His gaze dipped to her mouth. It was right there.

Right. There.

All he had to do was move his head, just a little, and he could claim her mouth with his. Then he wouldn't have to wonder anymore. He could know, finally know...

Even as his head started to drop, there was a familiar nudge against his leg, dragging him back from the edge of disaster and into cold, hard reality.

Holy shit.

Had he just been about to kiss Alexandra freaking McKenna? Where the fuck was his brain?

In his pants, obviously, judging by the fact he'd gone from semi-hard to railroad spike in five seconds flat.

Swallowing hard, he stepped back. Alex didn't move, but her gaze never left his, tracking his movements like a cobra watching a mongoose.

Or maybe *he* was the cobra, he thought, taking another step back. Because suddenly he felt a little hunted.

Bailey nudged his leg before pushing against it in her herding gesture, trying to make him walk away from whatever was making him anxious, just as she had earlier at the park.

Giving in to the dog's insistent push, he walked over to drop the cotton ball in the trash. Then kept going until he'd reached to the scarred wooden table on the other side of the room. Stepping behind one of the chairs to help camouflage the erection straining at his fly, he squeezed the back of it in a crushing grip, trying to ground himself. The carved wood dug painfully into his palms.

He squeezed tighter.

Anything to keep himself from reaching for her again.

Slowly, Alex seemed to pull into herself, the bright gleam in her eyes dimming as she picked at the drying edges of pink coating her arm as she mumbled, "Thank you."

There weren't enough functioning brain cells in his head to form a reply. Even so, Alex dipped her head in a jerky nod, as though he had.

"I should go. Sorry. I...sorry." Without meeting his eyes, she turned and practically bolted toward the kitchen door.

He knew he should let her go. It was better for both of them.

But the very last glimpse of her expression as she turned had him chasing after her, beating her to the screen door just as she pushed to open it.

His body crowded up against hers, his hand covering hers on the latch. They were so close he felt as well as heard the shocked gasp she drew in. But she didn't try to push her way out or pull away.

She also didn't look at him.

Using a bent knuckle under her chin to tip her face up from where she was staring far too intently at their stacked hands, he saw again what sent him on his intercept course.

Humiliation.

Damn it to hell. He'd done that to her.

"You really have to stop apologizing for things that aren't your fault." He gave in to the urge to run his thumb over the contours of the stubborn little chin he'd spent the last year admiring.

Her eyes widened in surprise. From the words or the touch, he couldn't be sure.

Maybe both.

"But I...we...you..."

"Almost kissed, yeah." He swallowed a groan as Alex's tongue darted out to moisten her lips. "But it's a bad idea," he told her.

Or maybe he was telling himself. Because suddenly he couldn't remember why he was so hellbent on denying himself a taste of those pretty pink lips.

"Oh." Her gaze darted from his eyes to his mouth and back again, as though she were wondering the same thing. When her teeth tugged at her lower lip, his erection jerked against his zipper in a painful surge.

Damn, the woman really was trying to kill him.

He moved his thumb up to rest over her lips to stop the erotic action. "You have no idea what that's doing to me," he rasped.

The gleam in her eyes had him reevaluating that statement.

"Minx." He moved his thumb in a soft caress over the petal-soft lips before cradling her jaw gently with his palm. "This really is a bad idea. You know that, right?"

"Do you want to kiss me?" Her voice was even huskier than usual.

This time, he did groan.

"Fuck yeah, I do."

"Then I think *not* doing this is the bad idea."

He wanted it. She wanted it.

So why the hell was he denying both of them what they both craved?

Like a man who couldn't swim gleefully jumping into the ocean knowing it was most likely going to kill him, but willing to drown for the pleasure of the experience, he brought his head down those last few inches and met her eager mouth with his.

Chapter 5

Alex wasn't entirely certain what had happened.

In the last five minutes, she'd fled from a swarm of vampire mosquitoes, been oddly turned on by Neil's ministrations with the Calamine lotion, been almost kissed, been mortified because of how *much* she wanted to be kissed, and tried to run away like a cowardly bunny when she realized how much Neil *didn't* want to kiss *her*.

Except, now he *was* kissing her, and it was...incredible.

His mouth was nothing more than a tentative press for a few brief seconds. But the pressure quickly increased until she willingly parted her lips for him. She groaned as his tongue swept in to caress hers. Then groaned again when he retreated.

No. No way was he getting away so soon.

Determined to hang onto this moment, she laced her hands behind Neil's neck to anchor him to her, ignoring the pain that shot up her arm when she banged her elbow on the doorframe. A small price to pay for more of his kisses.

She gave a happy hum when he complied, nibbling at her lower lip before taking her mouth with his again. The soft scrape of his evening stubble only added to the erotic intensity of it all.

As enjoyable as the kissing was, though—and she could feel just how enjoyable Neil thought it was—they both eventually had to come up for air.

Not that he stopped. Neil continued to kiss the corners of her mouth, then her cheek. And was about to move down to her neck when he stopped and reversed himself, bringing his lips to her cheek and stopping there to rest, his breath short, heavy pants against her skin.

She wanted to ask why he'd stopped, then remembered what had started all of this in the first place.

Dang it. Nothing ruined a sexy moment like being coated in pink crap.

"So, still think it's a bad idea?" She was panting a bit herself, but was determined to get this straightened out between them before things either went any further, or they ended entirely. Encouraging Neil to kiss her had been a gigantic leap of faith for her. If she'd made a mistake, she needed to know that before she humiliated herself any further.

"Probably." But the gentle butterfly kisses he laid along her cheekbone and jaw said he didn't care.

"Do you think we should stop?" Her breath caught when he nipped her earlobe lightly.

"Definitely." More kisses, teasing the corners of her mouth, her chin.

"Are we going to?"

"God, I hope not."

She laughed as the bubble of tension in her chest eased. It didn't disappear entirely, but for now, she was certain Neil was as in the moment as she was. Tomorrow...well, she'd worry about whether or not he had a change of heart then.

Right now, she wanted to enjoy every second of what she had been dreaming about in secret for months.

Her fingers ran lightly over his rough cheek, enjoying the freedom of finally being able to touch him. There was a small patch of scars there, like pale threads that flared out in a tiny starburst. She'd often wondered about them, but never felt she could ask. And she certainly wasn't going to now.

She wasn't stupid.

She did lay a gentle kiss on them, though. Her unspoken vow that she honored him for his pain and sacrifice, however he'd come by them.

He went still at the touch.

For several long heartbeats, she thought she'd ruined everything.

Not giving him the chance to pull away, she took his mouth, using her admittedly rusty skills to take his mind off what she'd done and shift it to what she was doing.

From the groan that rumbled in his chest, he approved.

Kissing had never been something she enjoyed a whole lot in the past.

In high school with her boyfriend, it had been awkward and a little bit sloppy.

In college, it had always seemed more of an afterthought, like a fee guys grudgingly paid in order to get to the main event.

And in all the years since, the only man she'd ever really enjoyed kissing had been the one who'd turned around and dumped her. Because he felt she was in a more committed relationship with her job than she could ever be with him.

Talk about irony.

But kissing Neil was an experience she'd never had before. It was all about lips and fingertips. Nothing else was involved. Even though his body pressed against hers, he wasn't grinding against her with the very impressive erection nudging her hip. Wasn't grabbing or groping anything, trying to stick his tongue in her ear or down her throat.

His lips were by turns firm and gentle, asking and taking, exploring and then still while he let her explore him back. Fingers stroked and caressed cheeks, eyelids, throats, and nothing more.

It was more sensual than the best sex she'd ever had.

She didn't know whether to beg for mercy or beg him not to stop when he finally broke away from her mouth for the last time. His lips were a little swollen, and an odd sense of pride—and possessiveness—slid through her at the sight.

She'd done that. Rusty skill set and all.

There were so many things that could have been said at that moment, but "Wow" was about the best she could manage. She might have felt awkward about it, but Neil didn't seem to have any better control over his vocabulary at the moment.

At least they were both equally wrecked by the experience.

After catching her breath, she leaned her head back against the doorjamb and smiled up at him. "That was...truly something."

"That was a lot more than just something." Neil placed a hand on the wall beside her head and leaned in a little closer, his expression serious. "You realize that, don't you?"

The fact he recognized how unique their connection was meant a lot. Probably more than he could possibly understand.

Raising a hand to his cheek, she asked, "Do you think we can do it again? Soon?"

Those delicious lips of his turned up in a smile.

The expression looked good on him. She made a mental note to do everything in her power to make certain Neil smiled more. A lot more. For various, and possibly even naughty, reasons.

It was a goal she looked forward to pursuing.

"I think," he said, pressing his cheek into her hand like a cat looking to be stroked, "that we'd be crazy not to." A soft whine from behind him changed the smile from satisfied to rueful. "But Bailey's right. It's getting late. You should probably be heading home. The roads around here can be dangerous in the dark if you don't know them."

It might have sounded like an excuse to get rid of her if she hadn't seen the reluctance and honest concern in his soft blue eyes.

"She said all that, did she?" She peeked around Neil's shoulder to where the golden retriever was lying on the wide-planked hardwood floor, her muzzle on her front paws as she paid unwavering attention to her human. "Pretty mouthy for a dog."

Neil chuckled, and she ate the sound up.

"I know this wasn't why you drove out here tonight, but I'm really glad you did." His gaze dipped back to her mouth. "*Really* glad."

She couldn't stop herself from moistening her lips as he watched. "Me, too." Before she could think about it too much, she added, "Would you like to come out to my place tomorrow? I could make us some lunch, something we could take down to the lake so Bailey can get the swim you promised her."

With how affectionately he'd been speaking to the dog when she first showed up, she wanted to show she understood the special bond they had. Even if it meant getting wet dog smell in her house.

"Uhm..."

Shoot. He was going to say no.

And once he did, he'd never change his mind.

Not giving him the chance, she said quickly, "Just think about it. I'll text you my address, so you have it. If you want to come by, come. If not, that's okay, too. It's just lunch." It was pushing her luck, but leaned up anyway to brush her lips against his. "I don't bite." She gave a teasing tug to his lower lip with her teeth. "Much."

The hiss that escaped him was quickly followed by another whine from Bailey.

Knowing when to retreat, she gave the dog a quick look of frustration before taking a step away from Neil and putting some much-needed distance between them. Clearly, she and Bailey were going to have some territorial issues to work out.

But for tonight, she'd leave well enough alone.

"So...let me know." She picked up her purse from where it had fallen to the floor at some point during their kiss. She hadn't even known she dropped it.

"I like fried chicken."

The abrupt announcement caught her off-guard. Then she realized what it meant.

A slow smile spread over her face. "I make great fried chicken."

Neil's head bobbed. "Well, okay then."

"Okay then. Make sure you come hungry."

Neil's eyes turned molten. "Count on it."

Count on it.

A day later, Neil's parting words still sent a shiver of anticipation zinging along her spine every time she thought about them.

There had been so much dark promise in not only his tone, but his eyes as well. The focus of a hunter locking onto his prey. And sweet baby Jesus, she wouldn't mind being eaten up by that man one least little bit.

Fanning herself with the paper plates she'd been about to add to the picnic hamper, she told herself to stop reading too much into it. They'd both been primed by their little kitchen necking session.

Well, she'd been primed.

Neil had been fully cocked and loaded, judging by the bulge in his jeans.

It was way too easy to let something like superheated hormones color what was said. To misconstrue an innocent comment as a declaration of intent. Which was why she'd made a whole lot of extra chicken for their picnic lunch.

Just in case she'd misunderstood his response.

And why she'd put on one of her favorite panty and bra sets when she'd gotten dressed. The one with the deep red roses on slick black silk.

Just in case she hadn't.

"This is crazy," she groaned, giving herself one last fan before dropping the plates into the hamper. Two days ago, she'd been reminding herself of all the reasons getting involved with this man was a horrible idea. This morning, she was wondering if the box of condom under the bathroom sink was expired or not.

Once again, Neil Crawford had managed to short-circuit her better judgment.

The difference was, this time she was guilty of being an active participant in her own downfall. *She'd* been the one to go to Neil's home last night. *She'd* been the one to follow him inside. Yes, she'd gone in to avoid being devoured by ravenous mosquitos. But the truth was, she would have followed Neil under any pretense, just to keep him from retreating from her the way he had.

And it had been a retreat.

For some reason, he had a problem with her calling him a hero. She didn't know why she'd chosen to use that particular term. To be honest, she knew nothing about his time in the military. It didn't really matter, though.

As far as she was concerned, anyone who donned a uniform and put their life on the line for others was a hero, be it military, fire, or police.

Folding the large red and black plaid blanket she used when out by the lake behind her house, she tried to shake off the doubts that started creeping back in. Okay, yes, she'd followed Neil inside. But he'd been the one to kiss her first.

Hadn't he?

It was all a bit of a hazy, sex-fogged blur. But even if he hadn't kissed her first, he'd definitely kissed her back.

Man, oh man, had he kissed her back!

Fanning herself wouldn't be nearly enough to combat the heat that flashed through her at the memory. Nope, this called for the big guns.

She went and stood in front of the open fridge.

Either she needed to stop thinking about Neil, or she needed to figure out how to control her reaction to him. Otherwise, she just might burst into flames before she ever got a second shot at seeing if his kisses actually lived up to her memories. And if they did...

"I *really* need to check on that expiration date."

After making sure she had everything packed that could be, she was left with nothing to do but wait. And worry.

Because Neil changing his mind about coming was still a real possibility.

One she wasn't sure how she'd deal with.

When she'd checked the hamper for the third time, she forced herself to go out to the screened-in porch to wait. Obsessively checking and rechecking things was one of her more annoying habits, even to herself. One she blamed on the chaos surrounding their first family trip to Disney, when her mother forgot to pack her favorite stuffed animal.

Maybe accidentally on purpose.

Her mother had been trying to dispose of Mister Fluffy for a while at that point. The bedraggled bunny had been her sleeping companion since she was two. At the ripe old age of five, he'd been looking pretty well used up.

She'd spent a miserable week crying herself to sleep and resenting her parents for not going home immediately to retrieve her bunny.

And had forever after been zealous about not forgetting anything ever again.

Of course, wanting to ensure her grandfather had zero reasons to be disappointed in her might have more to do with her perfectionist nature than a forgotten childhood stuffy. Knowing her every move, her every decision was being watched and judged had made her the teensiest bit neurotic these past few years.

Dionne might well poke fun at her over it, but Alex had seen what happened when someone disappointed Colin McKenna.

It wasn't pretty.

Colin wasn't a big believer in second chances. If she couldn't measure up to his expectations...

Thankfully, the crunch of a car coming up the gravel driveway drew her back from that sucking whirlpool of what-ifs. She jumped to her feet, running her hands down the summer-weight jeans she wore.

Then sat down again, not wanting to appear too eager.

Stop overthinking it.

She leaned back and crossed her legs, hoping to look cool and unaffected, but her foot wouldn't stop bouncing like a runaway yo-yo. She stood back up as Neil's SUV came to a halt beside her little Rav4, dwarfing it.

Another time, another man, she might have thought something snarky about the need to overcompensate. But she now possessed firsthand knowledge of how much that *wasn't* the case. Neil had more than enough to be proud of.

Quite a bit more.

Swallowing against a suddenly dry mouth, she met him at the screen door, holding it open as he and Bailey came through. "Hi."

"Hi."

They stood there like two awkward teenagers on their first date, neither one knowing what to do next.

"I, ah, just have to throw the food in the hamper, then we can head on down to the lake."

"Sure."

"You can come on in if you want."

"Okay."

Dying a little more inside with every step, she left him to follow or not as she went in and headed for the kitchen. Where had the chemistry from the previous night gone? The easy banter? Was Neil regretting kissing her? Had he only come because he'd said he would, and couldn't think of a polite way of backing out?

Was she ever going to learn?

This was such a huge mistake.

Fine, then. If he didn't want to be here, she would just treat this like a business lunch. They could talk about the digital album he was working on, ignore what had happened last night, and she'd send him on his way before he ever realized just how stupid she felt.

She snapped the lid of the hamper shut and turned, only to find her mouth suddenly involved in a kiss she felt all the way down to her pink-polished toes. With a groan, she held on to the man who evidently walked like a ninja since she hadn't heard him come up behind her, returning the kiss with every relieved ounce of passion she had.

Finally releasing her mouth—with obvious reluctance—Neil touched his forehead to hers as he sucked in a breath. "Hi."

"Hi."

"I thought maybe we needed to get that out of the way."

"Excellent thought."

"So, we good now?"

"Oh, we're way past good." Now that the universe had realigned itself.

She had to stop being so quick to believe Neil would change his mind at every turn. It wasn't fair to keep painting him with the brush of other people's flaws.

He eyed the hamper on the granite-topped island behind her with interest. "Food all ready to go?"

"Yup. I just need to get the drinks." She paused in opening the fridge to watch his biceps flex as he lifted the hamper.

Yum.

Grateful for the blast of cold air, she transferred a mix of Cokes and waters to the small cooler on the counter. Her hand reached for the bottle of wine chilling on the top shelf, then hesitated. After a few seconds of dithering, she left it where it was.

For now.

They could always have it later, if things went the way she hoped.

The grassy backyard was wide and open before sloping gently down toward the lake. There was a boathouse and small dock to the right, next to a crescent of sandy beach. She stopped walking right before the grass ended and the sand began, and sighed.

Darn it. The weather wasn't cooperating. Normally, the sunlight bouncing off the water made it sparkle like a million little twinkle lights at a high school prom. Today, though, rafts of clouds were playing peek-a-boo with the sun. It was still pretty, but she'd wanted to show off her little slice of paradise at its best.

Neil, however, didn't seem to care about the clouds. He stood looking out at the lake for a long moment, his face tipped up into the light breeze blowing off the water. He closed his eyes and drew in a deep breath.

"Nice," he said as he sighed the breath back out again.

He turned to help spread the blanket, and she smiled. From anyone else, the single word would have seemed an underwhelming observation. But in Neil-speak, it had been high praise. It wasn't just his words that mattered. You needed to watch his whole body to get the entire conversation.

After a year, she was finally starting to crack the code.

She slid off her sandals and knelt on the blanket, where she set to work unloading the hamper. "It is nice. I've loved this place since I was a kid. Colin built it for my grandmother as a vacation home," she said when he looked confused. "Not that *he* ever took a real vacation. But the rest of the family would come here as often as we could every summer. My grandmother absolutely adored the water. Well, looking at it, anyway. Getting wet was another matter entirely."

Her lips twitched at the memory of her normally easy-going nana screeching like a banshee when she'd gotten caught in the crossfire of a water fight between her, her brother Lyle, and their cousin Richard when they were kids. They'd been using their sand pails, too, not some piddly little squirt guns.

Nana was *not* amused.

"I don't think I ever met her." Neil hesitated, then toed off his sneakers and joined her on the blanket while Bailey settled on the grass nearby. It was large enough for them, the hamper, cooler, and all the food with room to spare. But he sat so close their legs were practically touching.

Not that she was complaining.

"She died about seven years ago." And was missed every single day. Her grandmother had been the heart of the family, the one who kept them tightly bound together. Since her death, they'd all sort of just...unraveled.

"I'm sorry."

She flashed him a quick smile to show it was fine. "After she was gone, it wasn't the same here. That year, when Colin had the place closed up for winter, he just never opened it up again."

"Did she pass while she was here?"

She nodded. "One night in her sleep. She wasn't alone, though. My uncle and his family were here that weekend."

"But your grandfather wasn't."

"No, which wasn't unusual. He hardly ever made time to come to the lake. There was always something he had to take care of at the network that was more important." It took a few seconds for the import of that to sink in. "Wait. You think he left the place to rot not just because she died here, but because he felt guilty he wasn't here when she passed?"

Neil shrugged.

"Huh." She hadn't considered that. Colin had never shown a shred of remorse for anything he'd done in his life. "He didn't have anything to feel guilty about, though. The doctors said it wouldn't have mattered if someone was right there with her when it happened. There was nothing he could have done."

"Yeah, nice if guilt worked that way," Neil muttered. So low she probably wasn't supposed to hear him.

But she did. And it sounded like he was speaking from experience.

It was tough, but she suppressed her rabid sense of curiosity and didn't ask.

Neil stared off at the lake for a long second before he reached for the container of fried chicken. "So, how did you end up with the place?"

She passed him a plate and napkin. "I wanted to move out of my apartment, and it was just sitting here, slowly deteriorating. So, I asked Colin about buying it. At first, he said no."

More like hell no. And more than once.

"Obviously, he changed his mind."

"Eventually." After some begging, hard negotiating, and a lot of promises she wouldn't let herself be distracted from work by the lure of having a "party house." As if she'd ever shirk her responsibilities to the network for *any* reason, much less that one.

A party animal she wasn't.

More like a hyper-diligent worker bee.

"It doesn't bother you? Living in the house where your grandmother died?"

"No." She shrugged. "I don't know, maybe it should. But honestly, I look at it the other way. I like living in the place she loved so much, and where I have so many wonderful memories of her. I guess it kind of makes me feel closer to her somehow."

"It's a lot of house for one person."

"Yeah, but I'm not home much during the week, so I barely notice." It was the weekends when things got a little lonely. Which was why she usually put in at least a few hours at the network despite there being a weekend producer on duty.

Her cousin Richard might have the McKenna name, but he lacked the McKenna news gene. Her looking over his shoulder had become part of their routine.

"Besides, I like having the room so everyone can come enjoy the lake whenever they want to. In fact, Lyle and Brax are staying with me when they come down from Nashville for Colin's birthday party."

"I know Lyle's your brother. And Brax is…?"

"Braxton Payne. Lyle's husband." A familiar wave of defensive anger flashed through her at Neil's silence. Times and attitudes were changing, but this was the bible belt, and some people were still a few decades behind in their views on gay marriage. If Neil was one of those people, she was going to be horribly disappointed.

Her chin inched up a notch. "Do you have a problem with that?"

"Put your claws away, momma bear." He grinned as he laid his hand on the fist she hadn't realized she'd made and patted it gently. "No, I don't have a problem with it. Your brother has the right to live whatever life makes him happiest."

"Yes, he does." Feeling foolish about preparing for a fight that wasn't going to happen, she deflated a little. "Sorry. I didn't mean to get all defensive about it, but…"

"But he's your brother, and you'd defend him to the ends of the earth. I get it. I'm the same way about my sister."

"You have a sister?" She latched onto that bit of personal information like a magnet.

"Mmhmm." He lifted her hand to his mouth and pressed a soft kiss to the knuckles. "Have I mentioned how sexy it is when you put that stubborn little chin of yours up when you're getting ready for a fight?"

A soft, squishy feeling raced through her at the strangely old-fashioned gesture. "I don't have a stubborn chin."

"Stubborn," Neil insisted, kissing her hand again. "And brave." Another kiss. "Always ready to take on everyone else's dragons." This time he ran his tongue lightly between her knuckles, sending a shudder through her. Their eyes met and held for what seemed like forever before he finally placed one last gentle kiss and relinquished her hand.

A bit jittery inside, she cupped her still tingling hand to her chest with the other. "Wow. You're good." She caught a flash of pleased satisfaction in his eyes.

After they'd finished eating and packed away the last of the food containers, Neil reached into the small backpack he'd brought and pulled out a dingy yellow tennis ball that had clearly seen a lot of use.

It was like a switch had been thrown.

Bailey, who'd been dozing on the grass off the side of the blanket nearest to Neil, popped to her feet, wide awake. She raced around the open yard, doing a few donuts as she chased the rush of scents coming at her on the breeze.

Alex laughed at her antics. "I've never seen her do that before."

"She knows when her ball comes out it's playtime." He juggled it from hand to hand as Bailey did the zoomies.

"Yeah?" That sounded to her like it might be petting time, too. She looked the question at Neil to be sure, though. When he nodded, she clapped her hands and called, "Bailey, come here, girl!"

Like a golden bullet, the dog streaked across the lawn and nearly landed in her lap. Laughing, she scratched and petted Bailey's sun-warmed fur, cooing silly words of admiration and praise to the squirming dog.

What was it about dogs that turned grown adults into baby-talkers?

Bailey reveled in the attention, bathing Alex's face with a wet, happy kisses. After only a few minutes, though, she abandoned her butt-scratch to sit expectantly at Neil's feet, tongue lolling and eyes bright.

Clearly, that ball trumped everything, even skritches.

Still juggling the ball hand-to-hand, Neil walked toward the water, Bailey dancing and weaving around him as she worked herself into a frenzy of anticipation. Alex stayed put, content to watch from the blanket.

If she'd had her eyes on the dog instead of the man, she probably would have missed it. The brief hesitation in his step before he transitioned from the grass to the sand. Such a small thing, but there was one possible reason for it that could be a big issue, one she hadn't considered when picking their picnic location.

Dang it.

She got up and went after him, trying not to seem like she was hurrying.

Neil stopped at the water's edge and cocked his arm back. Bailey froze, her eyes locked on the ball. The second it left his hand, she gave a bark of delight and chased it, bounding into the lake with a splash.

Alex couldn't help but laugh at the dog's obvious pleasure. "She loves the water, doesn't she?"

"Retrievers were bred to be water dogs, so she's in her element." He accepted the soggy ball from Bailey on her return, drew his arm back, faked a throw, then let it go, sending it even further out into the lake than the first time. "I should take her for swims more often than I do, but she'd got so much fur it can take hours to get her clean and dry afterwards."

She wrinkled her nose. "Wet dog smell. Yummy." She kept her eyes on Bailey, who was paddling back to shore with her prize, as she asked, "Does the beach bother you? The sand, I mean?"

"Not really." This time when he accepted the ball, he offered it to Alex to throw.

She did, but she didn't need the disappointed look Bailey gave her to know it was an underwhelming effort. "That was a little weak."

"It was a decent throw," Neil said diplomatically.

"It sucked, even the dog knows it. But I was referring to your deflection from my question." Just like he'd done after mentioning he had a sister by kissing her hand.

A disappointing realization.

"If you don't want to talk about something, all you have to do is say so. I understand personal boundaries." And would much prefer a straightforward "none of your business" to evasion or manipulation.

He said nothing for a long moment as Bailey slogged out of the lake, water streaming from her fur. The dog didn't even glance her way before dropping the ball at Neil's feet.

Alex exchanged a rueful look with him at the unsubtle snub.

This time Neil lobbed the ball in a high arc, keeping Bailey guessing where it was going to land. As soon as it splashed down, she was after it like a shot.

"It was over two years after I got back before I could walk on sand without breaking into a cold sweat." The words were so soft she had to strain to hear them. "It still bothers me sometimes, but the water helps. It keeps it from being too much like...over there." He gave a thin smile. "Not a lot of lakes over in the desert."

Unsure if she should, she laid a hand on his arm. He only flinched a little. "You don't have to tell me. That wasn't why I asked."

Was it?

"Yeah, I do." He stared down at the wet sand beneath his bare feet almost angrily before his gaze shifted to her and softened. "I want to. I want you to understand there are things...*wrong* with me. Things I can't always control. Things I'm sometimes not even aware of. Bailey helps. Therapy helps. But...I'm broken, Alexandra. In ways I don't think will ever really heal."

Those words, spoken with such an undercurrent of self-loathing, made her stomach clench. No one should ever feel that way about themselves. For any reason. And especially not the ones Neil had given.

"There's nothing wrong with you," she said with a fierce scowl. "Yes, I know, you have post-traumatic stress. There are things that trigger you, that will maybe always bother you. But it doesn't define who you are. It doesn't make you broken, or any less worthy of having a good life or being loved than everyone else. I won't let anybody ever say that about you, so I don't want to hear you say it about yourself, either. Got that?"

It was the surprise on Neil's face that made her realize she might have started out speaking, but she'd ended on something a little more forceful.

His lips pressed together in a firm line. She couldn't tell if he was trying to keep from saying something, or from laughing at her.

"Always with the dragons," he said finally with a small huff of air that might have been a laugh. When she angled her head up defiantly at the sound, he tapped his finger on her chin. "I warned you about that. Can't say I didn't."

And with that, he took her mouth with his in a hungry kiss, muffling any protest she'd been about to launch at him.

It took all of two seconds for her to melt into the kiss. Which turned into an embrace.

Which might have turned into more if Bailey, evidently tired of being ignored, hadn't chosen that moment to jump on them, sending them both crashing into the water.

Chapter 6

Damn sand got *every* damned place.

Even after a quick rinse in the outdoor shower and a more thorough one in one of the guest bathrooms, a few irritating grains were hiding in places they didn't belong. Pulling on a pair of sweatpants that belonged to Alex's brother, Neil could only be glad it was regular sand, and not the stuff they'd nicknamed "moon dust" that had been the bane of every soldier's life over in Afghanistan.

So finely grained, moon dust had stuck to everything—tents, vehicles, people—staining clothes and sucking every drop of moisture from your skin in a place where you had little to spare in the first place. Equipment stopped working, vehicles broke down, and not a damn thing you did could get rid of the stuff. Some of the guys in his unit started calling it Satan's baby powder.

So, strange as it was, he could sort of appreciate the discomfort of a regular sand wedgie.

The sweats were a little short and snug, but the t-shirt was so tight it might pop a seam if he moved the wrong way. Evidently Lyle was a lot leaner than he was.

Still, the only other option while his own clothes were in the dryer was to go shirtless. And with Alex in the same house, that didn't seem like a smart idea.

Hell, *nothing* with Alex was a smart idea.

And yet, he kept on kissing her. Every time he told himself it was a stupid, stupid idea to allow whatever this was between them to continue, he found himself going back for another taste of that amazing mouth.

He had to be crazy. It was the only explanation.

Why else would he risk the as close to normal as he could get life he'd built here by sucking face with the boss's granddaughter?

Maybe because, for the first time since he'd gotten his head sort-of screwed on straight and started dealing with his PTS instead of self-medicating it with booze, he found himself wanting something more than just close to normal.

He wanted…well, he wanted his life back.

To experience the satiny skin of a woman again. Breathe in her uniquely female scent and feel her soft hands all over his hard body. He wanted to lose himself in the ecstasy of making wild, passionate love. Watch her eyes dilate in passion and then go soft with climax, to feel his body explode with hers around it, deep inside.

He wanted all of those things.

And God help him, he wanted them with Alex.

He didn't understand it. There were other women he could have gone after. There were a few who'd shown interest since he moved to Shelby, despite the fact he tried his best to fly under everybody's radar.

The problem was, he hadn't felt any interest back. Not a twinge. Not the slightest stirring. To be honest, he'd begun to worry that all the anti-depressants and anti-anxiety meds the VA had pumped him full of when he went into treatment had somehow chemically castrated him.

The first time he'd seen Alexandra McKenna bending over the bottom drawer of her filing cabinet had proven that wasn't the case.

Thank God.

But it had left him fighting what was turning out to be a losing battle between his body and his brain. His body wanted all of that long-legged goodness wrapped around it. His brain knew it would be career suicide.

Not to mention the fact he was absolutely terrified that if he were to let it happen, if he let her get close, he might end up totally losing it in front of her someday.

Oh, she'd seen yesterday's mini panic attack and not been turned off by it—a miracle in itself. But she'd never seen the real deal, complete with shakes, choking, and the absolute certainty he was about to die.

Worse, what if she was with him when he had a flashback?

The panic attacks might turn him into a sweaty, hyperventilating idiot, but the flashbacks were something altogether different.

No, the smart thing to do was thank her for a nice day at the lake, get in his truck, and drive the hell home where he belonged. Alone. Just him, his dog, and his ghosts.

With that plan firmly in his mind, he went in search of Alex. He found her in the great room. There really wasn't any other word for it, with its soaring ceilings and timbered roof with beams that looked like they'd been hand hewn a hundred years ago. The house wasn't that old, so Colin must have brought them in from some old farmhouse somewhere.

Or hell, maybe a castle, by the size of them.

Alex was just closing the screen over the fireplace, where flames were beginning to lick at the logs set there. Made entirely of river stone, it soared all the way to the ceiling. Colin might have built the place for his wife, but he'd definitely put his own stamp on its bones.

Dusting her hands off, Alex turned and smiled when she saw him standing there.

"I thought I'd get a fire going to help Bailey dry out."

He held back a wince. Rinsing the dog off in the outdoor shower had been a hell of a lot easier than wrangling her into the bathtub like he usually had to. Afterward, he'd dried her as best he could with the old beach towel Alex provided. But he knew from experience she'd still be leaving little wet spots everywhere she walked or sat for some time.

Yet one more reason to leave.

Alex continued before he could say anything. "I also grabbed a couple of hair dryers from the bathrooms, but I wasn't sure if she'd freak out about that or not. I know dogs sometimes react badly to loud noises."

Not just dogs.

He pushed the grim thought aside. "You didn't have to go to all this trouble."

"It's no trouble at all. So, which will it be, dryers or fireplace?"

Say neither, dumbass.

But she looked so adorably expectant he didn't have the heart to turn her down. Or maybe it was the balls. Either way, he gestured at the hair dryers on the sofa. "I use one on her all the time, so it won't bother her."

It was a mistake to prolong his stay, but he could suck it up for a little while longer. They were going to be drying the dog. Nothing could be less sexually charged than that.

Boy, was he wrong.

He hadn't counted on the number of times their fingers would tangle as they ran them through Bailey's thick fur under the warm air.

Or how close they'd be as they knelt on the floor together.

Or how strongly the sight of Alex's bare neck would affect him.

She'd pulled her freshly washed hair up into a damp ponytail, something she never did at work. And as ridiculous as it seemed, that stretch of vulnerable skin usually hidden from everyone's view struck him as outrageously erotic.

He was so screwed.

By the time Bailey's double coat was reasonably dry, Neil was uncomfortably aware he wasn't wearing briefs under the borrowed sweats. His erection pressed freely against the snug-fitting material, something that would be impossible for Alex to miss when he stood up.

If he could stand.

"I think that's as good as we're going to get with these," Alex said as she sat back on her heels with a sigh. "The fire should take care of the rest." She seemed to take Neil's lack of response as agreement, because she got up and tried to coax Bailey over to the fireplace.

After waiting for the release signal, which he reluctantly gave, the dog followed and collapsed in a graceless heap on the woven hearth rug with a loud groan of contentment.

With Alex's attention elsewhere, he used the opportunity to get up.

But not fast enough. As she turned back, grinning at the dog's theatrics, it took only a second for her to notice his condition. Her smile kind of froze as her eyes did a quick trip down, away, then down again.

And stayed down.

It seemed silly to try and hide it at that point. Still, he turned away and walked to the sofa, winding the hair dryer's cord around its handle while wishing a hole would open in the floor for him to fall into.

"Um, thanks for helping with Bailey, but we should probably get going. You invited us for lunch, and we've already wasted half your day."

"There wasn't any time limit on the invitation." Alex hesitated. "Unless you want to leave."

"I probably should."

He wasn't sure if he meant he probably should go, or should *want* to go.

Because he really didn't.

"But you don't have to." Smart woman that she was, when she closed the distance between them, she didn't come up directly behind him where he couldn't see her.

She put a hand on his arm. "I thought we got all of the shouldn'ts and can'ts straightened out last night. And," she added, her tone and expression turning smug, "unless you've got some seriously deviant kink on for your dog, although I did catch you two getting pretty cuddly at your place yesterday so who knows, I'm pretty sure that hard-on you're sporting is for me. So, I don't see what the problem is making a decision here."

He didn't know whether to laugh at her outrageous comments or groan in embarrassment. He chose to do neither.

Instead, he turned and took her sassy mouth with his, drawing a deep moan of satisfaction from her. She wrapped her arms around him, pulling herself up tight against his body.

His body was totally on board with that. Nudging into the v of her thighs as though he belonged there, his erection gave a hard pulse as it pressed in against the soft give of the sweat shorts she'd donned.

Gasping at the sensation, Alex pulled back from the kiss far enough to look at him without either of them going cross-eyed. "No more arguments. You're staying."

No, no more arguments.

Not even with himself.

Now that he had Alex's soft body tucked up tight against his, he'd be the biggest kind of fool to stop what was happening. Later he might remember all the reasons this was such a bad idea, but for now, logic had been replaced by sheer, molten need.

Turning them both, he pulled her down with him onto the nearest sofa, thankfully roomy enough to lie out on without the risk of falling off if either of them moved.

Which was good, because he planned to be doing a lot of moving very soon.

First, though, he took his time exploring, starting with the mouth that had haunted him since last night. It was just as sweet as he remembered. But this time...this time it wasn't only mouths and fingertips involved in the kiss.

No, this time his hand swept slowly down Alex's side until he cupped her hip and pulled their bodies together again. As he rocked his hips in a torturously slow rhythm, the heat of her seared against his erection through the fabric between them. How much better would it feel when he was finally inside her?

His imagination went wild with the possibilities.

A warning throb in his balls left him no choice but to back off from his teasing. The last thing he wanted was for this to end too soon.

It had taken them a year to get here. A year of dancing around each other, and around themselves and their own issues, to finally both work up the nerve to give in to their desires. He wanted everything about this to be perfect.

Sliding his hand from her hip to her ass, he gave the firm cheek a gentle squeeze before sending his journey of discovery back up her body. Gliding along her ribs, up under the faded baby-blue tee that barely covered her bellybutton.

She trembled a little at the touch.

Then he was the one trembling when he realized she didn't have a bra on under the tee and his thumb was nestled against the soft side of her bare breast. He moved it once, twice, stroking against the sensitive skin. Luring them both further down this path of insanity toward the point of no return.

Alex groaned into his mouth when he finally spread his fingers over the firm little globe he'd discovered, the point of her nipple hard against his palm. She groaned again when he gently kneaded, his palm rasping over the sensitive tip again and again.

Finally, he couldn't take any more.

He had to see her.

Pushing back, he grasped the bottom hem of the tee and tugged it up. Alex readily helped, raising her arms so he could strip the shirt over her head and off. He dropped it to the floor and just...looked.

The picture she made, splayed out below him like an offering, her mouth kiss-swollen and her hard-tipped breasts just begging for more attention, was almost too much. He touched one finger to the rosy nipple nearest him, drawing tiny circles as her breath stuttered in and out in uneven pants.

"They're small," she said, then gasped when he gently pinched her nipple between his fingers.

"They're perfect. Whoever said anything else was a jackass."

Knowing she was about to argue, because that's what Alex did, about *everything*, he forestalled her protest by replacing his hand with his mouth. He worshipped at first one breast, then the other, showing her exactly how perfect he did indeed find them. By the time he eased off, she was writhing so hard she practically bucked him off the sofa.

"Perfect," he said again with quiet deliberation. Daring her to disagree.

"Gah," was the best she got out.

That brought an arrogant grin to his face. Being able to reduce the always loquacious Alexandra McKenna to a wordless state was a rare triumph.

The smile was probably a mistake.

Because the next thing he knew, Alex sent her questing fingers straight down past the waistband of his sweats and wrapped them around his painfully hard erection. The unexpected sensation of her hand combined with the exquisitely gentle caress she gave him was almost enough to make him blow.

Only sheer will and dumb luck kept it from happening.

"Fair is fair," she taunted when he caught her wrist in a restraining grip.

"Sweetheart, if you touch me like that, I'm going to come in my pants like a horny teenager dry humping his prom date."

Instead of being put off, she had the nerve to look intrigued by the idea.

He half-groaned, half-laughed. "Freaking Christ on a crutch, woman. Are you *trying* to be the death of me?"

"I'm *trying* to make you feel good." She wiggled her fingers, earning a tortured gasp from him. "Let me." Her tone was sweet and cajoling, but with an undertone of steel-willed command. Typical Alex.

Well, he was going to hell for today anyhow. Why not enjoy the ride?

Aiding and abetting his own downfall, he released her wrist.

The sunny smile she gave him was completely at odds with the wicked things her nimble little fingers were doing down below. Her thumb ran over the sensitive tip to gather the bead of moisture that had emerged, making his eyes roll back. Using the moisture to jack her hand down his dick brought his hips up in an unconscious thrust, although whether he was looking for her to stop or keep going was beyond him.

All he knew was that at this rate, he had about thirty seconds before he reached the point of no return. If he was going to stop her, it had to be now.

No way in fucking hell was he stopping. He couldn't if he wanted to.

And God help him, he didn't want to.

What he *did* want was to bring her with him.

Thankful for the sweat shorts Alex was wearing, he slipped his hand under the elastic waistband and the silky edge of the panties she had on, eliciting a surprised squeak.

"Wha-what are you doing?"

"Fair is fair," he said, giving her own words back as his fingers followed the delicious curve of her body to the source of the heat that had been scalding him. His finger stroked along the soft lips, making her hips jerk, and sent up a prayer of thanks she was as wet and primed to go over into the abyss as he was.

It took a few seconds before Alex focused back on the task at hand. When she did, she seemed determined to give better than she got. The restriction of the clothes they still wore hindered them both, but neither suggested stopping to do anything about it, too caught up in the rush to climax.

Being limited just made them both get more creative.

The end approached swiftly. His balls pulled up tight in anticipation, and he redoubled his efforts to bring Alex with him, sliding a second finger inside her as he increased the pressure of his thumb on her clit. She let out a mewl as her body contracted around his fingers in the first wave of her orgasm.

There wasn't time to savor that accomplishment, though. His own climax swept over him in a crashing surge, body bucking against the sheath of her hand as his head tipped back and he roared out his pleasure.

He was still coming back to earth and catching his breath when a wet nose intruded, pressing between his chest and Alex's to the accompaniment of a distressed bark.

Alex squealed in surprise, recoiling against the cushions.

"Bailey, no. Down, damn it. Place," he said sharply when she didn't move.

He felt like a shit at the confused hurt in the dog's eyes as she backed off and sat. But damn it, he'd just had his first non-self-service orgasm in almost three years, and he hadn't even gotten to bask in the fucking afterglow.

"You know, I *was* kidding before about you and your dog," Alex said, sounding more disgruntled than amused this time. "But now I'm not so sure. Is there a reason she doesn't like me getting close to you?"

He realized it must look that way to her.

Damn.

"It's not you," he said, uncertain exactly how to say it. "It's—"

"If you say 'it's not you, it's me,' I swear to God, I'll hit you."

Strangely, her fierce scowl while she was lying half-naked beneath him, the intoxicating scent of her climax still fresh on his hand, helped ease some of the tension that had filled him. Not just that he was going to have to talk about his PTS, but that he had to do it *now*, of all times and places.

Somehow, he even managed a rueful grin. "Actually, it *is* me."

The look in her eyes made it seem she might just follow through on her threat. Then the gleam changed to one of speculation. "Explain."

Where to start?

Especially when he didn't want to.

"One of Bailey's primary jobs is to head off any anxiety or anger she senses me having before it can escalate into a panic attack. She can identify small changes in my body language or voice to know when something isn't right, or smell the rise in stress hormones. When she does, she's trained to intervene and distract me. To break my focus on whatever is causing the distress, or to try and get me away from where it's happening."

"Like at the ballpark," Alex said, clearly connecting his words with when Bailey had mouthed his hand and tried to pull him away. Only he'd ignored her, not willing to leave Alex to face those two idiots alone.

He nodded.

"Does that mean..." She bit her lip. "Did something happen? Now, I mean? Were you...?"

"No! Now was...well, I won't say it was perfect. That would be a lie, because perfect would be having you entirely naked and all to myself in an actual bed. But I think I can honestly say now was a pretty damn good start." He looked down his body with a rueful twist of his lips. "Although I do owe your brother a new pair of sweats."

As he'd hoped, some of the apprehension seeped from her expression.

"It was well worth the price."

His satiated dick twitched in agreement. "Yeah, it was."

"So, if you weren't feeling anxious or upset or anything, why did Bailey react the way she did? She *was* trying to separate us, wasn't she?" Her brow crinkled. "She's not, I don't know, jealous or something, is she?"

"I don't think that's it, exactly." He hoped not, anyway. "She's probably just a little confused. I'm not giving her the usual cues to say I'm starting to stress out, but maybe stress hormones and...other hormones smell similar to her."

Not to mention the yell of ecstasy he'd bellowed out. That might have sounded like something the dog would be concerned enough about to alert on.

"Oh." Alex glanced at Bailey, who was still watching Neil with singular focus. "So, um, I guess this has happened before, then."

"No. First time."

"Oh," she said again in a small voice. "Then it *is* me."

"What? No." Realizing he'd given her the wrong impression, he said, "This is the first time it's happened because you're the first woman I've been with since Bailey and I became a team."

"The first? Really?"

"No need to sound so surprised. I'm not exactly someone who's in high demand with women."

"Are you kidding? Have you looked in a mirror?" Alex widened her eyes comically. "You do know that women drool whenever you walk by, and talk about your excellent backside all the time, right?"

The fuck?

"I really hope you're joking."

A secretive smile was all the answer he got.

"Anyway, I'm not talking about looks," he continued. But seriously, they talked about *his ass*? What the actual hell? "I'm talking about being too screwed up to be with a woman and not worry I'll suddenly lose it and do something…terrible."

Flashes of two tiny faces filled his mind, contorted in fear and wet with tears. Quickly followed by the equally tear-stained but furious face of the woman who'd told him in no uncertain terms exactly what kind of monster he really was.

His stomach clenched. Like he needed to be told after what he'd done.

"I'm not a good bet, Alex. You need to know that."

"What I need to know is what bitch put that idea in your stupid head in the first place," she shot back. "Because it's bullcrap."

"You don't know how bad it's been. I've really screwed up."

"Okay, you're right, I don't. But I do know who you are *now*. Whoever you were before, you're not that person anymore."

Her continued defense of him when he damn well didn't deserve it both frustrated and touched him deeply. "But I could be. At any second, something could make me snap."

"But Bailey—"

"Can usually help pull me out of it. But there's no magic pill that will keep it from happening in the first place. Believe me, I've taken enough of them to know."

"Oh, Neil…"

The pity in her voice was like acid on a raw nerve ending.

"What I'm trying to say is there's no cure for PTSD, Alex. I can manage it, to a point. But I'm not going to someday just be all better. It's a part of me. It's always going to be a part of me, for the rest of my life. How can I expect someone to want to be a part of that? To take on that kind of hell?"

God help him. There went that little chin of hers into the air.

"You expect someone to accept the bad with the good," she shot back. "That's what people who love you do."

There was a moment of almost eerie silence as the L-word sort of hung in the air between them. He had no illusions she'd meant it that way. Besides, he had little faith in the word, or the strength of the bond that supposedly went along with it. In his experience, it was far too easy to tack a *but* onto the sentiment and use it as a weapon.

You know we love you, Neil, but we just can't risk having you around the children being the way you are.

Of course I'll always love you, Neil, but I just can't be with you anymore.

I love you like a brother, man, but I don't think it's a good idea for you to come by the house again. You're just...well, you understand.

Yeah, he understood all right. In his opinion, love pretty much sucked.

Sex, on the other hand, was a lot less painful, carrying all of the benefits with none of the risk. As long as he kept things—kept this—all about the sex, maybe it would be okay.

Maybe no one would get hurt.

Alex was the first to shake free of the oddly frozen moment.

"Okay. So. What should we do about Bailey getting all over-protective or whatever this was the next time we get up close and personal? Because that *is* going to happen again."

Her expression dared him to disagree.

"Oh, it is, is it?" He knew he shouldn't, but he kind of enjoyed the possessive certainty in her voice. And the fact she didn't just suggest they put Bailey in another room. She understood his needs without making a big deal out of them. It felt...good.

Sex, dumbass. Keep it about the sex.

He cleared his throat. "Well, I'm not exactly sure, but I do know all her other training was done by repetition."

Her lips curved in a sexy grin. "Was it?"

"Mmhmm." He glanced at Bailey, who had relaxed but still watched him with those scary-smart eyes, like she knew they were talking about her. "She's a fast learner. I'm sure if we, what was it? *Get up close and personal* a few more times, she'll figure out there's nothing to worry about in no time."

And if not, he'd have to contact Another Step Forward, the training center where he'd first been paired up with Bailey, and see what kind of advice they could offer. He should probably start with that, actually.

But his way would be a lot more fun.

"I don't know." Alex frowned like she was mulling it over even as her hand settled on his shoulder. "Having sex in front of the dog. Sounds pretty kinky to me."

"Are you up for it?"

"I don't know." Her hand began traveling southward down his chest. "Are you?" Before she could reach her destination to find the answer to that question, her cell phone let loose with the theme song to The Walking Dead. Alex froze. Fisting her hand, she let it drop away just short of his waistband. "For the love of Pete."

"Ignore it." Even as he said it, he knew from her expression she wouldn't.

"That's Richard's ringtone," she said by way of apology as she reached blindly over her head towards the end table for the phone. "If he's calling on a Sunday, it probably means there's a problem at the station."

"He's in charge on weekends." He shifted to let Alex get up when she pushed gently at his chest. "He should be handling the problems that go along with the job."

"He should, but he usually can't." She reached down and grabbed her shirt off the floor, dragging it on even though it was inside-out before she swiped the screen. "Hello?"

Personally, Neil thought it was more a matter of he never had to, rather than he couldn't. Richard McKenna needed to be allowed to fall on his ass a few times instead of always being rescued by his cousin whenever he screwed up.

And if it wasn't Alex doing the rescuing, it was his father. Roderick McKenna had come roaring down to the network more than once since Neil had worked there to pull his son's butt out of whatever sling he'd gotten it into.

"What do you mean, it's gone?"

He winced at the shrill tone that had crept into Alex's voice. Whatever happened, it wasn't anything good. Which didn't bode well for how it had seemed things were heading for him and Alex tonight.

"No, the Founders Day repeat was already cued up and set to play tonight at seven. Yes, I'm sure." She pinched the bridge of her nose. "Did you look... Okay, no, I know you're not an idiot. It's just..." She threw a sorrowful look at Neil. "Okay, yes, I'll be there in about twenty minutes. Just, keep checking, okay? And let me know if you figure it out before I get there." She hung up and dropped the phone into her lap. "Crap on a cracker."

"Is it even possible for him to have deleted an entire digital file?"

"No, thank God. He said something about the system rebooting, though, and...I don't know what happened. I have to go take a look."

He sighed. "I know."

"I'm sorry."

"Me, too."

"I'll make it up to you." Leaning closer, she pressed a lingering kiss to his lips. "Promise."

As Alex scurried off to change her clothes, he leaned forward on the sofa, grimacing in distaste at the sticky situation in his pants. Bailey inched closer, scooting her butt along the floor, tail fanning the hardwood like an uncertain dust mop.

Knowing he'd confused her and hurt her feelings by snapping at her earlier, he reached out and gave her ears a good scratch. "I'm sorry. I know you were only doing what you're supposed to. Don't worry, girl, we'll figure it out."

They had to. Because dumb move or not, it looked like he'd just committed to being involved with Alexandra freaking McKenna.

Chapter 7

Monday mornings never bothered Alex.

For her, it was weekends she dreaded.

Time away from the station meant time when things could happen that she wasn't around to control. True, she was only ever a phone call away. But the control freak gene she'd evidently inherited from her grandfather sometimes made even that too far for comfort.

Or maybe it was just because she'd never had anything more interesting in her life to do with all that free time on her hands. Because yesterday, for the first time ever, she'd actually considered blowing off Richard's SOS call so she and Neil could finish what they'd started. Yes, they'd both had orgasms, but they had been nowhere near done.

Not even close.

She blushed like a lighthouse every time she thought about it. Good God. She'd put her *hand* down his *pants*. Her! The woman her friend Dionne liked to call the born-again virgin. What had she been thinking?

Well, she *hadn't* been thinking. That was the problem. She'd been feeling.

And oh, the things she felt...

No man had ever worshipped at her breasts like that. Ever. In her *life*. In fact, they'd more often than not been overlooked entirely. A pat, a stroke, a few squeezes—why did men seem to think women actually enjoyed having their boobs squeezed?—and then it was on to other things.

She'd long ago accepted her breasts were small and therefore of little interest. Just a simple fact of life.

Neil evidently hadn't seen that memo, because he'd been all kinds of interested in her girls, tiny or not. She was pretty sure she'd whimpered the first time he'd sucked on her nipple. The sensation had streaked all the way down to her other girly parts and gotten them involved in the party. Who knew breast play could be so exciting?

Well, she did now. And damn it, she wanted more.

More tingles, more orgasms, more *Neil*.

So today, instead of her usual reasons for being glad it was Monday, she had the added enticement that at some point during the day, she would see Neil again. He'd been so wonderfully understanding when she basically abandoned him for Richard yesterday. Frustrated, but understanding. For that alone she wanted to kiss him.

Well, that and a few other reasons, too.

Practically buzzing, she plowed through the usual Monday paperwork, determined to get ahead and carve out a good solid hour of free time for lunch, something she never did. Lunch was a half hour at most. Or better yet, eaten at her desk while she worked.

But the prospect of eating it with Neil made the expenditure of non-productive time much more appealing.

About forty-five minutes in, the low rumble of Neil's voice came from outside her closed office door. She'd recognize that gruff good morning anywhere. Probably spoken to her assistant Joy, who had the tiny office across the hall.

The knowledge he was right there, mere steps away, one small knock from entering her space, put all her senses into hyperdrive. Breath quickening in anticipation, she forced herself to focus on the computer rather than the door as she waited for him to knock on it.

It took a long minute to realize he wasn't going to.

Was, in fact, already gone.

Annoyed at being so disappointed by that, she threw herself back into her work with renewed vigor. There was no reason to feel snubbed. No reason at all.

Heck, he'd probably only been returning Joy's greeting. He was polite that way, a true southern gentleman. Initiating conversation wasn't really his thing. And besides, Joy's door was always open, while hers was closed. He'd likely thought she was busy, because she always was. Much too busy to interrupt to say hello. It was as simple as that.

It should have been as simple as that.

But doubts continued to gnaw at her confidence with the steady determination of a hound with a bone as she made her way through the weekend programming reports. Which were actually Richard's responsibility, but she always did them herself. It was easier than rechecking his work and having to redo what he inevitably got wrong.

The first stirrings of resentment tickled inside her.

If Richard hadn't called yesterday for what ended up being a simple five-minute fix *he* should have been able to make, would Neil have still bypassed her office this morning without a single word?

No. She was reading too much into it.

Wasn't she?

Needing to shake off the uneasy mood, she grabbed her mug and headed for the break room. Her heart did a quick little pitty-pat when she spotted Neil standing at the coffee pot, filling his battered travel mug. Just the sight of his broad shoulders and denim-clad butt were enough to cheer her right up.

"Morning!" She practically chirped the word as she all but skipped across the room. At the last second, she caught herself before reaching down to pet Bailey. Despite all their playtime the day before, the dog's blue service vest was a reminder she was currently on duty. A distinction Alex understood well.

There was a time for play, and a time for work.

Although she had the strongest urge right then to cross that line for the first time and give in to the desire to kiss Neil silly. Only the fact Penny was sitting at one of the small tables scribbling on a yellow legal pad held her in check.

"Morning," Neil mumbled, closing his travel mug with a snap.

Penny gave a distracted "good morning" as well, barely looking up from her notes.

Neil stepped away to give her room at the coffee pot. She took his place with a broad smile and filled her oversized ceramic mug. In her head, she rehearsed how to ask him to join her for lunch in a way that wouldn't peak Penny's inherently nosy journalistic interest. By the time she'd stirred in sugar and milk, she knew exactly what she was going to say.

When she turned around to say it, though, it was too late.

He was already gone.

Again.

Disappointment soured her stomach. She almost dumped the coffee down the sink, then glanced at Penny's downturned head and took it with her instead. No need to raise questions she didn't want asked.

Or know the answers to.

All the way back to her office, she tried to convince herself she was overreacting. Neil had not just snubbed her for the second time that morning. He hadn't known she wanted to talk to him, was all.

Besides, they sometimes went entire days without more than a hello-goodbye conversation. Their break room interaction hadn't been out of the norm for them in the least.

Logic didn't help much. Not against the little doubt devil poking at her brain, pointing out how this was exactly what happened the last time she'd gone after what she wanted.

No, after *who* she wanted.

The avoidance, the silent rejection. The only thing missing now was the huge public humiliation.

Caught in a spiral of dread, she started to pick apart everything that happened between her and Neil over the last two days.

She'd decided to join him on the assignment Saturday.

She'd shown up unannounced—and uninvited—at his house that night.

She'd been the one to ask him to come to her place Sunday.

She'd also been the one to kiss him first. And the one to stick her hand down his pants without so much as a how-do-you-do and take possession of the very happy prize she'd found there.

All facts.

As was the knowledge her judgment, when it came to men and sex, wasn't always reliable.

Had she been pursuing Neil?

She didn't think so. Not consciously, anyway. Yes, she'd gone to his place, but only to assure herself he was okay after what happened at the park.

She hadn't had ulterior motives. Not even when he'd kissed her in his kitchen. Or she'd kissed him. Whichever it had been. It had all just...happened.

The same went for what they'd done on her sofa. It had started out innocently enough. The fact it had escalated so quickly wasn't her fault. It wasn't like she was some kind of sex fiend or something, just waiting for an opportunity to pounce.

No. Everything between them had been entirely mutual, up to and including their orgasms.

Which left her no closer to a good answer for why Neil seemed to be avoiding her.

Only bad ones.

With a grim sense of déjà vu, she slogged through the rest of her work, opting to skip lunch in favor of one of the protein bars she kept stocked in her desk. She just couldn't bring herself to leave her office and risk running into Neil again.

One more snub would be more than she could handle.

Eventually, though, she had to emerge from her sanctuary. Much as she'd rather skip her weekly two o'clock upstairs with Colin, you had to be bleeding from the eyes before he'd excuse you from a meeting.

A warm and fuzzy boss, Colin wasn't.

More like demanding and prickly.

And a stickler for promptness. With a curse at the time, she grabbed her tablet and scooted out the door. Bypassing the lone elevator in the building, she headed for the stairs. Not only was it the only exercise she got most days, but it was also faster. Although nobody else seemed to think so, since she never ran into anyone else while using them.

Until today.

Today, there was someone waiting for her on the second-floor landing as soon as she pushed through the heavy fire door.

He was damn lucky her body recognized him before her brain did as he grabbed her and crowded her up against the wall. Otherwise, he might have been sporting some damage to his balls courtesy of the self-defense moves her brother-in-law the cop had taught her.

Instead, her body instantly softened against his as she was kissed near to senseless by the man who'd been tormenting her all morning, whether he knew it or not.

When Neil finally came up for air, he pressed his lips to her temple, breathing hard. "God, I've been wanting to do that all damn day."

"You have?" Doubt and hope clashed inside her.

Evidently sensing her uncertainty, he lifted his head to look at her. "All. Damn. Day."

She swallowed at the heat in his eyes. It was like staring into a supernova.

"But you barely said a word to me in the break room. And then you left." She hadn't meant it to sound like an accusation, but even to her ears that's how it came out.

Neil's mouth twitched with the hint of a grin.

"I left because we never got around to discussing if you wanted this thing between us to be common knowledge at work. And there was no way I could sit there and have a cup of coffee and a conversation with you without Penny figuring out all I wanted was to strip off your clothes and lick you from head to toe."

The image scrambled her brain. "Oh."

"Yeah. Oh." He cocked his head with a frown. "But you were thinking it was something else, weren't you?"

She bit her lip, not wanting to lie, but not wanting to tell him the truth, either.

"Okay. It can wait."

"It?"

"The explanation of whatever it was you thought was going on. That's probably not a discussion we want to be having on the stairs at work."

It wasn't a discussion she wanted to have anywhere at any time, but there really wasn't any way to avoid it. Not when Neil got that look in his eyes that turned them from soft denim to blue ice. He might not be a reporter, but he sure knew how to sniff out when there was a story to be had.

"Do you want to come by my place tonight?" he asked. "You've fed me twice now. I owe you a dinner."

And she owed him an explanation, like it or not.

She could have said no. But it would have only been putting off the inevitable. Besides, she wanted to see him tonight. Even if it meant exposing her most humiliating secret to him.

Her stomach clenched in protest at the thought.

Yeah, that was going to be a whole lot of fun.

"Sure," she said finally. "What time should I come over, and what can I bring?"

"How about six? And you don't have to bring anything. Unless," he added with a wicked grin, "you want to bring your toothbrush."

Heat flashed through her so hot and fast at the intent in his eyes, they were lucky the fire sprinklers didn't go of. Thankfully, Neil didn't seem to expect an answer. He just kissed her lightly and stepped back. Her body immediately followed of its own accord, the kiss ending with a tiny nip to his chin that made his entire body jerk against hers.

He groaned. "God, if you didn't have a meeting..."

Reality sliced through the haze of lust that had been wrapping itself around her again. With a yelp, she jumped away from the solid warmth of Neil's much-too tempting body.

"My meeting! Crap on a cracker!" She took a step, then pivoted and pressed her lips to Neil's for one more kiss. "Six," she promised before turning and bolting up the stairs. As she hit the midpoint turn between the second and third floors, she looked back.

Neil still stood there, Bailey at his feet, watching her with hungry eyes.

She didn't know what devil made her say it. Maybe she wanted to see him as rattled as she felt by his toothbrush suggestion. Or maybe it was because she'd finally gotten around to checking that box under the sink after she'd gotten home last night.

Whatever the reason, she found herself saying, "Make sure you have condoms."

As she raced up the next half of the stairs, she heard a low growl rising from the landing below. But God help her, she couldn't tell if it had come from the dog or the man.

Alex's excitement wound tighter with every step up the walkway to Neil's front door.

So did her anxiety.

Yesterday had been wonderful. A dream. But also spontaneous. What they were doing now was completely and totally premeditated. Between Neil's suggestion and her taunt, she knew they were both expecting the same thing to happen here tonight.

Hot, sweaty, incandescent sex.

She gave a quick double knock on the door, then pressed the chilled bottle of wine to her cheek. Though it did little to stave off the sudden rush of heat that shot through her. Man, oh, man, she needed to stop thinking about it or she was going to burn up from the inside out before she got to enjoy the experience.

And she *was* going to enjoy it. In fact, based on the sampling she'd already had, it was probably going to kill her.

But, oh, she'd be going out on a cloud of bliss.

The door opened, and her pulse jumped along with her body. Neil had changed his clothes since she'd last seen him at the station. He was still in jeans, but gone was the white button-down shirt with the sleeves rolled to his elbows that was so incredibly sexy on him since it showed off his muscular forearms.

One of her weaknesses.

She might have been disappointed if he hadn't exchanged it for a blue t-shirt that hugged his body and showcased his broad shoulders instead. The color was almost a perfect match to his eyes, really making them pop.

"Hi," she said, realizing she'd been standing there eating him up long enough to be obvious. She shoved the wine at him. "Here. I know you said not to bring anything…" *But a toothbrush.* She cleared her throat. "But I was raised to never show up empty-handed."

After a brief hesitation he took the bottle, barely looking at it. "Thanks. Come on in, dinner's just about ready."

It was impossible not to be nosy and look around as he led her through the small house to the kitchen in back. There wasn't a lot of clutter, which surprised her since he was a single guy living alone.

In fact, there wasn't a lot of anything in the house. Nothing personal, anyway.

No pictures on the walls. No awards on the fireplace mantle, and she knew he'd won more than a few in his career. There weren't even any of his own photographs displayed anywhere.

"I took a chance that you like steak," Neil said as they reached the kitchen. Two large ribeyes sat on a plate on the counter, glistening with a dark marinade that, from the sweet scent of it, included molasses and brown sugar. "Some women aren't big on red meat, but since you seem to be a fan of Babe's, I thought maybe…"

Mouth watering, she put aside her curiosity about his lack of décor and smiled.

"You thought right." Her mother had always despaired of her "unladylike" appetite. Helen McKenna ate like a sparrow, favoring salads and haute cuisine. Alex ate like a draft horse, and any lettuce that passed her lips was usually on top of a bacon cheeseburger.

Just one more reason she was a disappointment to her mother. But one she'd long since come to terms with. There were a lot of things she was willing to compromise on to keep the peace.

Giving up food with actual flavor wasn't one of them.

Neil looked relieved.

"Good." He grabbed the plate and barbeque tongs. "The corn's already done. So are the potatoes. I was just waiting on you to put these on the grill. How do you like your meat?"

It was such a loaded question that they both just stared at each other for a long moment before bursting into laughter.

Nervous laughter, she realized. For them both.

Knowing that helped some of her own nerves settle.

"Um, medium is fine."

But large would be even finer.

Somehow, she managed not to burst into laughter again.

Or flames.

Perhaps wisely, Neil led the way out into the backyard without comment. While Bailey flopped onto the grass in a patch of waning sunlight, he slapped the steaks onto the charcoal grill, sending up a loud sizzle. She chose the chair at the small wrought-iron table facing out at the yard so she could watch him. The yard was narrow but deep, and heavily ringed on all three sides by large trees.

"It was so dark the other night, I didn't realize how totally surrounded you are by trees," she said as Neil dragged the second chair around to sit beside her.

Though she wondered if being close to her was the only reason. She'd noticed similar seating choices in the past, like in her office. Neil never left his back exposed if he could help it. Leftover habit from the Army?

Or something else?

"How much property do you have?" she asked, trying not to think about it.

"A little over an acre. But there's not another house for at least a quarter mile in either direction, and behind me is state land, so it seems like a lot more."

"It's pretty." And it was. But looking out from the back of the house, it felt a little like they were inside a big, green box. She much preferred the openness of her yard overlooking the lake.

"Thanks for inviting me for dinner. It's a relief not having to decide between cooking or takeout for once. Especially after an afternoon of listening to department heads tap dance around the wrath of Colin about why ratings and revenue are down, and what we're going to do to turn things around."

Neil's brow furrowed. "Is the network in trouble?"

"Not even close. But you'd never know it to hear Colin rattle his Claymore and demand perfection. I swear, those meetings are enough to drive me to drink."

Neil popped back to his feet. "Dang, I forgot drinks. What can I get you?"

"Some wine would be nice. It's already chilled, and it doesn't need to breathe, so you can just open and pour it."

"Ah..." He grimaced. "I don't have wine glasses. Sorry."

Of course, he didn't. She kicked herself for not thinking that far ahead. What single man had wine glasses in his kitchen cupboards?

"Any glass is fine." Her inner vinophile whimpered at the lie.

He hesitated again, then nodded and went back in the house, Bailey trailing close at his side. Leaving her to worry she'd just somehow put a foot wrong. Was it the wine? He'd been kind of off about it from the start. Did he think she was being snooty by bringing it instead of having a Coke or a beer or whatever else he had on hand?

She groaned. Darn it, she'd grabbed the bottle they didn't get to enjoy last night because it was handy. She didn't mean to make things awkward.

Scraping back her chair, she hurried to the door and let herself into the kitchen. Neil was standing with his back to her, hands braced on the counter, staring at the unopened bottle of wine. His exposed back tensed when she came in.

She hovered uncertainly just inside the door. "Neil? Everything okay?"

His body heaved as he took a deep breath before turning. "I don't own a corkscrew."

"Oh!" Well, of course he wouldn't, just like he wouldn't have the right glasses. "That's okay, we can—"

"I don't own a corkscrew," he interrupted with strained intensity, "because I don't drink. Anymore. I don't drink *anymore*."

"O-kay," she said slowly. She was obviously missing what he was trying to tell her, but she needed a little more to go on.

"Remember when I told you things had gotten really bad? Back before I got the PTS diagnosis? Well, a lot of that was because I'd crawled into a bottle of Jack to try and escape the crap in my head that I didn't understand and couldn't control."

A sick feeling churned in her stomach.

"I'm gonna guess it didn't really help."

The noise Neil made had little in common with a laugh. "You could say that. I lost my job. I lost my fiancée. I alienated my family and friends. I ended up in the emergency room more than once to get my stomach pumped. The last time it happened, my blood alcohol level was so high I nearly died. Which, I guess, was the point. I just didn't realize it at the time."

A chill slid down her spine. The picture he was painting wasn't a pretty one. In fact, it was pretty damn bleak.

Neil had almost died.

Whatever hell he'd been facing, it had been so bad he'd wanted to escape it any way he could, even if that meant drinking himself to death. "I see."

"Do you? Do you *really* see me?"

She bristled. "Are you trying to scare me off or something?"

"No. God, no." He pinched the bridge of his nose. "Hell, maybe. I don't know. I just wanted you to know that..."

"That you were an alcoholic," she finished when he trailed off. She gave a definitive nod. "Okay, I get it."

"I *am* an alcoholic," he corrected. "A recovered one, but still and always an alcoholic. I haven't had a drink in over two years. Not that I haven't wanted one, but I know all it takes is one sip to undo every good intention."

And she'd brought a bottle of wine into his house.

She shot a horrified look at the offending bottle sitting on the counter.

Following the direction of her gaze, he managed a small grin. "It's okay. You can drink your wine. It won't bother me. Just...don't leave the bottle behind if you don't finish it. I might not have had an urge bad enough to tempt me in a long time, but I also don't believe in thumbing my nose at fate."

She was already shaking her head.

"No, I couldn't. I'm fine with whatever you have in the fridge."

"Alex..."

"Besides, you said you didn't have a corkscrew."

"I could probably figure out something that would work."

"No, it's okay." She crossed the few feet separating them and put her hands on his chest. His heart was thrumming like he'd just run a marathon despite his calm exterior. Smiling up at him, she tried to reassure him. "Really. I don't want the wine. I just want you."

He studied her face, his eyes still holding some of the wariness in his voice as he'd confessed what he clearly saw as a black mark against him.

"Okay," he finally said softly. The last of the uncertainty slid away, replaced by something that looked a lot like relief.

"Okay." She gave him a quick kiss, then patted his chest again and stepped back. "Why don't you go check on the steaks, and I'll grab whatever you have in the fridge to drink and bring it out for us?" She could have suggested the opposite division of labor, but was wise enough to know that men were usually more territorial about their grills than they were about their refrigerators.

The kiss Neil laid on her before he went outside sucked the breath right out of her lungs and had her clinging to the counter for support when he was gone.

Holy Moses, could that man kiss!

As she got out the pitcher of sun tea which was a staple in almost every southern kitchen during the summer, she worked hard to not let herself think too much about everything Neil had said. But it was an impossible endeavor.

Her mind kept circling back to the fact he'd nearly *died*.

It was stupid for that to bother her so much. He'd been a soldier, for pity's sake. Been in combat. He could have died then, too.

But somehow, that it happened after he was a civilian again, back home where he should have been safe, just made it seem worse.

She found the cupboard with the glasses, a mismatched grouping that looked like they came from a garage sale or maybe the clearance shelf at the five-and-dime in town. She took down two and filled them with ice from the tray in the freezer.

The crackle and snap of the cubes as she poured the tea over them echoed the thoughts popping around inside her head. Okay, so Neil was a recovering alcoholic. Reformed alcoholic? Well, whatever term he'd used, it had taken a lot of trust for him to tell her about it. Just like it had to discuss his concerns about his PTS the day before.

Picking up the glasses, she threw a baleful glare at the wine before heading outside, one last thought still knocking around in her mind.

Neil had been *engaged*?

He had included a fiancée in the list of things his drinking had cost him, hadn't he? She was pretty sure he had. For some reason, that shocked her almost as much as the news of his alcoholism had.

Becoming involved with Neil Crawford was getting more complicated by the minute. The problem was, she was already too far in to care.

Chapter 8

"I seduced my roommate's boyfriend."

The calmly spoken statement came as they sat at his slightly scarred kitchen table enjoying the excellent peach cobbler he'd picked up at the store. He would have much rather stayed outside, but when Alex had surreptitiously slapped at the first mosquito, he suggested the move.

"Okay," he said slowly, lowering his fork. "So, what, we're trading deep, dark secrets, is that it? I told you about my alcoholism, and you tell me about your naughty sexcapades?"

"What? No!" She looked chagrined, then laughed and shook her head. "Okay, that was a little out of left field, wasn't it?"

"Kinda." He liked the sound of her laughter, even if it was self-deprecating. Or maybe because it was.

Not a lot of women he knew were comfortable laughing at themselves.

"You asked me a question earlier today, in the stairwell, and I was just trying to give you some background so I could explain. Maybe I need to back up a little more, though." She tapped the side of her fork on the plate a few times as if gathering her thoughts.

He sipped his coffee and waited. Listening to people confess their darkest deeds and feelings was something he was used to from his AA meetings.

But Alex sleeping with her friend's boyfriend?

That was so far out of character for the woman he was coming to know that he'd wait as long as she needed to force the story out.

Plus, he'd be lying if he said he wasn't a little intrigued.

"When I was in my last year of college," she began again, evidently having found her starting point, "I had a new roommate. Claire. We didn't really have a lot in common, but we rubbed along okay. Neither of us was dating anybody at the beginning of the term, so we spent a lot of time hanging out together, going to parties and movies and campus events. Kind of like the buddy system, you know? So we never had to go anywhere alone."

"Smart." Too many horror stories were coming out of college campuses these days about assaults on young women who didn't have anyone watching out for them.

"Then, about halfway through the year, Claire started seeing someone. Orlando Mattise."

Just from the wistful way she said his name, he knew he wasn't going to like this guy. "And she left you hanging," he guessed.

"No, actually. Just the opposite. They made sure to include me, so I *wouldn't* be left on my own. We became a threesome. Not sexually," she added with a short, mortified laugh at his sharp look of surprise. "Just, we were almost always together. Like the Three Musketeers. That's what Orlando called us. Looking back, I can see now that Claire wasn't as thrilled about that as I was. But whenever she suggested to Orlando they go off on their own, just the two of them, he'd insist on including me. It was...flattering."

Yeah, he definitely wasn't going to like this guy.

"I'd always thought Orlando was attractive. God, he was like the best parts of Johnny Depp, Liam Hemsworth, and Kit Harrington all smooshed into one guy. *So* hot."

She looked like she wanted to fan herself, causing him to grit his teeth.

Really. Didn't. Like. Him.

"Everything was great for a while. But the more time I spent with him, with *them*," she corrected herself, "the more attention he started paying to me. At least, it seemed that way to me. I know now he was just doing things like buying me drinks and dancing with me so I wouldn't feel left out."

Neil had his suspicions there was a lot more to it than that, but he didn't interrupt Alex's story to point out the red flags.

"I buried how I felt about him, because no matter how hot he was, he was still Claire's guy, and friends don't poach each other's boyfriends. But then he started coming by the dorm room when she was in class or at work, just to hang out so I wouldn't be lonely. And I started to think maybe I hadn't been imagining things after all. That maybe he really was as attracted to me as I was to him, and he didn't know what to do about it, either."

Fury surged through his veins.

The bastard had known *exactly* what he was going to do about it. He didn't need the rest of the story to know how it would end.

"Then one night he came by the room when I knew he was well aware Claire was away for the weekend, with a six-pack of wine coolers and a movie on his laptop. It was almost the end of term, and I decided that if I was ever going to find out if Orlando felt anything for me besides friendship, it was now or never. So...I seduced him."

"And he let you."

The expression Alex gave him was pure exasperation. "I threw myself at him, Neil. No strings sex, free for the taking. What guy could be expected to say no to that?"

"Any guy with a moral compass bigger than his dick." Did she seriously not understand that? "He should have said no."

"He was attracted to me. Or, I thought he was. Either way, I tempted him into betraying Claire, *intentionally*. That makes me the bad guy, not him."

"Wow." He sat back in his chair. "He really did a number on you, didn't he?"

"What does that mean?"

It meant he really wanted to hunt this Orlando asshole down and kill him.

Rather than answer, he said, "Tell me the rest."

If it was possible, Alex looked even more embarrassed as she poked at the remains of her cobbler, crumbling the crust into a flaky mess.

"I thought because we, you know, slept together, that it meant something. That we were going to be a couple. I felt horrible because I knew it would hurt Claire, but I thought maybe once she knew Orlando and I were actually in *love*, she'd understand. Turns out, I was the one who didn't understand."

And the only one who was in love. His fingers tightened around his fork, turning white. With care, he placed it on the plate before he snapped it.

"I waited to hear from Orlando the next day, so we could decide together how we were going to break the news to Claire. But he never called or came by. I thought maybe he was busy with work or something, so I didn't worry too much. I left him a couple of messages to call me when he could. But by the next afternoon he *still* hadn't called me back, and Claire was due back that night, so I finally went looking for him."

She tipped her head back with a mirthless laugh.

"God, I was so stupid. I didn't even bother waiting until I could get him alone to approach him. I saw him out on the quad with some of his friends and went right up to him and tried to give him a kiss."

"What did he do?" he asked quietly, heart bumping heavy in his chest because he knew it would be bad.

"He couldn't push me away fast enough. He said sleeping with me was an accident. That it never should have happened, and it was never going to happen again."

"An *accident*? So, what? He just tripped and accidentally fell into your vagina?"

Alex slapped a hand over her mouth, stifling a horrified giggle.

"What else did he say?"

"Um, that he'd been drinking, so he wasn't really thinking straight when I started taking my clothes off, which is the only reason it happened." She looked over at him with a worried expression when he couldn't contain a growl of frustration. "He was right. I was the one who went after him. It wasn't his fault."

"Which I'm sure he made very clear to all of his friends, who were right there listening to every word."

She winced, but said, "It was nothing but the truth."

"It was establishing his defense. What else? How did he explain the fact he'd gone to your room to see you, and not his girlfriend?"

"He said he just wanted to keep me company since Claire was away for the whole weekend. That he worried about me being alone in the dorms."

"Right, he was just doing you a favor."

"He was."

He couldn't decide if she was really that naïve, or just that stubborn.

"Sweetheart, he set you up."

"What? No."

"He probably saw you were attracted to him right from the start. And he made sure you were always around where he could use that. Either to stroke his own ego, or, who knows, maybe to keep Claire on her toes by showing her he always had you to fall back on if she didn't work out."

Alex's mouth dropped open. "That's an awful thing to say!"

It was. But it was probably a hell of a lot closer to the truth than whatever bullshit Alex had been telling herself all these years.

"You never mentioned having a boyfriend in all this. Why not?"

"I was too busy with school for one," she replied, chin starting to rise.

"But not too busy to hang out with Claire and Orlando," he shot back. "I'll bet every time some other guy started to pay attention to you, your buddy was right there bringing you a drink or asking you to dance, wasn't he?"

"No...he..." Alex rubbed her forehead. "It wasn't like that."

He would bet every dime in his meager bank account it had been *exactly* like that.

"You said yourself you were starting to think maybe he was into you. That wasn't an accident, any more than him fucking you was." He was immediately sorry for the choice of words when Alex flinched.

Deliberately softening his tone, he continued no less relentlessly. "If all he cared about was keeping you company that night, then why bring the booze?"

"He was being nice. He knew I liked them."

"He'd been angling to get into your pants all year, and he knew you well enough to realize you'd need a little liquid persuasion to loosen your morals up enough to go along with his plan."

"My plan. I seduced him, remember?"

"Oh, I'm sure he made it seem that way. But who touched who first? Who made the first move? I'm willing to bet it wasn't you."

"I...don't remember. It doesn't matter," she argued doggedly.

"Of course it matters. That's how bastards like him operate. He got you tipsy, took advantage of your attraction to him, and then blamed the whole damned thing on you."

"No. You're twisting it all up."

"Untwisting it," he disagreed.

"Why?" Alex slapped her hands onto the table, making Bailey jump where she'd been dozing near his feet. "Why would he do something like that? He had Claire. Why would he go to that much trouble just to get me into bed once?"

"For the challenge."

It was the wrong thing to say.

He knew it as soon as the words left his mouth, even if it was probably the truth. He didn't need to see the stricken expression in Alex's eyes before she scraped her chair back from the table and bolted down the hall toward the bathroom.

The door slammed a second later.

Chest tight, he looked at Bailey, who'd come up on her haunches at Alex's hasty retreat and was now looking at him with her "what the fuck?" expression. Tossing her a chunk of the cobbler left on his plate, he sighed.

"And that, my girl, is how you ruin a date."

For the challenge.

Back pressed tight to the closed bathroom door, she couldn't keep the words from repeating in her head like a Greek chorus.

A challenge. She'd been a *challenge*?

No. Everything inside her rejected the idea. Orlando hadn't been some kind of cold, calculating creeper. He was a sweet guy that she'd put in a horrible position. He'd never been anything but nice to her. Attentive. Protective.

He hadn't let her be by herself at any of the parties they'd gone to as a threesome. Never let any other guy buy her a drink, so she didn't have to worry about date rape drugs or someone feeling she owed them anything in return. Too many college guys were asses who thought buying a girl a drink was equivalent to an all-access pass into her pants.

Orlando had protected her from that.

Just like he'd protected her from anyone getting handsy with her on the dance floor. Most of the time, no one asked her. But sometimes they did, and Orlando was always right there to warn them off if he thought they weren't someone safe.

Mostly she danced with him, or Claire, or sometimes with him *and* Claire. The three of them would shake it up, Orlando between them, making sure they *both* had a good time.

She hadn't cared at the time about him chasing off other guys, because she'd really wanted to dance with him anyway, not them. She hadn't cared then, but now...

Now she started to wonder.

Was it possible? Had his motives been other than he claimed? Had he been warning other guys off not to keep her safe, but to keep her from finding someone of her own? Were the guys he'd deemed "safe" merely ones he'd known she'd never go for?

Claire had made more than one comment about finding Alex a boyfriend so they could all double-date. But Orlando had always been quick to ask why do that when things were already perfect the way they were? Alex had taken it as a sign he was interested in her.

Oh, God.

She dropped onto the closed toilet lid.

What if Neil was right? What if Orlando hadn't been protecting her so much as isolating her? Making sure she was always around, always alone, always willing to tag along and do whatever he suggested because she didn't have any better options?

If that was true...

She began to examine those months they'd been the Three Musketeers through a different lens, this one no longer fogged with the rosy cast she'd always viewed Orlando through. So many incidents came into shocking clarity.

The drinks. The dancing. How he'd put his arms around both of them as they walked around campus. All calculated to mark her, not as under his protection like she'd always believed, but as his territory. He couldn't have made it any clearer if he'd put a stamp on her forehead.

Clear to everyone but *her*, of course.

Groaning, she buried her burning face in her hands. What an idiot! How had she not seen what he was doing?

Because he'd made sure she didn't.

With her new, painfully sharp take on the past, she could see exactly how he'd played on her obvious attraction to him.

And oh, dear lord, she'd been *so* obvious. She could see that now, too.

As well as how he'd stoked that attraction with small touches as they all walked around campus. His smiles and the jokes whispered in her ear like an intimate secret. The little presents he'd bring for both Claire *and* her, who he sometimes jokingly referred to as "his girls."

Or maybe not so jokingly.

Once she accepted it was possible—no, probable—Orlando had been manipulating her the entire time she'd known him, she was ready to take a closer look at That Night. The incident which had been her source of personal shame all these years.

Only now, it was so clear things hadn't happened quite the way she'd thought, that she couldn't believe she'd ever bought into the lies.

Neil was right about the wine coolers. If she hadn't been pleasantly buzzed, she never would have found the nerve to act the way she did. Impossible to remember exactly how many she'd had, but the six-pack had been empty the next morning. And Orlando usually only had one since he didn't really care for them, leaving the rest for her and Claire.

Only Claire hadn't been there.

Hell's bells. No wonder she'd been buzzed.

Probably closer to drunk.

Just the alcohol alone wouldn't have done it, though. It had been the movie Orlando brought up on the computer for them to watch that had really been the catalyst. Usually they watched action movies, some sci-fi, or even a chick flick once in a while when Orlando was feeling magnanimous.

But that night had been something else entirely. Not porn, exactly, but darn close.

Seeing all of that bare flesh, watching the people getting hot and heavy on screen, the simulated sex, had definitely put her body into arousal overdrive. She hadn't been a virgin, but it had been a long time since she'd had sex. And her body had been more than ready to have it with the man she'd *thought* she was falling in love with.

Stupid, trusting fool.

Yes, she'd taken her own clothes off, but had that been her idea, or his? She'd never been certain. He'd made it sound like it was hers, but was it really?

And what about the condom he had in his pocket? It wouldn't be unusual if Claire had been there. But he'd known she was away. It was his reason for coming over. So why would he have brought it with him?

The answer was pretty obvious.

Now, anyway.

Back then, she hadn't questioned anything. She'd been too happy having Orlando all to herself. Finally able to touch him and love him the way she'd been wanting to for ages. All the restraints she'd put on herself to stay a good friend were suddenly gone, and she'd been a little drunk on the experience as well as the wine coolers.

For the challenge.

Well, she hadn't really been all that much of one in the end, had she?

She'd given the bastard exactly what he wanted, and he'd taken it then used it to cast *her* as the villain of the piece. And she'd swallowed the lie.

Every deceitful word.

She'd accepted the blame and the humiliation, and spent the years since doing her damndest to learn from the experience and never repeat it.

Except now it seemed she'd learned the wrong lesson.

She wasn't a bad person. Weak, maybe, but not bad, and certainly not the amoral bitch-in-heat Claire had made her out to be once she found out what Alex had done. Things had gotten pretty ugly for that last month before graduation. But she'd stayed in their room and taken every nasty word flung at her, because she thought she deserved it.

Well, no more.

It was tough to readjust your whole life's perspective in a matter of minutes. But as the belief Neil was right about Orlando and That Night sank in, a rock she didn't know had been tethered to her heart was suddenly cut loose.

The freedom left her almost weightless.

So much of her identity, so many of her choices, were inexorably linked to that one horrible loss of control. Only it wasn't one. It was a reaction to cold-blooded manipulation.

If only she'd been smart enough to figure all this out back then, she could have spared herself ten years of self-recriminations and loathing.

Well, she hadn't been. But she *was* smart enough to take the gift of freedom Neil had given her and not squander it by hiding in the bathroom any longer. After splashing some cool water on her face and wrists, she squared her shoulders, blew out a breath, and went back to the kitchen.

Neil was still sitting at the table, but he'd cleared the dishes away and refilled both of their coffee cups. The ancient dishwasher's humming and gurgling were the only sounds in the room as she retook her seat.

"I'm sorry," they both said at the same time.

She held up her hand, needing to go first.

Neil hesitated, then deferred to her with a dip of his head.

"I'm sorry I stormed out of the room like a two-year-old having a tantrum. It was just really hard to hear what you were saying, and I needed a little time to process it."

"I should have kept my big trap shut," Neil interrupted. "What do I know? I wasn't there."

"Exactly. You have the benefit of seeing it through unbiased eyes and stripping away all the emotional garbage I'd been blinded by. Plus, you think like a guy."

"Now, why don't I feel like that's exactly a compliment?"

"It is. Mostly." She offered him a small smile in apology. "I never once considered that Orlando had deliberately set out to get me into bed that night. But once I did, all the little pieces started falling into place. You were right. I think he'd been toying with me all along, either for his own amusement, or for some sick power trip, or who knows why. And that night...that was part of it. The big finish. I was just too busy feeling guilty about *what* happened to ever question *how* it happened."

"Because you trusted him."

And that was what hurt the most. The first person she'd actually entrusted with her heart had been the one least deserving of it.

"But now you can place the blame squarely where it belongs," Neil continued, reaching to lay a hand over hers, "and stop feeling guilty about it."

"I'm not entirely blameless. I did lust after my friend's boyfriend."

"All that makes you guilty of is being human."

She wasn't sure she agreed with his total absolution, but it wasn't worth arguing over. Like she'd said, Neil thought like a guy. He didn't get the unspoken girl-code about the sanctity of boyfriends and husbands.

"So," he said, rubbing his thumb over the back of her hand, "I'm gonna guess since you told me all this, what happened with this Orlando guy has something to do with why you were upset with me at work today?"

"Yes. You are *nothing* like him," she said quickly, the flash of hurt in his eyes landing like a blow to her chest. "But we, you know, did what we did yesterday, and then today it seemed like you were avoiding me in the break room—"

"I already explained about that."

"I know. But before you did, I didn't know why, and, well, it felt so similar to what happened with him that I started to question whether or not I was doing it again."

"It?"

She dropped her gaze to their hands. "Throwing myself at a man who didn't really want me."

There was a long, scary moment when Neil took his hand off of hers and she wondered if she should have just kept her big mouth shut about everything. Then he pushed his chair back and stepped over Bailey, taking her hand again to pull her to her feet.

"Let me correct two misconceptions you seem to be working with here." He took her other hand, so he held them both as he stared into her eyes with piercing intensity. "One, you haven't done a single thing that could be considered throwing yourself at me."

"I stuck my hand down your pants," she blurted, then wanted to bite her tongue.

A slow smile stretched his lips. "Yes, you did. And if I didn't do it yesterday, let me take this opportunity to thank you for that." He chuckled as her face heated. "And I do believe I'd already gotten half your clothes off at that point, so I think it's safe to say I made the first move, not you. If we're keeping score."

Much as she might have wanted to dispute who had made what move when, she found the small circles being traced on her palms by his thumbs distracting enough to lose her train of thought.

"Um, okay. And the second thing?"

His smile grew more sensual. Tugging on her hands, he urged her a step closer.

"The second thing," he said, his voice a velvet rumble that made her legs tremble, "is thinking that I, at any point, didn't want you." He didn't give her a chance to reply, or question. Just put his lips to hers and showed her he meant every word.

The kiss was slow and sensual, yet so carnal she wouldn't have stayed on her feet if not for the steadying hold he had on her. Neil led the dance, but didn't control it, allowing her to respond and play and drive him just as crazy as he was driving her.

It was like the first kiss they'd shared in this very kitchen, only lips and hands touching. But instead of a slow burn, the sensations cranked up to blast furnace hot.

When his hands finally slid under her blouse to the bare skin of her back as he pulled her closer, deepening the kiss, it was like being marked by fire. Everywhere he touched, her skin grew hot and achy, until finally she thought she'd burst into actual flames.

Was it possible to spontaneously combust from sexual desire?

Breaking the kiss with a gasp, she stared up at him, dazed.

"I want you," he repeated. "I want to be over you. Beneath you. *Inside* you." He punctuated each statement with another hungry kiss.

"Yes," she managed to pant. "Yes to all of it. Just do it *now*!"

Chapter 9

The Alex of a week ago would have been mortified by the demand she just made.

The Alex of now was simply impatient about even the short time it took to move from the kitchen to Neil's bedroom.

He stripped the covers from the bed with a vicious yank, sending everything to the floor in a tangle of sheets and blankets. A small thrill reverberated through her at the barely restrained violence.

Oh, yes. He definitely wanted her.

That same impatience made her fingers clumsy as she tried to tackle the button and zipper on Neil's jeans. In a move of self-preservation, he brushed her hands aside and took care of it himself, shucking jeans and underwear to the ground with a single shove reminiscent of how he'd taken care of the bed sheets.

Wow.

Her hands stilled on her own zipper as she took in the sight of him. He was so erect, his penis curved back slightly towards his belly, the crown engorged and already damp. She had touched him before, stroked him to climax, but this was the first time she was actually seeing him. And the visual more than lived up to the promise of what she'd held in her hand the day before.

All of him did.

She drank in the sight as he stripped off his tee and stood before her unabashedly naked. She'd known he had broad shoulders. Now, unencumbered by clothing, she could see the muscles that made them that way, bunching in reaction to her scrutiny. His chest was smooth, with a smattering of hair mostly centered down his sternum into a tight arrow along his belly, right to his...

She swallowed. The term "happy trail" had never been more accurate.

"Do you want me to turn around so you can see the whole package?"

Rather than be embarrassed by the wry question, she smiled like he was a genie granting her first wish. "Yes, please."

He lifted a brow, but did a slow three-sixty, arms straight out so she could get a good look at him. The man had no shame about his nudity. But then, he really didn't have any reason to. He was gorgeous.

And, for tonight at least, he was all hers.

Show over, Neil dropped onto the bed, bunching the pillow up behind him before crossing his arms behind his head in a very deliberate manner. His smile was both a dare and a promise. "Your turn."

Giving him back a smile exactly like his own, she slowly lowered the zipper on her jeans, hips moving in a naturally sensual rhythm as she eased the denim over them and down her legs. She kicked them off and stood for a second, well aware her top was long enough to almost but not quite keep her panties out of view.

Slowly, she brought her arms up over her head, raising the hem of her top like a curtain to reveal the almost-not-there white satin panties that tied in a dainty bow at each hipbone.

The groan Neil released at the sight was gratifying, but not nearly enough.

Grasping her top, she pulled it up and off. Leaving her standing there in only the sexy panties and bra—which was even less there than the panties—she'd put on just for him.

Extending her arms as Neil had, she didn't bother to ask if he wanted the show, just did a slow pirouette. By the time she came full circle, the sound she got from him was less groan and more feral growl.

"Take them off and come here," he demanded.

Unable to resist tormenting him just a teeny bit more, she slid her thumbs under the straps of the bra and teased them off her shoulders. "Don't you want to do it for me?"

"Not if you ever plan to wear them again."

Laughing with the unexpected thrill of absolute sexual confidence, she dispensed with both the teasing and the underwear. Which had been well worth every penny, judging by the strained expression of masculine hunger on Neil's face as she joined him on the bed.

She expected him to pounce. Instead, he rolled to his side as she settled beside him and ran a gently reverent hand down the curves of her body.

"You are...perfect."

Not hardly.

Too tall, too skinny, too small-chested. She'd heard the list of her deficiencies far too many times from other men to ignore.

He must have seen the rejection of his words in her eyes, because he touched a finger to her lips as though she'd made her protest out loud.

"For me," he said in a firm, sure voice. "You're perfect *for me*."

He couldn't have come up with any more precious words than those.

Heart swelling with emotions she didn't want to examine just yet, she kissed him, using her body to push him over onto his back until she was straddling him.

Kissing her way down his chest, she tongued his nipples with quick flicks, making the points stand hard and aroused, before moving downward. Tongue circling his navel, she gave the taut skin there a small love nip that made his abdomen ripple in reaction.

She dared a look up his body as she continued her southerly quest.

Eyes that had heated to blue flames watched her, sending a pulse of need straight to her core with their intensity. Never breaking eye contact, she slid down until his hot, hard erection was cradled against her flushed cheek.

His entire body twitched.

With deliberate slowness, she turned her head, just a fraction, and ran her tongue up the length of him, from root to tip, in one long, hot swipe.

Still watching him watch her the whole time.

A short squeak erupted as she suddenly found herself on her back. No longer in charge, but more than willing to cede control. Especially when Neil's mouth unerringly found the tight bud of her aroused clit and almost immediately sent her crashing up and over the peak of her climax.

She gasped through the first one, groaned at the second that followed closely on its heels. By the time he'd brought her over the rainbow for the third and final time, she was thrashing and squirming and using words she'd never once in her entire lifetime used while making love to a man before.

Panting, with barely enough strength to keep her eyes open, she collapsed against the pillows. "That was...you...wow."

Still kneeling between her legs, now splayed like limp noodles, Neil gave a low, masculine chuckle. "Always a sign you've done things right when you can leave a lady speechless."

She wanted to make some kind of smart aleck remark, but she honestly didn't have enough brain cells left to think of one. Instead, she settled for giving him two thumbs-up, which made him laugh.

"Ready for round two?" He ran his fingers lightly over the sensitive flesh of her inner thighs.

A shiver ran through her. "Do you think I'm stupid enough to say no?"

Another chuckle as he ran his hands up over her hips to her belly, and then suddenly he muttered a curse under his breath and was gone. Startled, she came up onto her elbows.

"What's wrong?"

"Condoms," Neil growled. He jerked open the drawer of the nightstand and pulled out a white paper bag bearing the name of the local pharmacy, nearly ripping it in half as he yanked out the large black box inside.

As he fought his way through the cellophane that encased the package with the words "Party Pak" emblazoned on its side, she couldn't help but laugh.

"What did you do, look for the biggest box they had?" she asked with a giggle as he finally tore the box open and withdrew the prize.

Ripping one foil packet open with his teeth, he said succinctly, "Yes."

She was still giggling as he sheathed himself and settled back between her legs. But it quickly became a moan as he pressed inside, filling and stretching her in all the deliciously right ways. He was slow but relentless in his advance. She was tight, but after three orgasms she was more than wet enough. Slowly, stroke by stroke, Neil finally reached both the end of her and him at the same time.

"Oh, my God," she said on a shivery moan. "You feel...so good."

Raised on his hands above her, he gave her the savage look of a conqueror claiming undiscovered territory. "I don't think I can go slow," he gritted out.

"I don't think I want you to."

It was all the permission he needed.

Still holding himself above her with those muscular arms, Neil set a pace that almost knocked the breath out of her. Or maybe it was the glowing blue eyes of a Viking berserker that never left hers that did it.

Never before had any man looked at her with such intensity during sex. It was somehow a thousand times more intimate than what their bodies were doing. The things she saw in his eyes...

It was finally too much.

Climax rising, there was no way she'd be able to come while he looked at her that way. Not without losing more of herself than she was certain she wanted to give. At the last second before the wave hit, she arched her back and closed her eyes, breaking the too-intimate connection, crying out as sensations pummeled and threatened to drown her.

Distantly, in another part of her brain, she heard Neil let out a muted shout as his hips stuttered and eventually stilled.

He hung above her, both of them gasping and breathless, but didn't collapse to the bed until she opened her eyes and was caught once more in his burning gaze. With a satisfied grunt, he finally withdrew and dropped beside her.

She hissed a little at his withdrawal, something he didn't miss.

"Was I too rough?" He placed a protective hand over her lower belly.

"No. No." Panting, she dragged in a few deep breaths so she could get out more than one word at a time. "It's just...after four times...I'm so sensitive. I'll be fine."

"You're sure?"

"Absolutely."

Another man might have been smug about making a woman come four times in less than an hour. Neil only seemed concerned with her comfort. When had a man ever been that solicitous of her well-being at the cost of his own ego-stroking?

Oh, right. Never.

Despite trying not to, she fell just a little bit deeper into what she was very afraid might be something like love.

Crap on a cracker!

She stared blindly at the ceiling as Neil rolled over to dispose of the condom. It wasn't that she was against falling in love. It was that she didn't trust falling in love this fast. It felt far too much like what had happened with Orlando, all hormones and no substance.

Even as she thought it, she rejected the comparison.

Neil was nothing like Orlando. Nothing.

When he turned back to her, he kissed her gently before pulling her against his body with a contented sigh. Or she thought it was contented, until he whispered in her ear, "You're thinking too much again."

Busted.

"I can't help it. It's the Scottish in me. We're worriers."

"And is there something to be worried about?"

"Do you think this is all happening too fast?" Being tucked up against him, she felt the way his breathing stopped for a second before resuming.

"No."

He sounded quite definite about that. She waited for him to ask if *she* thought it was too fast, then realized just by bringing it up it was obvious she did.

She really wished she could see his face, to try and get a read on what he was thinking. Dang it, why hadn't she kept her big mouth shut? They'd just enjoyed what was the absolute best sex she'd ever had in her life, and then she had to go and ruin the whole mood by starting in with her ridiculous insecurities.

But the only alternative would have been to lie when he asked if she thought there was something to worry about. And that would have been even worse.

"*I* think," she said slowly, "that I don't want to do anything to screw this up."

"Neither do I."

"Then what do we do now?"

"We take every day as a gift, one day at a time, and go from there."

A wry grin touched her lips. "In other words, don't overthink it and worry."

"Exactly."

Easier said than done for her. But she was willing to try.

Once again proving how well he knew her, he said, "Don't worry, I'll let you know if your Scottish starts to show too much."

She gave him a pinch on his delicious butt for that. As he laughed, her hand and gaze drifted over his body in a lazy perusal, enjoying the landscape. Even sweaty, the man was a yummy treat for the senses.

Her gaze drifted past his long legs, and caught on the furry head propped on the mattress at the bottom of the bed, dark eyes focused and intent.

"Um, Neil? Your dog is giving us the stink-eye."

He looked down at Bailey, who gave a short whine. At the click of his fingers, she pranced along the side of the bed to where Neil could reach out and run a hand over her head. His ear rub elicited a doggy moan of approval.

"She didn't try to interrupt or jump on the bed," he said, using his other arm to gather Alex close while he petted the dog. "I'll take that as a good sign. That she's starting to figure out this—you and me—isn't anything for her to worry about."

The look on Bailey's face had seemed more possessive than worried to her, but maybe she was projecting.

Still, knowing the dog had probably been watching them the whole time they made love was a little disconcerting. Even if it *was* her job to stick close to Neil at all times.

Something she hadn't taken into consideration until just now.

Well, as long as Bailey didn't stick a cold nose up her butt, she'd just have to learn to ignore her presence during intimate moments. Hopefully Bailey would return the favor.

But then another potential problem popped into her head.

"Does Bailey usually sleep on the bed?"

"No. She only comes up if...she needs to wake me up."

There was something in that small hesitation that made her really think about what he'd said.

And what he didn't.

"Does she have to do that a lot?" she asked quietly. The possibility broke her heart a little.

"Not as much as she used to, but often enough." He hesitated. "I won't lie, Alex. I haven't spent the night in the same bed with someone in years for a reason. I can't predict when the nightmares will hit, or what I'll do. Sometimes, I yell. Or scream. At least, that's what my neighbors in Tiptonville told me."

Suddenly, the house with an acre of trees and nobody living next door took on a different purpose. It wasn't just the tranquility he craved.

It was the seclusion.

"It would probably scare the hell out of you, waking up with me yelling in your ear like that," he continued, beginning to sound grim. "Or worse."

"You're not trying to talk me out of spending the night, are you?"

"I think I am."

"Neil..."

"You said you don't want to do anything to screw this up." Abandoning Bailey's scratches, he took Alex's hand and pressed it to the hot, damp skin of his chest. "Well, neither do I. Spending the night, the whole night, together might not be such a good idea."

"We could try it and see what happens."

"Maybe. Eventually. But...can we just sort of ease into it? Please?"

She would have continued to argue if his heart hadn't started to jackrabbit beneath her palm like it was trying to escape. This was clearly a huge issue for him. And the last thing she wanted was to push him past his comfort zone.

Burying the painful pinch of disappointment, she gave a small smile and leaned over to kiss him. "Okay. We'll do it your way."

For now.

When she started to get up, though, he held her to his side with an almost desperate grip. "Don't go yet. Please. Let me hold you like this a little longer."

Who was she to argue when this was right where she wanted to be?

She nestled into the crook of his arm, head pillowed against his shoulder, her hand still held tightly against his chest by his. His heart slowly settled back into a strong, even rhythm there. From beside the bed, the soft jingle of Bailey's tags said she'd moved to the other side of the room where the dog bed was.

All was right in the world again.

Almost.

Because as nice as it was being cradled in Neil's embrace, inhaling the musky, masculine scent of his skin, there was also a lingering sense of dissatisfaction. She wanted to fall asleep like this, darn it. And wake up the same way.

Going home to her cold, lonely bed was definitely *not* how she'd thought this night would end.

Life was looking pretty sweet.

He wouldn't have thought it possible, but the last two weeks had gone by with no sign of his PTS rearing its ugly, unpredictable head. No panic attacks, no zoning out, and, most important as far as he was concerned, no nightmares.

It had nearly killed him to tell Alex he didn't want her to spend the night in his bed, when the truth was he couldn't have wanted anything more.

But Bailey and her watchful gaze had brought him down off his endorphin high long enough for reality to seep back in. As much as he wished otherwise, he couldn't just have a normal relationship because he wanted one.

There were things any woman he included in his life would have to take on and deal with. None of them things he wanted Alex exposed to. But he'd already accepted he was too damned selfish to stay away from her.

Especially now that he'd had her.

More than once.

The best he could do was protect her from becoming collateral damage to his demons.

Pulling into the parking lot for Coulter's Corner Grocers, he toyed with the idea he was maybe being a little *too* protective. Alex certainly seemed to think so. On the nights they were at his place she'd been staying later and later. And on their nights at the lake house she was constantly finding new and more interesting ways to take his mind off of leaving.

They hadn't spent a complete night together in either bed, but they'd dozed a few times from sheer exhaustion and nothing bad had happened.

Yet.

That was the fear that continued to make him get in his truck or walk her out to her car, when all he wanted was to stay wrapped in the cocoon of Alex's warmth and affection. Nothing had happened *yet*, but the possibility hovered there. Always. Like a wasp's nest just waiting to break open over his head and rain all kinds of painful badness over them both.

Though with every night that passed without a nightmare dragging him gasping and fighting from the arid hell of Afghanistan, he began to have hope. That maybe, just maybe, his life was finally settling into something that might actually be considered normal.

Or as close to normal as he was ever going to get.

Grabbing a cart, he nodded a greeting to the owner and manager, who was stocking the giant pyramid-like display of barbeque staples that dominated the front of the store. Big Tom Coulter, as he was always referred to—to differentiate from his son, also named Tom—was one of the few business owners who hadn't given him a hard time about Bailey when they first moved to Shelby. More than a few had.

Some still did, although they were a lot more subtle about it than they used to be.

But Big Tom had welcomed him with a handshake and a brusque "thanks for your service" despite Neil not putting any military embellishments on Bailey's working vest like some vets did.

It might make his life easier in the long run if he did, too. But somehow, even with no patches or pins to give it away, Big Tom had somehow known.

It hadn't taken long to figure it out, though. Like recognized like, and it didn't surprise him to learn Big Tom had done a stretch in the Marines back in the day, before returning to Shelby to dig in his roots and start a family.

His oldest, who'd luckily avoided the moniker Little Tom, had continued the family tradition. Neil hadn't seen him yet, but he'd heard through the small-town grapevine Tom the younger had recently returned home after completing his second combat rotation with the National Guard.

First was a quick trip through the produce section to grab some fresh string beans and a few peppers to grill with the chicken they were having for dinner. Tonight was Alex's turn to cook, but she'd gotten stuck late at the station in a last-minute meeting with Colin and Vanessa. So, she'd texted him the list of groceries to pick up and bring to her place.

It was all just so damned coupley, and he was loving every minute of it.

As she always did, Bailey ranged slightly ahead whenever they came to the end of an aisle. She would step out and scout before turning back to either indicate the coast was clear or that there was someone out of sight around the corner.

It was one of the hundred little things that reminded him that as normal as he might sometimes feel his life was getting, it wasn't. Without that warning, there was a real possibility the simple act of walking blindly around a corner without knowing someone was there could trigger a fight-or-flight reaction.

Surprises were not his friend.

Usually, he shopped at odd hours to help avoid such problems, but that wasn't an option today. Luckily, there weren't a lot of other people in the store at the moment, so he had most of the aisles to himself. But then he heard the high-pitched squeal of at least two kids who had evidently spotted Bailey as she ranged around the corner.

Damn.

Kids loved dogs, and it was almost impossible to explain to them why they couldn't play with Bailey. Some parents tried, but some just gave him dirty looks when he calmly asked their children not to touch Bailey unless he allowed it since she was working.

Discretion was sometimes the better part of valor.

Or, in this case, retreat.

He backtracked down the aisle and scooted around the back of the store, away from the kids. After grabbing the package of chicken breasts, he detoured down the snack aisle for a bag of the blue corn tortilla chips Alex liked, even though it wasn't on her list.

As he contemplated the various salsa options, a loud squeal and high-pitched laughter came from the front of the store. Followed by a woman's strident voice saying, "get back over here now!"

Good. If he was having any kind of luck at all, they were on their way to the checkout and would be gone by the time he finished getting the last two things on the list.

As he reached for the jar of medium spice chunky salsa, there was another squeal, this one more like a scream, really, and then an explosion that ripped reality right out from under his feet and heaved him straight back into hell.

Chapter 10

INCOMING!

Instinct kicked in with no hesitation or time for rational thought. Neil's body knew what to do, and did it, muscle memory throwing him to the ground, arms raised protectively over his head to shield himself from the debris that would be raining down any second.

There was another explosion. And another. And all he kept thinking was that they'd walked right into an ambush and there was no way in hell they were going to get out of this without losing men.

Cover!

He needed to find shelter, but there was nothing. Nothing but crumbling buildings that didn't look like they could stand up to a good, stiff wind, much less an RPG. So, he stayed where he was, face pressed to the hard, gritty ground, and prayed.

Lots of guys found God when they were on the battlefield. Some lost Him the same way. Neil had never much cared either way. But in a situation like this when the shit really hit the fan, it seemed he came down on the side that didn't want to risk leaving this life with the sins of war on his soul.

Move!

The explosions had stopped, but even though he felt someone shoving at him, trying to get him moving, he couldn't unlock his muscles. Couldn't slow his heart rate. Could barely catch his breath as he panted into the sand.

No. Wait.

Not sand. It didn't scorch his skin or fill his mouth and nose with its fine grit, trying its best to choke him as he fought for air. No, the ground beneath his cheek was smooth, and blessedly cool, and smelled like bleach and lemons rather than camel shit.

That made no sense at all.

The next shove was more like someone pounding on his back, and damn it, that *hurt*. He forced his head to turn, to tell whoever the hell it was to leave him the fuck alone, and had a cold, wet nose shoved into his now exposed face for his troubles.

Well, shit. Why was there a dog jumping on him? It should have run for the hills when the shelling started. Instead, it was trying to burrow under his prone body like he was the dog's own personal safe zone.

Dog.

Safe.

Bailey.

The burrowing nose finally found Neil's neck as his arms come off from over his head, the familiar *whuffle* by his ear and wet tongue on his clammy skin slowly bringing things back into focus.

For a moment, there was the strangest sensation of being in two places at one time. Part of him knew he was in Coulter's market. Part of him was just as certain he was in Afghanistan. It took his brain a minute to process which of those beliefs was false.

Shit. *Shit!*

Embarrassment got him off his face, but his muscles were still too frozen to manage more than rolling to a sitting position. A quick look confirmed the aisle was empty.

Thank God. Nobody had seen.

Then again, he had no idea how long he'd been lost inside his own screwed up head, so it was entirely possible someone had.

Bailey pawed at his arm with a whine, then tried to take his hand in her mouth.

Right. He needed to move. Needed to get the hell out of here, breathe some fresh air, get somewhere safe before the crash that always followed a flashback sent him into a tailspin.

He needed Alex.

No.

The denial was as swift as it was furious. He wasn't ready for her to see him like this, cowering on the floor like a frightened child because, what? There had been a loud noise? Oh, boo-fucking-hoo for him.

She might say she could handle the reality of his PTS, but he suddenly didn't believe that once she was faced with the real deal, she'd actually stick around. Really, what woman would? His fiancée hadn't. Hell, neither had his sister.

Why should Alex?

In the tiny corner of his brain where logic still lurked, he knew he wasn't thinking rationally. But the hormonal chemical cocktail that terror had sent coursing through his body didn't care. It overrode everything except the most basic of impulses.

And that was to protect himself at all costs.

It took two tries, but he got to his feet. Bailey tucked in against his legs, lending him not only emotional support as they staggered down the aisle, but physical support as well. Keeping him moving and headed in the right direction.

He probably would have done better using the cart for support, he realized as they got to the front of the store. But he wasn't going back for it now.

All he wanted to do was get the hell out.

Which was going to be more of a problem than he thought. Shattered bottles from the once impressive barbeque display now littered the floor between him and the exit, the sharp scent of pickle brine filling the air making Bailey sneeze.

The bitter smell on top of the jitters from the adrenaline made his stomach tighten as nausea hit hard and fast. He swallowed the saliva that pooled in his mouth. No way was he going to puke inside the store. No way.

But he had to get *out*.

On the other side of the disaster zone, Big Tom was squatting down in front of two subdued kids, probably no more than five or six, talking to them softly. Or as softly as that big, booming voice ever got. Their mother stood with her hand over her mouth as she surveyed the damage her offspring had evidently caused.

At Bailey's second sneeze, Big Tom turned his head in their direction. With a last pat on the kids' heads, he got up and headed right for them, hand up like a traffic cop.

"Hold up. There's too much glass for Bailey to make it through here safely." He picked his way around the jagged remains of the heavy pickle jars, sliding a few times in the puddles of brine despite his rubber-soled boots. "It'll take me a couple few minutes to get this cleaned up if you want to keep on shopping. Or if you're done, I can get your things rung up and then you can go out through the back."

He knew Tom was talking to him. Heard the words. They just didn't all fit together into any kind of sense that mattered. He tried to concentrate, but his eyes kept sliding past the man and seeking the exit. Out. He needed to get *out*. Nothing Tom or anyone else had to say was more important than that.

"Neil?"

The sharp tone drew his attention to the man standing in front of him. But only for a second, before he was once again looking at the glass doors that led to freedom.

With a soft curse, Big Tom reached out to touch Neil's arm, then drew his hand back as if reconsidering the wisdom of such an action. Instead, he pointed. "We can go out through the back."

Out was the magic word.

Without any argument, Neil followed him back down the aisle, past his abandoned cart and through the dark brown door marked "Employees Only." The narrow hallway beyond it made his adrenaline pump again, the sensation of being closed in with no means of escape nearly choking him.

"If you want to wait in my office..." Big Tom took one look at Neil's face and changed his mind, walking down the hallway and out the emergency exit door at the end, Neil so close behind him he nearly stepped on his heels.

As soon as he hit fresh air, he sucked in a great big lungful of it. Then another, and another, until finally the vise around his chest loosened, and he was able to breathe without having to fight for it.

"There's a bench for employees who want to come have a smoke. It's pretty private back here. No one will bother you. Just...take as long as you need."

Like a puppet, Neil dropped onto the wooden bench as the other man went back inside. Bailey whined and all but climbed into his lap so she could lick his face. He pushed her away half-heartedly, then grabbed her in a tight hug and buried his face in her soft, familiar fur.

God.

What a fucking nightmare.

Reality had fully realigned itself, but that only made everything worse. A few fucking jars break, and he's hitting the deck and practically wetting his fucking pants.

Normal? Had he actually been thinking his life was getting back to *normal* when he'd gotten here? What a fucking joke.

He was screwed up. He was always going to be screwed up.

That was his new normal.

By the time Big Tom came back outside, Neil had managed to calm down enough that Bailey wasn't trying to crawl all over him anymore. Instead, she lay at his feet panting, but she jumped up and immediately put herself between Neil and the other man in her blocking stance when Tom approached.

It wasn't a threatening pose. Just a stance that allowed Neil the personal space people sometimes unintentionally encroached on.

Non-threatening or not, Tom gave the dog a respectful distance as he placed the two plastic bags he was carrying on the bench.

"I rang up what you had in your buggy. Not sure if you were done, but I figured you wouldn't be coming back inside to finish even if you weren't, so..."

It took two tries for him to unstick his tongue enough to croak out, "How much?" As he fished out the right amount of cash from his wallet, he debated before asking the question that pressed most heavily on his mind. "How did you know? That I needed to get out?"

Tom took the bills without counting them.

"I've seen that same look a few times on my Tommy since he came home this time 'round." His voice was grim and his bulldog face infinitely sad. "A car door slamming, a helicopter passing over-head, and suddenly he's got eyes that are a million miles away and it's all he can do not to run out of the room. I figured those jars hitting the ground were probably enough to do it for you. I know they sure scared the ever-lovin' spit outta me."

Neil gave the barest nod.

"You can stay back here for as long as you like until you feel you're okay to drive. Or I can call somebody to come get you if you want."

For the second time, Alex was the person who popped to mind.

And was just as quickly rejected.

"I'll be fine on my own, thanks," he lied. "I just need a few more minutes."

"Well, whenever you're ready, you can go around the back of the building to the left there. If you follow that little alley between the buildings, you'll get to the parking lot."

"Thanks."

With a nod, Big Tom started to leave, but stopped when he got to the door and turned back to ask with quiet desperation, "Does it ever get any better?"

He knew the man was asking because he was worried about his son, but Neil just didn't have the answer he wanted.

"Depends." He was going to leave it at that, because it was the truth. Everyone processed their issues differently.

But Tom had really saved his ass by recognizing his state of mind. And not only getting him out of the store, but doing it quietly before anyone else realized how close he was to totally losing his shit. He owed him something more.

"Tommy should talk to someone. It helps."

"What, like a shrink you mean?" Big Tom sounded doubtful. "I don't know. Never put much stock in all that navel-gazing crap."

Neither had he until he'd had no choice. "What could it hurt for him to try?"

Big Tom made one of those noises in his throat that could be anything from an agreement to a sign of disgust before heading back inside. Once the door closed behind him, Neil tipped his head back and sighed.

Chances were, Tommy wouldn't call the VA for help. His father's attitude would likely influence his own. Folks in small towns didn't put much stock in the benefits of sharing your problems. Going to a shrink ranked right up there with walking down Main Street with your bare ass hanging out of your pants for all the world to see.

Which was really a goddamned shame, because he knew he owed his life to his therapist. It had taken nearly dying to get to where he was ready to let Isaac help him, but once he'd found that lifeline, he hadn't let it go. He still drove up to Tiptonville twice a month to see him.

In fact, he'd been there just two days ago. Isaac had listened with apparent pleasure while Neil talked about his budding relationship with Alex. He even wanted to meet her.

Well, that was never going to happen now.

He scrubbed his hands over his face and stood. Bailey got to her feet and gave herself a full-body shake before locking on him with eager eyes. As horrible as the past half hour had been, she still looked at him with the same nonjudgmental adoration and acceptance. He gave her head a quick rub in appreciation.

He seriously doubted he'd get the same look from Alex if she'd been the one here to witness his inglorious face-plant in the middle of the store.

Driving home was done on auto-pilot. Normally, he wouldn't have gotten behind the wheel so soon, but he rationalized he lived so far outside of town there was little chance he'd even pass another car, much less crash into one.

A theory that ignored all the traffic he had to navigate on his way *out* of town. But logic had no place in his current thinking. Like a wounded animal, his brain was focused on one goal and one goal only.

Getting home and going to ground.

Closing the front door behind him was a relief. But within seconds, the house felt too confining, forcing him to escape out the kitchen door to the backyard. He collapsed into the chair by the fire pit and just breathed, trying to let all the lush, green life surrounding him suck away the too-visceral memories of heat and sand and endless shades of brown.

At some point, his phone rang. He ignored it.

When it rang again a few minutes later, he pulled it out and turned it off. Not long after, the phone inside the house began to ring. It rang on, and on, and on, until finally, somewhere around the twentieth or so time, it fell blessedly silent.

It didn't ring again.

The light faded, and the frogs started their evening serenade from deep within the trees. He shivered. There was no wood laid in the pit for a fire, and he couldn't drum up enough interest to go and get some.

So, he just sat in the gathering dusk and ignored the chill. The bugs. The thousand self-defeating thoughts circling inside his head like vultures waiting to dive in and tear a chunk from his already scarred and battered soul.

A sudden flood of light erupted behind him as the patio motion sensors were triggered. Something which would normally have him on his feet and spinning around in alarm to protect his exposed back. Now, though, so lost in his own head, he barely cared.

Someone taking him out might be a relief.

Bailey stood from where she'd been all but laying on his feet to face whoever was coming up behind him, but didn't bark or block.

"Neil?"

Shit. *Shit!*

Alex.

Why was she here?

Wait. He'd forgotten...something. Something he was supposed to do.

"Neil, are you okay?" When he didn't answer, she came closer. "When you never showed up at my house I called, but you didn't pick up on either phone." Another pause he didn't fill. "I got worried something was wrong and finally decided to drive over and check on you."

Her words were getting more clipped, betraying her growing annoyance. But he still couldn't figure out how he was supposed to answer.

"Damn it," she finally exploded. "Do you have any idea of all the horrible things going through my head about what could have happened to make you just drop off the face of the earth like that? I thought maybe you'd had a car accident, or fell and hit your head and were lying somewhere unconscious, or, or, got attacked by a bear or something! And you're just sitting here in the dark, ignoring me? Seriously?"

"You're right," he said in a hollow monotone. "I'm a real shit. Sorry."

"Sorry?" She took a breath as though to tear a well-deserved strip off his sorry ass, but hesitated. Then stepped even closer.

Bailey whined and shifted restlessly, though not to block her.

More like she was asking for help.

Alex bent down and took a good look at his face. Her entire demeanor shifted immediately. "Oh, Neil." She gently cupped a hand on his cheek.

The warmth of her touch was so delicious against his chilled skin he almost moaned. He put up no resistance when she took his hand and urged him to his feet, letting her lead him like a child to the house, which was ablaze with light.

He was pretty sure he hadn't turned any of them on. Had he?

No. It had still been daylight out when he got home. Alex must have gone looking for him inside before finding him in the yard. Which meant he'd left the front door unlocked. Left his home, his safe space, vulnerable and unprotected.

The thought should have horrified him.

He could barely work up the effort to care.

"Oh, sweetie, you're freezing." Alex chaffed his goose-fleshed arms as he stood docilely in the middle of the living room. More of that sweet, comforting heat seeped into his body.

Alex grabbed the thick chenille blanket from the back of the sofa, the one she'd brought over to cuddle under with him while watching TV. She wrapped it around his shoulders and urged him to sit before she knelt on the floor in front of him and rubbed her hands against his denim-clad legs to generate some warmth.

In some part of his brain, he knew the icy numbness encasing him had nothing to do with the temperature. It wasn't shock, exactly, but something damn close. Some kind of primitive survival instinct to hold reality, and the pain that came with it, at bay.

Too bad it wouldn't last much longer.

Because now he had not only the humiliation of what happened at the grocery to contend with, but also Alex finding him surfing the space cadet zone.

Fucking hell.

He managed to make his arms work and put his hands lightly on Alex's forearms to make her stop. Any other time, having the woman of his dreams kneeling between his legs, hands on his thighs, looking up at him as she bit her lip with those straight, white teeth would be the stuff of erotic fantasies.

Instead, he was about as far from hard as he'd ever been in his life.

Humiliation wasn't much of an aphrodisiac.

"Are you okay?" she asked, her wide green eyes so filled with concern he was afraid she was going to cry.

"Better. Thanks." It came out gruffer than wanted, but his throat was still so tight he was lucky he'd gotten out actual words.

"Can you tell me what happened?"

He gave a mirthless laugh. "Me. I happened. Me and my broken brain. Ow!" He stared at her in disbelief at the pinch she'd given his thigh.

"You are not broken," she said, hitting each word hard. "So stop saying that." She added another pinch to punctuate the command.

"*Christ!*" He let go of her arms to rub his abused flesh. Good thing jeans didn't have that much give to them. He stayed wary as she got up to sit on the sofa beside him.

"Okay, let's try this again. Tell me what happened." She took his hand in hers and stroked her fingers over the back of it. "Please?"

He didn't want to. God, he really didn't.

But in fits and starts, with a lot of stumbles and mumbles and a few crude words he didn't realize he'd let slip until it was too late, the story came out. He didn't skip or gloss over anything. He laid it all out there, naked and raw.

Every mortifying second of it.

The flashback. The panic. The primitive need to run, hide, get away from a danger that didn't exist. From a place thousands of miles away that was sometimes so real in his mind's eye his body could feel it, taste it, smell it.

The lost time. The inability to think clearly, to make good decisions. Forgetting about her, and their plans, and everything that mattered in the *now*, because he was so trapped in the imagined hellscape of his *then*.

If Alex wanted to know the truth, he'd give it to her. Then they'd see if she still thought he wasn't as broken as an over-wound tin soldier.

She was quiet when he was done, though the fingers making small circles on the back of his hand the whole time he talked never stilled. That soothing contact had helped him get through his confession.

Now, it was all that kept him from crawling out of his skin.

"I'm not sure if you're waiting for me to run screaming from the room, or tell you we're through, or what," she said finally, her tone ridiculously conversational. "But if so, I'm afraid I have to disappoint you. I'm not going anywhere."

His gut tightened even as his heart beat a little harder.

"You heard what I just said, right? I was lying on my face in the middle of the market because of some damn broken jars."

"I heard you."

But she wasn't understanding. She couldn't be.

"And what if something like that happens when we're out together somewhere?" Because she wouldn't be able to ignore the humiliation when she had a front-row seat.

"Then you'll have to tell me the right thing to do if it does, so I can help and not make things worse, like at the ballfield."

He just stared at her, unable to process her matter-of-fact answer.

What the fuck was happening?

In response to his obvious confusion, she took his face in her hands. "I'm. Not. Going. Anywhere. Got it?"

The look in her eyes was earnest and filled with something rarely seen before. Not even from the people who were supposed to love and care about him unconditionally because they were blood.

Simple acceptance.

It made no sense. Not after what he'd told her. She should be distancing herself.

Saving herself.

But God help him, he believed her. Alex always meant what she said. She wasn't going to leave him. She was willing to stick, despite the crazy.

It was so much more than he'd expected. More than he could have hoped for.

Probably a lot more than he deserved.

But she was here. It was all that mattered as he wrapped his arms around her and held her tight, his face burrowed into the warm crook of her neck as he breathed in her unique scent of fresh air and Alex. There was dampness on his cheeks, and *goddamn it* he was crying like a friggin' two-year-old, but he couldn't stop. His body needed that final release.

And in her undemanding embrace, he had the strength to take it.

Eventually, he loosened his hold and pulled back, both physically and emotionally wrung out. He swiped his face against his sleeves to erase whatever betraying moisture was still there. If Alex noticed, she had the decency not to say.

He rested his forehead against hers with a quiet sigh. "Thank you."

It might have been the position, or maybe his brain was finally kicking on all cylinders again, but he suddenly got his first good whiff of himself.

Holy roadkill.

Fear sweat had a whole different level of potency than regular perspiration.

He pulled away from her as he gave a horrified laugh. "God, I stink!" Alex didn't comment, but the way her little nose scrunched up was as good as an agreement. "I, uh, think I'll go take a shower."

"How about I make dinner while you're doing that?"

"Sure." A hazy memory trickled in. "I, ah, might have left the groceries out in the back seat."

"Go." She shooed him away. "I'll take care of it."

He went. Now that he'd smelled himself, he couldn't get clean fast enough.

The stench of terror was a sharp, bitter reminder of the day, and he was more than ready for it to be gone.

With a pat of apology, he closed Bailey out of the bathroom, something he usually never did. He stripped, leaving his rank clothes in the middle of the floor, and stepped under the water while it was still warming up. The quick chill, followed by the soothing warmth, sent prickles along his skin.

Ducking his head under the spray, he stood with his hands splayed on the shower wall, letting the water wash over him. Sluicing away the horror of the day to disappear with a gurgle down the drain.

Alex stayed.

The knowledge terrified him as much as it thrilled him.

She'd stayed, and that meant something. Something important.

Alex was a woman of integrity, and once she committed to something, or someone, then she was all in, no matter what. By making it clear she wouldn't be chased off, she was declaring he meant enough to her to suffer through potential humiliation for.

That she cared about him. Cared for him.

Maybe...could even love him?

He barely had time to consider the question when the shower curtain was pulled aside by the very woman who inspired it as she stepped in to join him.

Chapter 11

ALEX DEBATED LONG AND hard about whether she should do this.

Neil had seemed more himself when he headed for his shower, but still not exactly *right*. Understandable, considering what he'd been through. Her heart felt like it had been through a meat grinder after listening not just to what he said, but the way he said it. Like he wasn't worth anyone's sympathy.

Like he wasn't worth anything.

But while he eventually seemed to accept that nothing he told her would change how she felt about him, she hadn't been sure her words alone were enough.

Now, seeing the stark need in his haunted eyes as he turned to look at her, she knew she'd made the right choice.

After tugging the curtain closed, she ran her hands gently over his chest, enjoying the firmness of the muscles he hid so well beneath his clothes. There'd been enough exploration over the past two weeks that she already knew the story his body told.

The scattering of scars, most of which he'd told her about when she asked. And a few he'd refused to discuss at all. The sensitive ridge of his hipbone that seemed the most unlikely of places to be ticklish. The swirl of hair circling his bellybutton—an adorable outie—in the complete opposite direction as the rest of his chest hair grew.

But admiring his delightful body wasn't why she was there.

With gentle pressure, she urged him to turn back around and put his hands against the wall again. The firm muscles on his back flexed and contracted as she lathered them with the fresh, minty eucalyptus bath gel he used.

Starting at the tops of his shoulders, she pressed into the knots, easing away the tension there. Slowly, methodically, she worked her way down his strong arms, his broad back, his trim waist. Fingers alternating between a deep massage and a light caress as each part of his body softened and yielded.

By the time she reached his luscious butt, she realized her mistake.

This wasn't supposed to be sexual. It was supposed to be about Neil. Making him feel worshipped and cared for. Special, and deserving of her complete and total focus. Not work *her* up into a needy ball of arousal.

Which was exactly what was happening.

Her nipples were so hard they ached, and her clit was in desperate need of attention, all tingly and tight. Practically begging for relief.

Well, too bad. This wasn't about her. She'd just have to suck it up.

A groan nearly escaped at the thought of dropping to her knees to do just that.

I think I'm in real trouble here.

Steeling herself for more torture, she ran her slippery hands over Neil's very fine behind, straying into the space between his slightly spread legs as she continued down to the tops of his thighs. Both thumbs grazed his testicles more than once, drawing a hiss and causing his butt and leg muscles to flex and tighten.

Her inner muscles did the same.

So, so much trouble.

Quickly moving on, she brought the massage down along those muscular thighs, enjoying the soft rasp of the hair there against her palms. She hesitated, but there was no other choice. Not if she was going to reach his lower legs to finish.

She went to her knees.

And knew she'd never make it through the rest of the massage without losing her mind. She just couldn't.

No woman was that strong.

Which was why she gave in to the urge that overcame her—because it was *right there* for pity's sake—to lean in and gently bite the firm globe of Neil's butt cheek.

He jumped. Probably more from surprise than pain, since she'd only taken a tiny nibble. But she immediately soothed the bite with her lips and tongue anyway.

Just in case.

She was altruistic that way.

With a groan from somewhere deep inside his chest, Neil slid from her ministrations and turned around. Judging by what he presented her with, she hadn't been the only one getting turned on by the massage.

Fantasy fulfilled, she wasted no time taking full advantage.

Humming in pleasure, her mouth slid over the head of his straining erection. She took him as deep as she could, over and over in a slow, torturous rhythm that slowly sped up as his urgency began to match her own.

Predictably, he tried to stop her before he went off. One consistent thing in their lovemaking had been Neil's personal policy of "ladies first" when it came to orgasms. It was sweet, and usually extremely satisfying, but tonight she was determined to keep this as much about him as possible. To put *him* first.

Somewhere, she had a feeling, he'd rarely been placed.

So, she ignored his hands as they tried to urge her to her feet. Instead, she took a firm but gentle grip of the base of his penis with one hand and his testicles with the other, anchoring herself. All while never missing a stroke with her mouth.

She could just barely angle her head enough to look up the long length of his body. Blinking against the water droplets that beaded on her lashes, she met his hot gaze. Told him without words that this time, she was in charge till the end and he'd better just sit back and enjoy the ride.

With another groan, this one of surrender, Neil's hands fell away.

She continued to worship him with her hands and mouth, ignoring the slight burn in her jaw from being open wide so long and the twinge in her knees from the hard porcelain. Both of which were forgotten as Neil slapped his hands against the wet tile and roared out his release, hips churning helplessly as he emptied himself into her.

Empowered, she stayed with him all the way through, determined to give every last second of pleasure possible.

Only then did she let his softening length slide from her mouth. Panting, she pressed her forehead to his belly, fighting to catch her breath, her own body still humming with unfulfilled need.

But the discomfort was minor compared to the sense of triumphant satisfaction that consumed her. From the way Neil's usually sturdy thighs were quivering, he was about thirty seconds away from sliding into a satiated puddle.

Well, okay then.

It wasn't what she'd planned when she first stepped into the shower, but the result matched her original intent, so she'd take it.

She had shown he was still every bit as attractive to her as he had been before his confession—if that was even the right word—about the flashback he suffered earlier. Not just physically, although *whoo-ee* he was a sight to behold, all naked and wet and *hers*.

No, she'd wanted him to know he was important to her.

Cherished, flaws and all.

Loved.

She was still afraid to say the word out loud, but she'd thought it more than once. And she was starting to come to terms with the truth. That somewhere in the last crazy, passionate, blissfully perfect two weeks, she'd gone and done the stupidest thing she possibly could.

She was falling in love with a man who didn't think he was capable—or worthy—of having a normal relationship because of his disability.

Well, it seemed she'd just have to figure out a way to prove him wrong.

"How do you like your eggs?"

As she nudged the refrigerator door shut with her hip, she directed her question at Neil. Who had just entered the kitchen and come to a dead stop when he saw her.

He was wearing a pair of cotton sleep pants and a wrinkled tee, his short hair messy with an epic case of bedhead. Probably because it had still been damp when they'd finally tumbled into bed the night before.

She bit her lip to keep from smiling at what had taken place in that bed after they'd tumbled into it.

The man had *more* than made up for breaking his ladies first policy.

Legs quivering in memory, she deposited the carton of eggs and nearly empty jug of orange juice onto the counter beside the rest of the potential ingredients she'd assembled. She'd wanted to surprise Neil with breakfast in bed, to celebrate the success of their very first sleep-over date, such as it was.

They'd shared lots of dinners and even some lunches these past weeks. But breakfast? Other than coffee, she was still in the dark about his preferences there thanks to his self-imposed rule about not spending the night together because of his nightmares.

A rule that was hopefully one step closer to changing.

But she didn't want to pressure him.

Or spook him.

And he definitely looked a little spooked, standing there in the doorway, staring at her with hooded eyes she couldn't quite read.

Because of that, she did her best to act like it was no big deal she was in the middle of his kitchen at seven o'clock in the morning, wearing nothing more than her panties and the t-shirt he'd given her to sleep in. She poured him a steaming mug of coffee, hit it with a large dollop of milk, stirred, and deposited it on the counter with a smile.

The promise of caffeine finally drew him the rest of the way into the kitchen. He mumbled his thanks and took a long sip, followed by another.

She didn't take offense at his lack of greeting. She'd learned the day of the softball game that Neil without his morning coffee was about as personable as a hungover porcupine with a hangnail.

Finally, after a good portion of the mug was empty, he answered her question. "Any way but runny's fine."

One more thing they agreed on.

She surveyed her food options, which were a little lacking. "How about an omelet?"

"Sounds good."

"Okay, I'll tackle that if you want to do the toast."

He grunted. "Be right back." Mug still clasped like a lifeline, he headed for the kitchen door where Bailey stood waiting. He followed her out into the backyard, the door closing behind him with a soft but definitive click.

Emotions knotted uncomfortably in her belly. Was joining the dog outside as she did her morning business the norm, or did he just want a minute away from her and this odd moment of domesticity?

She blew out a breath. Whichever it was, her course was set. There was nothing for it but to stick with the plan and see what happened.

By the time Neil and Bailey came back inside, she'd finished shredding some cheddar cheese and diced up one of the bell peppers from last night's original menu. The chicken had to be thrown out after being left in his truck for hours. So, when they finally emerged from the bedroom in search of sustenance, they'd feasted on boxed macaroni and cheese instead.

There was something to be said for simple comfort food.

Without a word, Neil topped off her coffee before refilling his own, brought both to the table, then came back and dropped two slices of bread into the toaster. By the time it popped, he'd given Bailey fresh water and a bowl of food she promptly buried her face in.

The silence was becoming almost unbearable.

Staring down at the frying pan waiting to flip the omelet, she nearly jumped when he padded up behind her on silent feet and slid his arms around her to nuzzle her neck.

"Good morning,"

The slight scratch of his unshaven scruff sent a delicious shiver through her as her body remembered the same sensation in other, more intimate places last night.

"Morning." She turned her head so his questing lips could connect with hers. With a happy sigh, she relaxed back against him, some of the knots in her tummy loosening. "Mmm, nice. I could get used to this."

The toast popped right then, so she couldn't tell if that was why he stepped away from her so abruptly, or if it was her words. Whichever the reason, the playful mood evaporated like it had never been.

"Don't," Neil said gruffly as he yanked out the toast and slammed another two slices of bread into the slots.

Well, that answered that question.

Rather than keep dancing around it, she asked straight out, "Why not? I was here the whole night and nothing horrible happened."

"We got lucky." He sounded as on edge as he had last night, when instead of going home after their post-coital cuddle, she told him she was staying.

After what he had been through, she hadn't wanted him to be alone. Plus, he needed to know she wasn't about to run whenever his PTS surfaced and threw his life into chaos. Staying the night was the logical solution.

Not that it had been easy to convince him of that. But short of physically removing her from his house, he'd been stymied on how to get rid of her. Sometimes all those gentlemanly southern manners really played to a woman's advantage.

A fact she'd been shameless about exploiting.

But only because it was for his own good.

"Did you hear what I said?"

After dividing up the omelet, she slid both halves onto plates just as the second round of toast came up. "You were either going to have a nightmare, or you weren't. You didn't."

"But I could have."

"But you didn't. And even if you had, I was all the way out in the living room." His condition when he finally relented. That, and not to come into the bedroom without his say so, no matter what she heard.

"I told you I'd take the sofa. There was no reason for you to be uncomfortable." He dropped the toast onto the plates and carried both to the table.

"And what if you *did* have a nightmare?" She tore off two paper towels from the roll and slapped them down next to the plates before taking her seat. "There's no way for Bailey to turn on the light for you in the living room."

An aspect of Bailey's training which had both intrigued and impressed her. Pawing a wall switch to light up a room when he had a nightmare. That way, he could see his surroundings and know where he was and, hopefully, pull him out of it quicker.

She glanced at the dog, lying relaxed but attentive beside Neil's chair. That was a good sign, right?

"The point is, you took an unnecessary risk." Neil forked some eggs into his mouth, chewed, and added in the same brusque tone, "This is good."

"Thank you. And no, I didn't." She put her own fork down without taking a bite. "Neil, sweetie, don't you get it? I know you might have nightmares. I know you might have panic attacks. But please stop expecting me to run whenever you do, okay? It's insulting."

That stopped him cold.

"I'm not trying to insult you, damn it. I'm trying to keep you safe."

She tossed her hands in the air. "You keep saying that, but I have yet to see any reason for you to think it. People have nightmares all the time."

"It's different."

"How? How is it different?" When he remained silent, her frustration percolated from simmer to boil. "Neil, how am I supposed to understand if you don't *explain* it to me?"

"I choked a woman."

The words were so low and harsh she wasn't sure she'd heard him right. "You…"

"I choked a woman. In my sleep. During a nightmare. *That's* how it's different."

Icy chills raced from her nape all the way down her spine. "Neil…" She swallowed. Hard. "You didn't…"

"Kill her? No. But I sure as fuck could have."

The fear of that was very real. It was plain on his face, in his haunted eyes and bloodless lips compressed into a hard, tight line.

Part of her wanted to just drop the subject and find a way to wipe that horror from his mind. But another part, the harsher, analytical one, said press on. If she was ever going to get to the root of his phobia about sharing a bed with her, if they were ever to find a way forward, it needed to be now.

Or it might be never.

"What happened? Neil?" She reached over to lay her hand on his, but he pulled away. The rejection stung. "Please. Talk to me."

"Want all the gory details, huh?"

She ignored the nasty tone, because it couldn't quite camouflage the underlying fear. "I want to understand."

The internal debate for fight-or-flight played out so clearly across his face that she saw the moment his body tensed for flight. "I'll just follow you," she warned.

Huffing out a soundless laugh, he shook his head in defeat.

"Yeah, you would, wouldn't you?" He shoved his plate away. "Okay, fine. You want the story? Here it is. I had a nightmare, and Laura tried to wake me up, but she got sucked into it instead. I have no idea what I was dreaming about, but when she shook me, it must have seemed like an attack and I...reacted. When I woke up, I had her pinned to the bed with one hand over her mouth and the other wrapped around her throat. I could have killed her."

The promise Neil demanded about not entering his bedroom no matter what she heard suddenly made a lot more sense.

Moistening her abruptly dry mouth, she said, "But you didn't."

"By the grace of God."

"Was she...hurt badly?"

There was an odd hesitation before he replied. "No."

"Neil?" She sat up straighter, instincts quivering. "How bad was she hurt?"

Again, he hesitated. "She had bruises on her wrists from where I grabbed her."

"But no bruises on her throat?" That didn't sound right.

"No. At least none I saw the next day."

"So, you didn't actually choke her."

"I had my hand on her throat."

"Not the same thing. If you'd used any force at all, there would have been bruises."

"She *said* I *choked* her." Neil's fist hit the table to emphasize the words. "Just because she didn't bruise doesn't mean she lied."

"I'm not saying she did. I'm just saying that everything probably happened really fast, and she was scared, and she might have *thought* you were about to choke her. But from the sound of it, you didn't actually hurt her."

"Whether I hurt her or not isn't the point. I *attacked* her. *That's* the point, and that's why we can't share a bed. I won't take the risk. Not with you."

"It's not your decision to make."

"The hell it's not!"

Trying a different tack, she asked, "I'm guessing Laura was your fiancée?" When he nodded, she continued. "So, this all happened back before you had Bailey. Before you were even diagnosed with PTSD, right? Or had any therapy? And were probably still drinking?" Talk about the perfect storm.

"None of that—"

"Did it only happen that one time?"

"Well, she sure as hell wasn't gonna stick around for an encore, was she?"

No, she'd evidently left him at the first sign he was struggling with something much worse than a simple drinking problem. Alex wanted to hate her for that, but couldn't. As far as Laura knew, she'd been escaping a potential domestic violence situation. Which was absolutely the right thing to do when you felt threatened.

But Alex didn't feel threatened. She knew exactly what she was facing, and why. And she planned to stick around and fight for Neil to the bitter end.

"Have you ever tried to sleep with someone in the same bed since then?"

"I've never even slept with someone in the same house since then."

"Until last night," she said, feeling smug. The look he gave her said he heard it, and wasn't amused. She didn't care. They'd crossed a threshold last night. Neil could be as annoyed with her as he wanted. He still couldn't take back the fact it happened.

And what happened once could happen again.

"It's not going to happen again," he said grimly.

Sometimes they thought way too much alike.

"Yes, it will." She brought a forkful of eggs to her mouth and chewed despite the tension knots that had destroyed her appetite. It tasted like old rubber bands, but she ate a second bite anyway, hoping to affect a sense of calm she was nowhere near feeling.

Neil scrubbed his hands over his face, fingers rasping against the harsh stubble. "Damn it, Alexandra…"

"I mean it. It's going to happen again. And again, and again, and again, until you realize that spending the night in the same house with me isn't the big, scary thing you've built it up to be in your mind."

"So, you're satisfied to be in the same house, even though it means never sleeping in the same bed?"

"For a start, anyway. Baby steps."

She sipped her coffee to wash away the taste of the eggs. Or was it the taste of fear? Because she might talk a good game, but she was working on instinct and sheer stubbornness here. There was no guarantee she was right.

Neil glared at her for a moment before shaking his head. "You have no idea what you're getting yourself into."

"Actually, I do, and that's the difference between me and Laura." She couldn't help the sour twist her lips gave when she said the name. "Face it, Neil, you're not getting rid of me. We're in this together."

She forced herself to eat another forkful of eggs as if she didn't have a care in the world when, in fact, the next few minutes could decide everything. In the long silence that followed, all she could hear was her heart pounding and the soft click of her tight jaw as she chewed.

Finally, Neil muttered something under his breath about stubborn Scots and dragged his plate closer again, digging back into his food with vicious stabs.

It wasn't exactly a victory. More of a temporary ceasefire, with the potential for renewed hostilities at a future time. Still, she gave herself a pat on the back for holding her own in the opening salvo.

As they cleared the dishes away a short time later, the tension had eased and things seemed to have settled back to their normal light conversation and mostly comfortable silences. Which was fine by her. If he could pretend nothing had changed, so could she.

For now, anyway.

"Do you still want to go up to Knoxville today?" She'd been looking forward to the trip all week. But a Saturday in June meant tourists by the busload. And after yesterday's incident at Coulter's, she wasn't sure if Neil was up to traveling that far from his comfort zone of home, or being around tons of people. "We could just go fishing on the lake or something."

She didn't know how they'd get Bailey into the small rowboat, but they'd figure something out.

"No, we planned for Knoxville, we'll go to Knoxville." He didn't look happy, but he did look determined, so she didn't argue. "You'll need to stop home first to shower and change, though. Do you want me to swing by and pick you up in, say, an hour?"

She hesitated.

"Would it totally freak you out that I have an overnight bag with toiletries and a change of clothes in my car?"

Neil's eyes narrowed. "So, you planned to spend last night here all along?"

"Not last night, specifically, no. But I planned to spend the night *some* night, and I wanted to be prepared. It's been there for about a week now." The confession could totally backfire on her, but she wanted him to know how serious she was about this.

No matter how embarrassing.

He looked like he had something he wanted to say about her premeditation to sleep over despite all his protests, but didn't. He just shook his head.

"Go take your shower. I'll take care of the dishes."

She didn't want to leave the room with him being annoyed at her.

Biting her lower lip, she looked at him through lowered lashes. "Sure you don't want to come share?"

As hoped, a flare of lust bloomed in his eyes, obliterating the last of the shadows lurking there. Dishes clattered in the sink. "Not if you want to get to Knoxville anytime today," he growled.

She was still a little tender from the night before, so retreat might be her wisest course for the moment. Then again, there were plenty of things they could do—

Richard's ringtone sounding from her phone jarred her right out of that train of thought.

Oh, crap on a cracker.

Throwing a look of apology in Neil's direction, she swiped the phone up from the counter and answered. "What could have possibly happened in the very few hours you've been there that would warrant you needing to call me on a Saturday morning, Richard?"

There was a long pause. "I, uh, have a problem."

Of course he did. Richard always had a problem. And he could never seem to solve them on his own. It was always Alexandra to the rescue.

And whose fault was that? asked a tiny voice that sounded suspiciously like Dionne.

"What kind of problem, Richard? Is the building on fire?"

"Uh, no..."

"Anyone dead or bleeding?"

"God, no! Why would you—"

"Is the network still broadcasting?"

"Yes. For Pete's sake, Alex—"

"Then I think you can handle whatever it is on your own." God, her stomach cramped just saying those words, but they were long overdue.

"You...*what?*"

"You heard me. You're an assistant producer. It's time you started acting like one. Take charge of the problem and handle it. I'm not going to come running to do it for you anymore." She looked at Neil, who was watching her with a hooded gaze. "I've got more important things to do."

"More important than work?"

It wasn't surprising her cousin sounded so totally incredulous. There had never once been something Alex put before the network since she started working there. Even before that, when she'd spent summers interning there during high school. She had brushed aside dates and parties and just plain having a normal teenage life in favor of whatever job cropped up that no one else wanted to do.

But standing in Neil's kitchen, watching him watch her with a resigned look that said he totally expected her to bail on their day—again—she saw all the lonely days and nights she'd spent focused on work. And knew she didn't want to live like that anymore.

She'd finally found something that was worth more to her than proving she was the best at what she did to everyone.

"Definitely more important than work."

"Who the heck are you, and what have you done with my control freak cousin?"

The only half-joking question made her grin. "Richard, you have the job because you can do the job. So, I'm letting you." She paused. "Unless you want to tell me you don't think you can?"

"No," he replied quickly. "I'm not telling you that."

"Good."

"Okay." There was a pause, then he said again with more assurance, "Okay. I'll handle it. But can I call you if I have a question?" he added in a rush.

He sounded overwhelmed and a little freaked out, so she didn't have the heart to set him entirely adrift on his own just yet.

"You can text me," she counter-offered. "But I'll only reply if I don't think you already know the answer yourself."

Richard sucked in a deep breath. "Fair enough."

"I'm hanging up now."

"Um, okay. Bye. And, ah, Alex? Thanks."

Thumbing off her phone, she was immediately caught between relief and panic. God, she'd never even asked what the problem was. What if it really was bigger than he could handle? How was she going to get through the day with that question mark hanging over her head? Maybe she should just call him back real quick and...

"Breathe," Neil whispered against her cheek as he slipped his hands over her hips and pulled her back against the lean, hard line of his body. "I can't believe you did that."

Swallowing, she leaned back into his comforting embrace. "Neither can I." She pressed a hand to her stomach. "God, I feel nauseous."

"You'll be fine." He kissed her temple. "But I don't think we're going to Knoxville today. You won't be able to enjoy yourself," he added when she started to protest.

She sighed. "No, I won't. I'm so sorry." She turned in his arms to face him and slid her hands slowly up under his tee along his warm skin. "What can I possibly do to make it up to you?"

With a wicked grin that sent shivers of delicious anticipation down her spine, he said, "Oh, I think we can come up with something."

Chapter 12

"I WANT TO DO a special about Bailey."

Neil looked over at Alex, who was bending to set the dog's water bowl in the raised tray she'd gotten to match the one he had at home. He took a long second to admire the curve of her ass as she did, not feeling the least bit guilty when she turned and caught him at it.

Interest stirred in her eyes, as well as his pants.

He might have even done something about it if the bacon hadn't chosen that moment to spit hot grease onto his hand and recall him to his task.

"Neil, did you hear me?"

"I did." He carefully turned the rest of the sizzling strips before sliding the spatter shield back over the pan.

"And? What do you think?"

"I think that while Bailey is extremely photogenic and would probably eat up being on camera, I doubt she'd have much to say in an interview."

"Neil."

"Alex."

Making sure the flame was low under the frying pan, he went to where she stood, arms crossed. With a gentle tug, he pulled her in against him so he could nibble on her neck.

God, she tasted sweet.

"That wasn't what I meant, and you know it," she grumbled even as she stroked a hand up over his chest. She let out a small moan as he nipped her earlobe.

"Then what did you mean?"

"I want to do a special about Bailey and *you*."

That's what he'd been afraid of.

"No." Abruptly, he set her away and stalked back to the stove.

"No? Why not?"

She actually had the nerve to sound surprised. And annoyed.

Damn it, if anyone had the right to be annoyed, it was him. After nearly a month of being together, she knew him better than just about anyone except maybe Isaac, and she still couldn't figure it out?

"I don't need to air my dirty laundry in public." He turned the bacon again and adjusted the flame higher. The sooner it was ready, the sooner they could occupy their mouths with something other than talking.

"Dirty..." She looked horrified. "That's not what I meant. At all. How could you think that?"

"So, you don't want me to talk about the PTSD and how fucked up my life is because of it? About the nightmares and panic attacks? Hell, why not throw in how I can't even share a bed with the woman I'm sleeping with?" He knew he was being obnoxious, but couldn't seem to stop himself.

It was one thing to share his issues with *her*. To ask him to expose them to the whole, wide world?

Fuck that.

"I was hoping you could talk about how having a service dog has impacted your quality of life since your diagnosis," she replied stiffly.

"Same difference."

"It is *not* the same." Alex took a breath. "Neil, I just want to raise awareness of the issues facing returning veterans, and especially the ignorant bias people seem to have about service dogs. Don't you want to be able to walk into a shop or restaurant and not have to explain yourself because someone doesn't know or understand what a service dog is or does, and what rights you both have?"

He groaned in sudden understanding. "This is about the movies, isn't it?"

Damn it. Of course it was.

When they'd finally gotten around to their day trip to Knoxville, they'd gone to one of the big cineplex theaters with the heated recliner seats Alex had been itching to try out. And been denied tickets because of Bailey.

He would have just left, but not Alex. Oh, no.

She'd put up such a ruckus the manager had to be called. Who'd apologized up and down about the "misunderstanding" and offered to comp their tickets. But the damage was done. Their pleasant day ended on a sour note, and Alex had fumed the whole ride home.

Truth was, it had ticked him off, too. But it wasn't the first time something like that happened. Wouldn't be the last. He'd learned to pick his battles when it came to the ignorance of the public about ADA laws. Some fights just weren't worth having.

Judging by the stubborn look on Alex's face, though, she didn't agree.

"It's about the movies, and the ballpark, and the snotty lady making all the nasty comments not-so under her breath at the restaurant, and every other time you've been given grief over having Bailey with you," she said. "You were injured serving your country, dang it. You deserve a heck of a lot more respect than 'you can't bring your dog in here' everywhere you go. It's just not right."

"Technically, I wasn't serving my country when everything went to shi—went sideways on me. I was civilian press."

"You served eight years before that. Don't you think every-thing you went through during that time was part of a cumu-lative effect?"

Maybe. Or maybe watching Jessie's brain get scrambled by a bullet as she reached out to him for help had been enough all on its own. Not like it really mattered. The result was the same. He was still one fucked up motherfucker.

"Vets aren't the only ones with service dogs, you know." Let her go interview one of them and leave him alone.

"That's right, and raising awareness of the problem would benefit everyone," she replied. Totally missing—or more likely ignoring—his point.

Damn, that chin of hers was starting to come up. He needed to nip this idea now, before she really sank her teeth in and it became some kind of crusade.

God knew he'd had enough of those from her already.

"I know you mean well, sweetheart, but I don't think a five-minute piece on a county news network will do all that much to change the world." He caught the flash of something in her expression that set off his "bad-shit-is-about-to-happen" meter.

Alex's chin notched a fraction higher. "That's why it's going to be a full half-hour special."

"*Going* to be?" Hadn't she been listening to a word he said?

"Well, when I pitched it to Colin, I knew—"

"Wait a minute." He waved his hands, tightness clawing at the base of his skull. "You already brought this to Colin? With-out talking to me first?"

"Well, I wanted to see if he would even go for the idea," she replied, sounding both defensive and guilty. "I never men-tioned you. I kept it totally in the abstract."

"Right. Because he'd never connect me with a piece on ser-vice dogs."

Embarrassment flashed over her face at the sarcasm, but she didn't back down.

"He thinks it's a good idea. So do I. It could help so many people."

"What you mean is, it could help you get ratings," he snapped back. "Weren't you telling me Colin was on everyone about that? Boosting ratings and revenue? Well, sorry, sweetheart, but you're going to have to find some other way to score points with the Old Man, because you sure as hell aren't doing it on my back."

"Neil, no! It has nothing to do with—"

The sharp shriek of an incoming mortar round sliced through the rest of her words.

Instinct kicked in.

He jumped forward and snagged an arm around her, pulling her with him to their knees against the cabinets, body curved over hers as a futile shield. His heart beat so hard in his chest, in his ears, in his throat, that he couldn't hear her right away. Then she frantically patted his arm. He tried to focus. She was saying…something. Something about letting her up.

The second he did, she scrambled to her feet and sprinted for the stove. With one hand she shoved the smoking pan onto one of the unlit burners, while the other hit the switch for the exhaust fan.

Frozen, he could only stare as she waved a potholder at the screeching smoke detector high on the ceiling, his breathing so fast and shallow he thought he might pass out. Bailey burrowed into his side, pressed tight, wet nose in his face as she whined. Doing her job despite the piercing alarm that had to be hurting her sensitive ears. Keeping him from slipping any further into something that wasn't real.

As abruptly as it began shrieking, the smoke detector fell silent, leaving only the low hum of the exhaust fan as it sucked the last of the hazy smoke from the room. With a clumsy hand, he gave Bailey's head a pat to praise her.

But his gaze stayed fixed on Alex, who was staring back with wide eyes.

The startled look of shock in them nearly gutted him.

And fueled the need to strike back.

"Not so easy to stomach when you see it firsthand, is it? Too bad you didn't have a camera handy. You could have filmed *that* for your special."

Without waiting for a reply, he got up and slammed out the door, moving as fast as he could without admitting he was running. Once on the deck, he continued walking, down the steps, over the grass, across the sand, and finally out onto the dock.

Which was as far as he could get from the house—from Alex—without climbing in his truck and leaving.

Which maybe he should do.

After that little show, he sure as hell couldn't face her again.

But leaving felt too much like giving up. Giving up on her, on them. On this chance he'd found, this miracle, to reclaim part of the man he'd once been. The one he wanted to be again. For Alex, yes, but even more for himself.

For that, he'd face the humiliation of apologizing for being an ass.

In a little while.

For now, he stood at the end of the dock, looking out at the water that stretched in a rippling horizon before him. Late morning sunlight danced along the surface. It was soothing. Tranquil. A balm to his soul, which was feeling pretty tattered. Nothing could be further from the endless sea of sand that formed the backdrop of his personal hell.

The faint jingle of Bailey's collar tags came from behind him.

Damn. He'd run out so fast he'd left her behind. Alex must have let her out.

Grateful to them both, he dropped his hand onto the dog's head as she sat beside him, leaning into his leg. Sharing the silent comfort of her presence. Like the water, it was soothing, but neither was enough to fully still the edgy restlessness just beneath his skin.

The need for something he couldn't quite bring himself to admit.

Because once the universe knew what was important to you, it could take it away.

The faint vibration of her footsteps echoed through the weathered planks, announcing Alex's presence before she slid her arms around him from behind. As she rested her head against the middle of his back, something loosened inside his chest and the restlessness receded.

"I'm so sorry." Her words were muffled, but clear. "You're right. I should have talked to you first. And I should have accepted it when you said no. It wasn't fair of me to expect you to talk about something so personal on camera. I didn't understand. I thought I did, but..."

But now she'd seen the real deal.

It hadn't even been a full-fledged flashback. More of a muscle memory reaction. Duck and cover when the mortars sang that high-pitched song.

But it had been enough to show her that the crazy never lurked far from the surface.

And yet...she was still here.

Touching him. Holding him.

He didn't know why, but he wasn't going to question it. Much as he wanted to turn and hold her close, breathe her into his lungs like she was a hit of pure oxygen, he settled for pressing his hand over hers where they crossed over his belly. He wasn't ready to face her just yet. "It's okay."

Her arms tightened around him for a second before she pressed a kiss to his spine and once more put her cheek on his back. "I'm so sorry," she said again, but this time he was pretty sure she was talking about something far different from their argument.

"So am I." Sorry he'd dragged her into his screwed-up life. Sorry she'd had to be a part of that mini-flashback. Sorry she felt she needed to fight so many battles on his behalf.

But he was nowhere near sorry enough to let her go.

"Okay, I see why you've been keeping him for yourself all these weeks." Dionne reached over and patted Alex's arm. "I totally forgive you for ditching me for him."

Sitting in the low-slung Adirondack chairs like Neil's that she'd bought for the grassy knoll facing the lake, Alex followed her best friend's gaze to where the man under discussion was standing on the dock. Fishing pole in hand, Bailey laying like a golden rug soaking up the sunshine nearby.

Next to him was Dionne's fiancé. Usually, Martel's ex-football player physique dwarfed everyone he met. But while Martel had a few inches on him in all directions, Alex thought Neil held his own rather well in comparison.

Not that she was biased or anything.

"He is pretty fine, isn't he?" She sipped her sweet tea, then added, "And I didn't ditch you. I've just been...busy."

"Mmhmm. Busy doing that boy until he can't walk straight, you mean. Oh, stop!" Dionne laughed at her sputtered objection. "I've seen the way you two look at each other whenever you get within touching distance. You've moved *way* beyond the hand-holding stage. And since I know for a fact you hadn't even kissed that man the last time we talked, that's some pretty fast moves for you. You usually think everything to death before you decide to jump in bed with anyone."

She wasn't certain she and Neil had ever had a hand-holding stage. And Dee was right. Things *had* moved pretty fast between them, right from the start.

Maybe too fast?

She shooed the nagging doubt away.

"Things are going good with us. Really good."

"There's a 'but' in that voice."

"But...I might have screwed up."

Dionne put her glass down on the grass and donned her teacher face. The one that never failed to put the fear of God into her students. And, though she'd never admit it, into Alex as well.

"Alexandra Aileen McKenna, what did you do?"

The skin on the back of her neck prickled at the triple name calling.

"I, um, did something that really hurt him. I didn't mean to," she added quickly, "but it did anyway, and, well, I'm not sure how to make it better."

Neil had accepted her apology and her promise to drop the whole idea about the special, but things had still been a little strained between them since yesterday morning. And for the first time since she'd broken through that invisible barrier of sleepovers, they hadn't spent the night in the same house.

She'd half expected him to bail on today as well, since it was the first time he'd be meeting her friends. Something he hadn't been all that enthusiastic about in the first place. But he had shown up as promised, and things between them had seemed almost back to normal.

Almost, but not quite.

"What did you do?" Dionne repeated.

"I told him I wanted to do a special that would bring attention to the importance of service dogs for returning vets."

"And?"

She squirmed. "And...that I wanted to focus on him and Bailey."

"Focus on Neil? Are you insane? I only just met the man and I know he'd never be comfortable having his life splashed all over the screen for people to gawk at. What were you thinking? No, wait, I know the answer to that. You were thinking of the story, just like you always do. Only this time, it's the person *behind* the story that should have been most important to you." She shook her head. "I don't blame him for being upset."

"I never meant to hurt him."

Just the opposite, in fact. She wanted to help.

But Dee had hit the nail on the head. She'd been thinking like a journalist rather than a girlfriend. Neil didn't need her to shout his story from the rooftops. She just had to be at his side when he needed her most.

And she would.

"So, what happened?" Dionne gestured toward where the two men were packing up their fishing tackle and rods. "He's here, so clearly you worked things out."

"I told him I'd kill the idea for the story."

It went against every instinct she had, but she'd do it. The reception that announcement would likely get from Colin wasn't something she looked forward to, but for Neil, she'd go toe-to-toe with her grandfather if it came to it.

Just like she had when he'd called her on the carpet for leaving Richard to fend for himself instead of dropping everything to run to his rescue. Thankfully, Richard had dealt with his "problem" with the aid of only a few panicked text messages and one phone call to talk him off a ledge, so Colin hadn't really had room to bitch.

Not that it ever stopped him if he felt someone hadn't performed as he expected.

Which was the way Alex was beginning to feel. That she wasn't so much doing her job as performing for the Old Man in the top office. He set the tune, and she danced to it. Oh, she still loved her job, but she was finally beginning to see why her father and uncle had stayed far, far away from their father's autocratic rule.

"Did you apologize, too?" Dionne asked.

"Of course." More than once. And it still didn't feel like enough.

"But?"

She sighed. "But things still feel...off. I'm worried that whatever this thing is between us, I might have damaged it."

"This thing?" Dionne echoed. "Really? You still can't say the words?"

Not out loud. But she'd been using them in her head for some time now.

She drew a deep breath. "I love him."

"There." Dionne picked her drink back up with a smug grin. "That didn't hurt too much, did it?"

More than her friend might think, since she wasn't sure if Neil felt the same way.

"This was your first big fight, wasn't it?"

"Yes," she replied after giving it some thought. They'd had minor skirmishes—a lot of them, actually, especially over sleeping arrangements—but yesterday's blow-up had really been the first time she'd call what they did an actual fight.

"Then don't worry too much about it. It's normal for things to take a little while to settle back in place. Give it a few days, maybe a week, and you won't even remember you were mad at each other."

Doubtful, given the topic. But she was willing to hope that was true. In any case, Neil and Martel had almost reached them, so the discussion was over.

Since the men had caught nothing worthy of being lunch, they settled for the burgers and ribs Dee and Martel had brought with them. Although 'settled' was a relative term, since the burgers were Dee's awesome inside-out cheeseburgers that oozed artery-clogging pepper jack gooey goodness with every juicy bite.

"Sorry about the ribs," Martel apologized as they dug in. "I know they're not as good as the ones we usually get from Coulter's, but they, ah, were sold out."

"You have to get there really early, especially on the weekend." She hadn't meant to sound like she was scolding, but dang, it was a disappointment to the tastebuds. These ribs weren't anywhere in the same league as Big Tom's.

Rumor had it some big restaurant chain in Nashville had offered him a pretty penny for his secret BBQ sauce, but he'd turned them down flat. Much to the delight of everyone in Shelby, who considered Big Tom's ribs a local treasure and preferred to keep it that way.

Dionne was frowning at her fiancé. "You told me there was something wrong with the refrigerator where they store all the meat, and *that* was why you got the meat for the burgers from the Piggly Wiggly when you know I prefer the way they grind it at Coulter's."

Rib halfway to his mouth, Martel froze. His eyes darted quickly to Dionne, then away. "Umm..."

Fingertips tapping against the table, Dionne demanded, "Martel Jeremiah Hunt, did you *lie* to me?"

"Ooh, you're in trouble now," Alex muttered under her breath. Or so she thought. The small nudge to her ankle from Neil had her looking down at her plate to hide the grin that wanted to blossom.

Busted.

Martel was in full-on deer-meet-headlights mode. "Umm..."

"Well?"

It shouldn't have been amusing to watch the poor man squirm. But she couldn't help but marvel at the way her friend could bring a six-six former collegiate all-star to the level of recalcitrant schoolboy with no more than a look and a tapping finger.

Would she ever have that kind of power over Neil?

Glancing his way, a tingle of awareness zinged through her as their gazes collided. A tiny grin quirked his lips and he gave his head a slow shake, as though he knew exactly what she was thinking.

Whoo-boy.

Alex quickly switched her attention back to the mini-drama playing out on the other side of the table. Sometimes it scared her, the way she and Neil seemed to think on the same wavelength. But she was beginning to like it more than it bothered her. No one had ever *gotten* her like that before. No one except for Dionne.

Who was still tapping that finger, waiting.

"Okay." Martel dropped the half-eaten rib to his plate and grabbed a napkin to wipe the sauce from his fingers. "Yes, I lied, but before you go ripping up at me about it, let me say my piece, okay?"

Mouth pinched, Dionne gave a regal nod for him to go on.

"I did go to Coulter's this morning right after church, just like I said I did. But it wasn't open. That's why I had to drive to the Piggly Wiggly for everything."

"It wasn't open?" Alex frowned. "That doesn't make any sense. I can't think of a single day Big Tom didn't have the doors unlocked on time."

"And why would you think you had to make up a lie about it?" Dionne added, looking as confused as Alex felt.

Strangely, it was Neil who Martel glanced at before he continued.

"I, ah, asked a few people who were there, too, looking to get into the store. And, ah, one of them said they heard that Big Tom and his family were all over at the hospital in Gatlinburg. That, ah," another glance, "Tommy, you know, the boy who just got back from overseas? That he, um...he tried to kill himself last night."

Shocked silence descended over the group. Alex sensed Neil go rigid beside her. She slid her hand over his on the table and squeezed. That he didn't show he was even aware of her touch worried her more than his silence did.

Dionne, meanwhile, had slumped in her chair, all the anger gone, replaced by sympathy and confusion. "Oh, my dear lord, that's *awful*. But, why didn't you just tell me that in the first place?"

"I didn't want to ruin your day," Martel replied. He reached out and took Dionne's hands into his. "I'm sorry, baby. I don't like lying, but at the time it seemed the lesser evil."

Alex might have bought Martel's reasoning if she hadn't seen the worried look he'd sent in Neil's direction. Oh, he may not have wanted to upset Dee, but there was more to it. More like if he'd told her, there was no way Neil wouldn't have found out. If there was one fault her friend had, it was that she couldn't keep a secret to save her soul.

And a secret as big as this one wouldn't have lasted ten whole minutes.

Much as she appreciated Martel's consideration for Neil, she still hoped the couple was long gone when Dionne figured that one out for herself.

"Did they know what happened?" Dionne asked.

"Dee!" Alex shot her a look of pure disbelief.

"What? I didn't want *details*. I was just wondering..."

Without a word, Neil shoved his chair back and left the table, heading down the steps from the deck to the yard, Bailey faithfully at his heels.

"Neil?"

"Need a minute."

The fact the dog wasn't pressed to his leg or trying to lead him by the hand was all that kept her from jumping up and following, despite his words. She did her best to convince herself this wasn't what happened in the kitchen the day before. This was just a man rocked by bad news who didn't want to expose his emotions to people he barely knew. Who needed to be alone to process things.

Again.

Okay, then. If he needed some space, she could give him that. For a little while, anyway. But she wasn't going to let him keep putting distance between them whenever something was bothering him.

They were a couple, damn it. They'd face their problems together.

Whether he liked it or not.

Dionne was also watching Neil's hasty escape, and her eyes suddenly widened in belated understanding. "Oh. *Oh!* I shouldn't have said that. I didn't mean to..."

"It's fine." Or at least it would be.

Hopefully.

"I wasn't sure how he'd take it," Martel said apologetically.

"I appreciate you worrying. It's probably best he heard about it now, and not tomorrow at work or something." That kind of news ran like wildfire through a small town like Shelby. She was actually surprised she hadn't gotten a half dozen texts already. Her hand went to her shorts pocket.

Oh, right. She'd left her phone inside the house. On purpose. Something she never did.

See what happens when you unplug yourself from the world?

"Will he be okay?" Dionne asked.

Alex glanced in the direction Neil had gone, but he was no longer in sight. "I think so. It's just..." How much to share? "He was just talking to Big Tom not that long ago about Tommy. I think that makes it hit a little closer to home, you know?"

Martel winced. "Yeah, it would."

They continued eating, but the conversation was awkward and sparse. By the time they were done with their plates, Neil's minute had stretched into twenty, he still hadn't returned, and her patience had reached its end.

Thank God for Dionne being able to read her like a book. She was quick to hustle Martel to the car with a hasty goodbye and a look that said 'call me' before they drove away. After waving them off from her front steps, she took a long moment to mentally steel herself, then went on the hunt.

He was surprisingly easy to find. Stretched out on the ground beneath the huge weeping willow tree she, Lyle, and Richard had once climbed like monkeys pretending to be everything from Tarzan to pirates to actual monkeys. Hands stacked beneath his head, he stared upward. Branches hanging like a droopy green umbrella blocked the sky, so his vision was likely turned inward.

Bailey thumped her tail in welcome as Alex sat on the ground next to Neil. She gave her a quick stroke, but all of her attention was for the man her heart was breaking for as he sat up, unable to hide the grief that was eating him whole.

Knowing without words what he needed, she reached for him.

There was such urgency to Neil's movements as he stripped them both of their clothing that she expected him to take her hard and fast in order to exorcise his pain.

Instead, he slid into her slow and sweet. And made the most tender, caring love to her beneath the cool branches of her childhood playhouse that when her climax burst upon her, setting off sparklers behind her eyelids, she knew this had been different.

More than sex. More than lust. More than distraction.

Tears pricked her eyes as he withdrew and pulled her gently into the curve of his body, her back to his front. Never had she felt so protected, so cared for.

So loved.

In that moment of peace and contentment, the last thing she expected him to say when he spoke softly against her neck was, "I'll do the special."

She stilled, not sure she'd heard him right. "Are you sure?"

"Yeah." Then he added, "On one condition."

"What?"

"You do the interview."

Familiar panic stabbed her, seizing her diaphragm. "Oh, no. Vanessa would do a *much* better job—"

"No. I'll only be able to get through it if it's you I'm talking to. No one else, and *definitely* not her."

Understanding allowed her to subvert her own anxieties in order to deal with the much bigger, uglier ones Neil would have to conquer to get through the interview. She might hate being on camera, but he would be baring a piece of his soul to the world.

Comparing the two, there was only one answer she could give.

"Okay."

"Okay." The subtle tension in his body eased as he pulled her closer, as though he'd crossed some inner Rubicon. And maybe he had.

She'd give him the chance to change his mind later, after the endorphin high had faded and she was certain he was thinking clearly. But if he didn't change it? If he really wanted to go through with the special?

She had some intensive work ahead of her, because this was one interview she couldn't afford to get wrong.

Chapter 13

"You didn't have to come, you know."

Following him up the walkway to Manor Hill, Alex replied, "No, but I wanted to." They both paused when they reached the front doors. "Gus is your friend, so of course I want to meet him. You met my friends."

"Yeah, but they were *nice*."

Alex laughed.

He wished he were joking. Gus was a pain in the ass on his best days. On his worst...he was a lot for even Neil to deal with. He had no idea how Alex was going to react to the uncensored stream of profanity that peppered the old bastard's vocabulary.

Most men raised by southern mothers, himself included, had an almost subconscious switch in their brain that blocked the use of foul language in the presence of women and children, except maybe under extreme duress. Either Gus's switch had broken with age, or he just chose to be offensive for reasons which were entirely his own.

Neil tended to lean toward the latter option.

Accepting he wouldn't dissuade Alex from the visit, he sighed and opened the door for her. She smiled and patted his chest as she walked in.

"Stop looking so worried. You forget, I've been dealing with a crabby old curmudgeon most of my life. If I can survive thirty-one years of Colin, an hour with your Gus will be a piece of cake."

He looked skyward and prayed she was right.

The sour expression on Gus's face didn't exactly buoy his hopes when they entered the common room. Despite the fact he'd seemed eager to meet Alex when Neil mentioned the possibility during their post-meeting chess game last week, the old man wasn't looking any too pleased now that the moment had arrived.

Neil's mood grew grimmer by the second. He'd always cut Gus a lot of slack, but he found he wasn't willing to do that now. Not if it meant subjecting Alex to his nasty temper and foul mouth. One wrong word and they were out of there.

At least Gus got to his feet as they approached.

A good sign, maybe?

"Alex, this is my friend, Gus Fazzalaro. Gus, this is Alexandra McKenna, my…girlfriend." He stumbled over the word a little, but only because he hadn't said it out loud before. Hell, he hadn't even said it in his head.

Not that he didn't consider them much more than fuck buddies or friends with benefits or whatever the hell they called it these days. They'd just never discussed what, exactly, they *did* consider themselves to be. Or where they thought they were heading. Everything had been more of a one-day-at-a-time kind of thing for them.

And today was evidently the day he committed himself to something more than he'd thought he'd be willing to risk with another woman ever again.

Not seeming fazed by him dropping the g-word, Alex extended her hand and smiled. "It's so nice to finally meet you, sir."

"Really? Huh. Can't think of why." Gus gave a perfunctory shake before scrutinizing her with an almost insultingly thorough perusal. "Bit on the skinny side, isn't she?" he finally said in an aside to Neil, as though Alex wasn't right there or had suddenly gone deaf. "I mean, she's pretty enough, I suppose, but she's barely got any titties at all."

"Gus!" *Son of a bitch!*

"What? It's true, ain't it? Man likes a little something to hold on to while he's getting 'er done."

"Judas priest, Gus, why would you...no." He put up his hands. "I don't care why. That was way more than just out of line, old man, and you'd better damn well apologize."

He risked a glance at Alex, expecting her to be all pokered-up and offended, the way her mother had looked on Founders Day when he'd dared to ask about borrowing the precious McKenna family albums.

Instead, he was shocked to see a grin twitching at the corners of her lips.

What the hell?

"Well, it *is* true they're small," Alex said with a shrug as she glanced down at her chest and sighed, "and that's a fact." She looked back at Gus, who was watching her with a confused pucker to his brow. "But it's kind of like guys with tiny...you know." She hooked her pinky and wiggled it.

"Oh? And how's that?" Gus asked.

Alex leaned in a little closer and replied conspiratorially, "We learn to compensate in other areas to make up for where we lack."

Both men stared at her, Neil in shock, Gus in a kind of awed admiration if his cackle was anything to go by. He shook his head and slapped Neil on the arm as the cackle grew to a full-out laugh.

"Damn, boy, you went and picked yourself a good one here. Not a prissy bitch at all. I like that."

"Why, thank you," Alex said in a very prissy voice, which made the old man laugh even harder.

Then he started to cough.

Neil took Gus's arm to steady him as he hacked and wheezed, while Alex hovered at the old man's other side.

"Should I go and get someone?" she asked anxiously.

"No, he should be okay in a minute." He hoped he was right. Gus had these coughing jags more and more often lately. It worried the hell out of him. But Gus had not-so subtly told him to mind his own damn business whenever he brought the subject up. So, he'd had no choice but to do exactly that.

Gus's wheezing slowly diminished to heavy breathing as he tried to catch his breath. He even grudgingly accepted Neil's help to sit back down in the wingback chair he'd been occupying when they first came in, though he couldn't hide the grimace that spasmed his face when he did.

Clearly, he wasn't having one of his good days.

"Maybe we should go," he said once Gus's breathing finally evened out.

"And leave me to the tender mercies of the Cougar Club?" Gus sputtered, sounding alarmed. "Hell, no!"

"The Cougar Club?" Alex repeated, looking to Neil for an explanation.

He bit back a grin.

"That's what he calls the group of single ladies here at Manor Hill who seem to have taken a special shine to him." In light of Gus's foul mouth and fouler temper, he couldn't fathom what the attraction was. But he'd been witness to several of the blatantly flirtatious exchanges firsthand, so he knew it was true.

Well, one half of the exchange had been flirtatious. The other half had been damn near offensive. And yet, the ladies kept coming back for more.

What did he know? Maybe they found grumpy assholes a turn-on.

"But a cougar usually means...oh!" Alex grinned at Gus, who was looking every inch of his seventy-three hard-living years. "Wow, the younger man, huh? Good for you!"

"Good for me hell," Gus snapped back. "I don't want those old biddies sniffing after me all the time. They all expect things."

"Things?" Neil exchanged a look with Alex, not sure he should ask, but unable not to. "What kind of things?"

A half-smirk lit the old man's face. "Well, now, let's just say I don't have to worry about doing no...compensating." He crooked his pinky as best as his arthritis would allow.

Alex slapped a hand over her mouth to stifle a laugh.

"Gus, for Pete's sake." But even he was fighting laughter. The man had absolutely no sense of boundaries.

A fact Gus proved when he winked at Alex and asked, "What about him?" with a jerk of his head in Neil's direction.

Before he could sputter out a single word, she said with a surprisingly straight face, "He holds his own quite nicely."

"He'd probably like it better if you held it for him," Gus returned.

"Okay, I think we can change the subject now." The last thing he needed was his friend and his girlfriend chatting about his junk and how well he used it.

Christ on a crutch.

Alex, at least, took pity on him.

"So, Gus, Neil tells me you're a pretty good chess player."

"Pretty good?" Gus snorted. "A fair sight better than that, I reckon. I beat his pansy ass more times than not." He eyed her speculatively. "Don't happen to play, do you?"

"I've been known to dabble."

"Hell, anyone can dabble. I asked if you could *play*."

Alex's chin rose at the challenge in his tone. "Well, I guess you'll just have to find out for yourself, now, won't you?"

"Well, now, I guess I will."

Two games later, Neil had no choice but to be impressed. He and Alex had played once, but he'd gotten distracted when she started removing bits of clothing, and, well, they'd never gotten around to actually finishing the game. So, he didn't know if her bold claim to Gus was true or not.

Seeing her play now, he knew she was more than a match for the old bastard.

Gus knew it, too, because he tipped his king with a grunt of disgust and glared at her from under his bushy white brows. "That's a game apiece. Set it up again. We'll go best of three."

Knowing they'd be playing all night if Gus had his way, he said, "Why don't we leave it a draw for now? It's getting kind of late."

"Oh, for fuck's sake, what are you, twelve?" Gus snapped. "Gotta get home before curfew or something? It's not even eight o'clock yet."

"Is it that late already?" Alex glanced at her watch. "Gus, I'm so sorry. It's my fault we have to call it an early night. But maybe I can come back another day so we can have a rematch? Maybe best of five, just to make it interesting?"

"Hmph. Fine. I suppose getting all naked and sweaty together is more fun than spending time with a lonely old man, so go ahead. I can find a deck of cards and play some solitaire until the cougar pack comes around and hunts me down."

Neil put his head in his hand with a groan.

"Actually," Alex said, coughing to cover a giggle, "we're going back to the studio to do some filming, so we're leaving because of work, not play."

The look she gave him from the corner of her eye promised play would come later.

It was that unspoken promise of blissful escape that would get him through the hell of what would come first.

"Huh." Squinting up at Neil, Gus asked, "So, you're really going through with it? Letting her film you while you vomit up all your feelings about how badly the war fucked you up, poor fucking you?"

Over the sharp breath Alex sucked in, he said as evenly as possible, "I told you I was."

Gus shook his head and muttered something under his breath.

"I don't know why you're so against the idea."

"Because talking doesn't do jack shit."

"We talk at our meetings all the time."

"Not about this," Gus said sharply. "What happened over there…that's what *we* talk about. Soldier to soldier. Nobody else gets it. They don't want to get it. They want everything all neat and tidy, only there's nothing tidy about broken-down soldiers who come back home fucked in the head because they suddenly got a face full of just how dirty and real war can be. Kids whose biggest worry one week was a zit on prom night, and the next was if they should blow away the ten-year-old kid walking over with a smile and a basket of bread because he might be carrying a bomb inside it."

There was raw anguish under the words, making Neil wonder just how acquainted Gus was with that particular head-fuck.

"Oh, Gus…" Alex whispered.

"Don't go all mushy and shit on me," he snapped. "That's not why I'm saying all this. I'm just saying plenty of guys have gone through the same, and worse. You don't see them crying about it all over TV."

"No," Neil said, his voice hollow, "they just crawl into a bottle under some overpass somewhere instead. Or put a bullet in their brain." Or down a handful of pills, like Tommy Coulter had done two weeks ago.

Only by the grace of God, and a mother with a gut feeling and a key to his room, had they gotten him to the hospital in time to save his life.

Whether there was any permanent damage remained to be seen.

"Which is exactly what we want to help keep from happening," Alex said. "We want them to know there are other options."

"By *talking*." Gus made it sound like a dirty word.

"Yes, by talking, damn it." Alex's tone was taking on a sharp edge of anger. "Stop being such a goddamn stubborn ass." She waved away the twin looks of surprise she got. "Oh, stop. I do know how to swear. I just don't do it unless I get really ticked off. And you—" she pointed at Gus "—are ticking me off."

"You're right, you know," Neil said, finally seeing where Gus was coming from. "Just talking about it won't fix it. There'll always be soldiers going off to war who come home screwed up in more ways than anyone can count, or fix. But it's those screwed up soldiers this whole thing is all about. We're losing over twenty guys a day to suicide back here at home where they're supposed to be safe, Gus. *Twenty!*"

He'd felt sick when Alex told him that stat. He still did.

"And all because they don't know what's wrong with them, or they do but don't know how to make all the shit in their head stop other than to just...stop everything." His tone softened. "Because they had to decide whether to shoot the kid with the bread or not. And nobody can deal with that shit without a piece of their soul bleeding. All you can do is find a way to stop the hemorrhaging before it drains you dry."

"You got that fucking right," Gus growled, swallowing hard as he avoided everyone's gaze. Neil thought he saw a wet glint in the old man's eyes before he blinked it away.

"So, if I can help one damn person decide to go see a shrink, or check themselves into the VA, or rehab, or *anything* other than eating a bullet because they know they're not weak or crazy, that they're not alone, then yeah. I'll damn well 'vomit my feelings' for the camera as many times as Alex asks me to."

She slipped her hand into his. He grasped it gratefully as Bailey leaned into his leg. He was nowhere near as blasé about offering up his personal experiences for public consumption as he made it sound, but he meant every word. If a little humiliation would help save a life, then maybe it would be worth the cost.

It took a few minutes before Gus had himself under good enough control to say anything. When he did, it was with a voice that was hoarse and raspy, like a man who'd been screaming for decades on the inside, only no one had heard him. Until now.

"I'm sorry. God knows I don't say it much, so don't get used to it, but you're right. If you really think you can bring some guys in from the edge, keep 'em from falling into the hell war makes for us in our heads...then maybe talking isn't such a bad thing."

That had to have been damn hard for him to say. He patted the old man's leg affectionately before he stood, bringing Alex up with him because he refused to relinquish her hand. "We'd better go."

"It really *was* nice to meet you, Gus," Alex said, her voice soft. "I'll be back for that rematch soon."

They'd only gone a few steps when Gus said, "Guys..." His voice cracked. When they turned back to look at him, he cleared his throat.

"Guys from my war...we didn't have all the fancy letters like you do to explain what was wrong with us. Lots of them...lots of *us* probably have that PTSD thing. Just nobody ever bothered to tell us about it when we got out, or that there was something we could do to help make it better. There's not a whole lot of us old fu—uh, bastards left now, but maybe...maybe you could mention something about us somewhere in your show. That it happened to us, too. You know, to let 'em know they aren't crazy."

Neil nodded, but before he could say anything, Alex said, "Maybe you could tell them for yourself. If you think you're up to it, that is."

Gus looked from her to Neil and back, his rheumy eyes sharpening and curved shoulders lifting as he considered the challenge thrown down before him. He nodded. "Well now, missy, I think maybe I just am at that."

"What flavor cone do you want?"

Neil looped Bailey's leash around the back of one of the wrought iron chairs set around matching tables outside the small ice creamery. "Strawberry."

Alex huffed and rolled her eyes. "That's what you always get. Don't you want to try something different?"

He shrugged. "What can I say? I like strawberry." His gaze dropped to her breasts, his thoughts on what they'd done with the last of the strawberry ice cream from his freezer two nights ago.

Oh yeah, he liked strawberry a lot.

Especially when it was served on top of smooth, creamy skin with two raspberry red nipples like cherries on his very own personal Alexandra sundae.

Under his hot gaze, those nipples suddenly puckered up tight under the thin top Alex wore. With a hitch in her breath, she crossed her arms over the evidence that she, too, remembered.

"Okay," she said, her voice half an octave too high. "Strawberry it is." She leaned in to kiss him and whispered, "Just remember when you restock your freezer that it's my turn next, and I like chocolate."

She strutted into the crowded shop without a backward glance.

He dropped into the chair, not so much claiming the table as needing to hide the reaction in his pants at Alex's parting comment. Still, he couldn't help a rueful smile.

The woman was a constant surprise and delight. She was always so straightlaced and put together at work, but when they were alone...he never knew what was going to come out of her mouth. He didn't think he'd ever seen her this lighthearted in the year he'd known her.

Hell, he didn't think *he'd* been this lighthearted.

Being with her was a balm to a soul he'd once thought hopelessly fractured. But Alex had somehow slipped into the spiderweb of cracks and welded them whole again with her humor and affection.

Well, maybe not whole, exactly.

Those remaining cracks were why he was sitting outside the ice cream parlor while she waited on the long line inside for their cones. Where the crowd had been just a little too big and the space a little too small for him to be comfortable in.

Baby steps, she kept telling him. Crowds and loud noises were still going to take some time to conquer. But he'd managed to get through the filming of the special reasonably well, despite needing numerous breaks. And he'd even survived all the Fourth of July fireworks without incident, thanks to the combination of noise cancelling headphones, and Alex and her very distracting body.

Baby steps.

All of his victories gave him hope. But hope was a dangerous thing, something he knew only too well. So, he accepted his time with Alex and the peace she brought him with a cautiously optimistic attitude. But in the back of his mind, he was always waiting for the moment the whole house of cards was going to collapse.

"Well, I guess the cat is out of the bag now."

Hell, shit, fuck, and damn.

If he had to pick a list of the three people he'd least want to make conversation with on a Saturday afternoon, Vanessa Scott would take all three slots. Putting up with her at work was bad enough. Having to deal with her on his own time was flat out cruel.

He gave his head the tiniest nod of acknowledgment. "Vanessa."

Unfazed by his less than welcoming demeanor, the blonde anchorwoman said, "It all makes a lot more sense now."

He didn't ask. He didn't really care. All he wanted was for her to go away.

Now.

But evidently Vanessa didn't need an invitation. She pulled out the other chair at the small metal table and dropped into it. "I always wondered why Alex sang your praises so hard. Guess now I know. Smart move, getting in bed with the boss."

"Watch your mouth," he snapped.

"Oh, defending her honor. How sweet." She offered a saccharine smile. "But if you were trying to keep it a secret, you should have been a little more circumspect about where you have your PDAs."

For one panicked second, he thought Vanessa meant at work, where admittedly they'd been less than discreet a time or two. Then he realized she meant the kiss Alex had laid on him a few minutes ago. Remembering what she'd whispered afterward, he couldn't keep the stupid grin off his face.

Looking annoyed at not getting the reaction she'd been going for, Vanessa said, "You really are a bastard, you know that? I should have been the one to do that special. The minute I heard Colin mention it, I knew it was my golden ticket right up to one of the big networks. They eat that wounded warrior stuff up. But then he tells me no, Alex is going to be doing it, because you insisted on it. *Alex!* She doesn't need the exposure. Hell, she doesn't even like to be on camera. She pokers up like an ironing board."

That much was absolutely true. It had taken Alex almost as long to relax as he had, and all she'd been doing was asking the questions. Still, true or not, he didn't like hearing anyone talking about Alex that way.

Especially Vanessa.

"She did just fine." He looked toward the shop door as the bell tinkled to announce someone coming out, but it wasn't Alex.

Damn.

"Just fine." Vanessa practically snarled the words, her attractiveness vanishing under her vitriol. "I wouldn't have done just fine. I would have earned a damn Emmy off it. And *you* took that away from me! Why, damn it?"

Because you look so much like the dead woman who haunts my nightmares that I can barely stand to be in the same room with you sometimes.

The words leapt to his brain and shocked him into silence.

Was that it? Was that the reason?

For over a year, he'd been itchy and uncomfortable whenever he was near this woman. He'd traded assignments to get out of working directly with her when he could, and sucked it up and done his best to get through it when he couldn't.

Vanessa always complained he did subpar work when he was handling the camera for her, and honestly, he agreed, although he could never quite pin down why.

Both Vanessa and Jessica had long, blonde hair. Their eyes were different colors, but the rest of the physical resemblance, from their height to the way they walked and talked, was astonishingly similar now that he thought about it.

And he always did his best not to think about Jessica.

He hadn't even brought her up during filming. He couldn't. She was a ghost he kept safely buried in the deepest part of his memory, who only escaped when she haunted his nightmares.

And Vanessa had been a living, breathing doppelgänger haunting his daytime ones.

Unaware of the stunned epiphany going on in his whirling brain, Vanessa scraped her chair back and stood, body stiff with outrage. "I don't care if you are banging the boss, Crawford. You'll be sorry you screwed me over. Just you wait."

As she stalked away, his brain superimposed another woman, dressed in dusty combat fatigues, who had walked away from him just like that more than once a million years ago on another planet called Afghanistan. The melding of those two images sent a violent shiver through him and brought Bailey to her feet.

She jumped, draping her front paws over his legs, and pressed her body weight into his chest. Dragging him back to the single vision of Vanessa, *just* Vanessa, disappearing down the crowded sidewalk.

He hugged the dog and pressed his face to her neck.

Fuck. Fuckfuckfuck.

"Neil?" Alex's comforting voice reached into the darkness and wrapped around him like a hand offering a way back to the light. "You okay?"

He took a long breath and sat back up, giving Bailey a quick ear rub to let her know the crisis was over.

"Yeah, I'm fine."

Now that you're here.

"Was that Vanessa I saw walking off in a huff? What did she want?"

"Nothing important." He gave Bailey her down command and stood, taking one of the cones from Alex's precarious grasp before wrapping an arm around her waist. For a moment he just held her close, absorbing her warmth, breathing in the uniquely Alex scent that had started to mean home to him.

"Why don't we walk while we eat these." He noticed the insulated bag tucked in the crook of her arm. "What else did you get?"

Alex tilted her head and looked at him from under her lashes. "Oh, just a little something for later."

Just like that, Vanessa, her grievances, and her likeness to a dead woman were all forgotten. Bailey's leash looped around his wrist, he wasted no time getting them moving toward his truck.

"Let's go. We can eat the cones on the way home."

Chapter 14

"YOU REALLY OUTDID YOURSELF on this one, sis." Swooping in from behind Alex and taking her by surprise, Lyle gave her a big, smacking kiss on the cheek before dropping into the folding chair next to her on the back lawn of Colin's estate. "Helluva party."

She might have been more pleased by her older brother's effusive praise if she didn't smell the whiskey on his breath.

Still, she didn't bitch at him about the drinking. It had been hard for him coming back for their grandfather's eightieth birthday celebration. Knowing it would mean subjecting himself and his husband to the chilly disapproval of some people in attendance.

Their mother included.

Surprisingly, for all his old-fashioned and slightly misogynistic ideals, Colin was *not* one of them. No, his beef with his grandson was that he'd chosen to take his fancy Ivy League degree and use it to become a high school English teacher rather than take his rightful place at the network.

Just one more McKenna who'd sidestepped the "honor" of following in the family patriarch's lofty footsteps. Leaving that path to Alex.

And Richard, God help them all.

Although even she had to admit that ever since she'd forced him to start taking more responsibility, he'd been doing a pretty decent job of it. Richard would never have the drive it took to handle sitting in the big office, but he might eventually make a not-so-terrible executive producer.

Maybe.

Someday.

A long, long way off.

"I didn't do it all myself," she told her brother. "Mrs. G would never allow it." The stout, gray-haired Scot had been Colin McKenna's housekeeper since what seemed like the dawn of time and ruled the household with an iron fist. A requisite when dealing with Colin.

A lesser woman would have quit decades ago, but born and raised in the Highlands, Hannah Gillespie was made of sterner stuff.

Since the only place large enough to accommodate the crowd Colin's birthday bash would entail was his own estate, by necessity Alex, her mother, and her aunt had teamed up with Mrs. G in the planning of it. Or, rather, her mother and aunt had made suggestions about the type of party *they* thought it should be.

Alex and Mrs. G had ignored them and planned what Colin would enjoy instead.

Looking around at the crowd on the manicured lawn framed by the nearby Smokey Mountains, she had to agree with Lyle's original assessment. They'd done one heck of a good job.

The weather had cooperated, thank goodness, with clear skies and a soft, steady breeze, which had kept the day from getting uncomfortably hot. Dinner was long past, but desserts were still being passed on trays by waitstaff. Two bars were set up on opposite sides of the expansive lawn. Between them, tables and chairs had been arranged in random clusters where people could mingle, talk, or just catch their breath.

Alex had been doing the latter when Lyle appeared. Even with Mrs. G riding herd on the catering staff, she'd spent most of the day on the move, making sure everything was running smoothly and everyone was having a good time.

Playing hostess was usually her mother's role at family parties. She thrived on it. But since most of her suggestions had been ignored, Helen McKenna had repaid Alex in kind by abdicating all duties to her, knowing she'd hate it.

Passive-aggressiveness at its dysfunctional best.

"What happened to Brax?" she asked, just noticing her brother-in-law was nowhere to be seen.

"He's busy pumping your boyfriend for information, while I'm supposed to be over here doing the same to you."

Panic flared at the thought of Neil getting the third degree. And it would literally be the third degree, since Braxton was a Nashville detective. "Lyle..."

"Alex," her brother sing-songed back with a grin. "Don't worry, your man was holding his own when I left. Brax won't chew on him too hard."

"He'd better not."

"For what it's worth, I like him."

She couldn't help but grin. "So do I."

Lyle looked at her for a long moment before collapsing back against the chair with a sudden exhalation. "Wow."

"Wow, what?"

"You really like this one. I mean, *really* like him."

"How can you tell?"

"Well, that goofy grin you're wearing, for one. I know that grin." He tapped his own mouth. "It's the same one I get whenever I think about how damn lucky I am I found the one person in the world who's absolutely perfect for me." His hand dropped to his lap. "You love the son of a bitch."

"A minute ago you liked him, and now he's a son of a bitch?" she asked with a laugh.

"A minute ago I didn't know my baby sister thought she was falling in love with him."

"Not falling. Fell." She'd been afraid this might happen. Lyle took his big brother responsibilities a little too seriously sometimes. "And I don't think, I know. I love him."

"You barely know him!"

"What are you talking about? I've known him for over a year!"

"He's *worked* for you for over a year," Lyle countered. "That's entirely different from *knowing* him."

"Well, I *know* him well enough to know I love him, no matter what you or anybody else has to say about it, so back off, big brother. I'm plenty old enough to know my own mind."

"He comes with a whole lot of baggage, you know."

She rolled her eyes. "No, really? And here I thought Bailey was just a fashion accessory."

"Okay, that was stupid," Lyle admitted with a self-deprecating snort. "Obviously, you know. But are you sure you're ready to take all that on? Maybe for the rest of your life? PTSD can be managed, but it'll never go away. That's a pretty huge commitment."

It was hard, but she did her best not to get annoyed with her brother. He was raising valid points. Ones she'd already thought about herself. For that reason, she was willing to cut him a little slack, since he had her best interests at heart.

But only a little.

"What would happen if, God forbid, Brax got shot on the job?" she countered. "What if he was paralyzed and couldn't walk, or lost his sight? Would it change the way you think about him? Would it make you stop loving him, just because it might make your life a little more complicated? Because he wouldn't be 'normal'?"

"Jesus, sis, you don't pull any punches when you're pissed, do you?" Lyle raked a hand through his hair, a lighter brown than hers but still glinting with the same red highlights. "No, of course it wouldn't change how I feel about him. I love him, damn it. For better or worse, and all that shit."

"And I love Neil the same way. So, you'd better get on board with this." She poked him in the arm to drive home her point. "Because I already have Mom and her stick-up-the-butt attitude to contend with, and I could use a few more people in my corner."

Lyle grimaced and shifted away from her, rubbing his abused arm. "Okay, okay, you win. You're a big girl. I won't give you grief over who you date."

"Thank you."

"But if he hurts you, I'll let Brax have some of his less savory acquaintances kick the shit out of him."

Planting a kiss on her brother's cheek, she replied, "Now that's the kind of backup I'm talking about." She stood and held out a hand to help pull him out of his chair with an exaggerated grunt of effort. "Now let's go rescue my boyfriend."

She'd meant it as a joke—mostly—but was pleased to see Neil and Brax having what appeared to be a friendly conversation when she and Lyle reached them. The biggest sign all was well was Bailey laying in a contented furry lump at Neil's feet, nose on her paws, apparently dozing in the last glimmering rays of the setting sun.

She slipped her hand into Neil's, smiling up at him. He gave her a somewhat distracted kiss on the cheek before continuing what turned out to be a lively discussion about, what else, football. Lyle jumped right into the fray.

She tuned them out, having not the least bit of interest in college ball despite that being close to a sacrilegious sentiment in this part of the country.

Instead, she focused on how damn happy she was. The party was a success. Her brother and brother-in-law, both of whom she loved dearly, were getting along with her boyfriend. And, most important to her, Neil actually seemed to be enjoying himself despite the worries he'd voiced that morning. About the possibility of feeling out of place and a little overwhelmed by the sheer number of people who would be there.

If the guest list had included only the snooty elite her mother had wanted, she would have worried, too. But there was a nice mix of people from all parts of Colin's personal life, as well as a large contingent from the network, so Neil hadn't felt like a total outsider.

He had, however, drawn more than a few speculative looks from their coworkers. The days of keeping their relationship private were gone.

Not that she wanted them to be a secret.

But she'd been enjoying the fun of Neil pulling her into a storeroom for a quick kiss. Or their clandestine rendezvous in the stairwell before Monday staff meetings. Now that people were aware they were dating, they'd have to be extra careful about any PDAs at the office.

Reporters were nosy by nature. The last thing she needed was someone snapping a shot of the two of them with Neil's hand up her skirt.

Colin would have an absolute cow.

Speaking of the Old Man...

She checked the time, and a bubble of excitement ballooned in her chest.

Showtime.

"I hate to interrupt what sounds like an absolutely fascinating argument," she said, not sorry in the least because, God, *football*, "but it's just about time for Colin's surprise. We need to get down to the wishing well."

As the four of them walked that way, a slow stream of other guests being instructed by the waitstaff to head in that direction joined them. Letting Lyle and Brax get a little ahead, she leaned into Neil, relishing the feel of his strong body enveloping hers as he put his arm around her.

"Sorry about Brax and Lyle," she sighed, snuggling against him.

"Nothing to be sorry about. It's what brothers do."

"Oh, so you gave your sister's boyfriends a hard time, too?" she teased, then immediately regretted it. She didn't know what part of what she'd said caused it, but Neil stiffened, almost but not quite pulling away from her.

Quickly, not wanting anything to ruin the day, she patted his chest and said, "I'm glad Brax didn't make you feel uncomfortable. He can be a little intense."

It took a few seconds, but Neil relaxed again. "It's the cop eyes. He's probably hell in an interrogation room. But no, it's all good. He knows how I feel about you."

And how is that?

She squashed the needy little voice. It wasn't important that he hadn't used the words yet. Neil had told her he loved her in so many different ways every day that she shouldn't need to hear him actually say it out loud.

But a tiny part of her, the insecure, once-burned part that remembered exactly how it felt to be in love with a man and think he loved her back only to be totally, humiliatingly wrong *needed* those words.

Needed to know she wasn't making the same mistake all over again.

Pushing her doubts and fears far, far down inside, she forced herself to focus on today. Today was wonderful, and tonight was going to be spectacular, and tomorrow would take care of itself. Like she told Neil all the time, *baby steps.*

They stopped when they reached the gazebo. She gave him a quick kiss. "I'll be back when it's over." She hesitated. "Are you sure you don't want to come with me?"

Neil shook his head. "You go on. Bailey and I will hang out here until the music's over. She's more of a bluegrass fan than bagpipes."

It was true he was hanging back from the evening's finale for the sake of Bailey's ears. But it didn't hurt that it would also keep him out of her mother's line of sight. Since realizing she and Neil were together, her attitude had gone from chilly to downright frigid toward him. Something they'd be having words about very soon.

But not tonight. Tonight was for Colin, and they'd all do their best to play nice.

Tomorrow, though, all bets were off.

Reluctantly, she gave him another kiss and continued on to where Colin and the rest of her family were waiting near the old wishing well that had been her grandmother's favorite part of the entire estate. Her way of including Gram in the festivities.

A sentiment Colin seemed to share as he ran a hand over the old stones he'd had shipped over from Scotland as a surprise for his beloved wife.

"So, what's this all about, then, Alexandra?" Colin demanded, his booming voice still carrying a hint of a brogue despite having left Scotland over six decades ago. "I was on the patio enjoying a dram of that excellent Glenfiddich your young man brought me, and the next thing I know, Gillie is telling me I need to come down here in the dark without breathing a word about why."

She stifled a grin that rose from several different emotions.

First that he'd called Neil her young man.

Second that Gillie, as Colin had always called Mrs. G, had managed to separate her grandfather from his Scotch. A feat few people would even attempt, much less succeed at. The woman clearly had superlative powers of persuasion.

"Well, sir," she said, visually collecting her brother and cousin to her side, "we have one more present for you to end the evening. This one's from Lyle, Richard, and me." She'd wanted to include Brax, but he, like Neil, preferred not to poke Helen's temper during the festivities. "We hope you enjoy it."

Before Colin could ask anything more, the lonely skirl of a single bagpipe split the air, bringing a hush over the crowd. Backlit on the hill by the last of the day's light as the sun disappeared behind him, the piper stood in all his kilted glory, his song low and haunting. The sound reverberated through her body like a physical touch.

It wasn't her favorite form of music, but it never failed to move her deeply whenever she heard it performed live.

Evidently, it affected her grandfather just as deeply. The look on his face was one of total rapture and contentment, something she wasn't sure she'd ever seen on him before, not even when her grandmother had been alive.

The last, lingering notes faded in perfect timing with the last of the light, leaving the piper as lost to the darkness as his song. After a moment's hesitation, the audience, as though waking from a trance, broke into applause.

Colin was still smiling when he embraced the three of them. A public display of affection that Alex hoped someone had gotten a picture of, since it would most likely never happen again. Wiping his eyes, Colin stepped back and shook his head.

"I know I said I didn't want any presents, but for once I'm glad no one ever listens to me," he said with mock annoyance. "That was the perfect way to end the party. Thank you. It was even worth dragging me away from my whisky," he added, to the chuckles of everyone assembled.

Vanessa appeared at his side and slipped her arm through his. "Actually, Colin, there's still one more surprise for the evening. If you'd just come right over here."

Fury swept through Alex as she watched Colin being led away by the smiling reporter.

"What's going on?" Richard asked, looking confused. "I thought the piper was supposed to be the capper on the evening."

"It was." She didn't miss the smug little glance Vanessa tossed over her shoulder as she brought Colin back to stand near the wishing well. This was payback, she realized. Vanessa was still pissed about being cut out of the special, so she was upstaging Alex's birthday present to Colin to get even.

"What is this bitch doing?" Brax hissed as he joined them.

"I have no idea," Lyle replied, scowling, "but I guess we're about to find out."

Basking in having the complete attention of every person there, Vanessa put on her best reporter smile. "Colin, everyone in the WMKN family wanted to give you a very special birthday present. It took a while to come up with something a man of your stature would appreciate and enjoy, but I think I managed to find the perfect thing."

Alex didn't miss how, despite starting out saying the gift was from everyone at the network, Vanessa had ended up taking sole credit for whatever it was.

Typical.

There was a distant pop, and a few seconds later, a giant starburst of gold exploded overhead. Several more pops in quick succession, and more fireworks filled the sky as everyone tilted their heads back, oohing and ahhing at the show.

"Well, damn," Richard said, sounding sulky. "No one's going to remember the bagpipes now."

She didn't give a damn about being upstaged.

She cared that Neil was all alone with no prior warning about the fireworks. He'd been very careful to avoid being anywhere near the Fourth of July shows and their constant bombardment of explosions. Being taken unawares like this could very well trip one of his flashbacks like the broken jars had.

She needed to get him inside the house. Now.

As she turned away, Lyle caught her arm and gave her a questioning look. All she had to say was "Neil" and he let her go with a nod.

She briefly considered asking him to come with her. But knowing how Neil felt about anyone seeing him while lost to his demons, even her, she discarded the idea. She'd find a way to get him to quiet and safety on her own.

Somehow.

She had only made it halfway to the gazebo when a hoarse shout sounded in a lull between fireworks exploding. The horrible certainty she was too late hit her like a wave of icy panic, but she kept going.

Neil came barreling through the crowd of guests, knocking them out of the way. One even stumbled to the ground with a cry of surprise. She tried to intercept him, calling his name, thinking he was looking for her, but he never even glanced her way. Still yelling words she couldn't understand, he ran right past her, shoving a few more people aside.

And tackled Vanessa straight to the ground.

Alex walking away without him was like a lead brick weighing in his gut.

Everything in him wanted to be at her side when she sprung the surprise she and her brother and cousin had come up with for Colin. But he had to think of Bailey and her sensitive ears. When he'd gone with Alex to listen to the piper before hiring him, the poor dog had all but howled in protest.

He could sympathize. He hadn't been fond of the music, either.

Then, too, there was Helen McKenna to consider. Alex's mother had not been at all happy to see her daughter arrive with him at her side. After the first few comments flung his way, he'd done his best to play least in sight with her, just to head off any unpleasantness that could mar the party.

Not for Colin's sake, but for Alex's. She'd put her heart and soul into making this a celebration that was remembered for years to come by everyone. He didn't want to contribute a single moment that might detract from her perfect vision.

Leaning against the side of the white gazebo, he grinned as Colin bitched about being dragged away from his Scotch. The Glenfiddich had cost him a bundle, but he figured it couldn't hurt to suck up to the Old Man a little. Especially since he hadn't yet given his blessing to Neil's relationship with his granddaughter.

Although, by referring to him as Alex's 'young man,' maybe he just had.

Some of the tension in his gut lessened.

As the piper played, he bent down and rubbed Bailey's ears, trying to help block out the sound and distract them both. Thank God Alex and the others had decided that a single song at sunset would have more impact than an entire repertoire, so it was over in just a few short minutes.

As everyone applauded, he gave Bailey one more rub and a few words of praise for not uttering any embarrassing howls during the performance. Now he just had to wait for all the guests to filter back to the house and leave, and then he could get Alex home to his place for a little celebrating of their own.

It took a moment to realize no one had moved yet. As he came down the gazebo's steps, Vanessa's polished, non-accented television announcer voice rang through the silence, saying she had another present for Colin. His temper spiked.

That sneaky bitch.

She was stealing Alex's thunder by making *her* surprise the last of the evening.

He took a step away from the gazebo to go find Alex, and quite possibly keep her from ripping Vanessa's hair out by its permed roots, when the soft *thud* froze him in his tracks.

There was an explosion overhead, and light filled the sky.

More *thuds* followed, the sounds hitting like physical blows as he struggled to comprehend what was happening. In quick succession, the rockets exploded almost directly overhead, their combined light filling the night sky and exposing everyone's position.

With a gasp, he slammed back against the building, looking for shadows as the light from the flares diminished, then was replaced as new ones were sent aloft. The sound of the mortars was distant, but he'd recognize it anywhere. Someone was shelling them. He had to get to cover. He had to get to—

Alex!

His heart gave a massive thump, louder than the mortars firing from out in the darkness. He had to find Alex. He had to protect her.

Save her.

Pushing away from the timbered hut, he lurched through the crowd of idiots who weren't taking cover. He yelled at them to get down as he went, but they only looked at him like he was crazy. Didn't matter. None of them mattered.

He had to find Alex.

She was counting on him to keep her safe.

Ignoring the stray dog running alongside of him, barking and almost tripping him up, he pushed his way through the gawking idiots. Flinching and covering his head as another barrage of mortars went off, so fast they almost became one long sound with no end.

More flares illuminated the night, their eerie light in gold and red and green turning people's faces into grotesque death masks, eyes vacant holes, mouths open in a soundless scream. And there, over by the well...

Jessie.

As he stared, she turned and saw him. A smile curved her lips as she tossed her blonde mane over her shoulder before turning back to talk to the LT.

No, no, no.

His body began to shake. He stood frozen, knowing what was going to happen. Knowing that any second, a bullet was going to slam into her brain and leave her staring at him with those lifeless eyes. Eyes that always accused him of not doing his job, not keeping her safe enough. He didn't have to hear the words to know it was his fault she was dead.

Her eyes told him so every night in his dreams.

Not. Going. To. Happen.

Not again. Not this time.

This time he'd be fast enough, move soon enough.

This time, he wouldn't fail.

Ignoring the mortars, ignoring the flares, and the dog, and the clueless idiots milling around in the middle of the attack, he launched himself across the seemingly endless distance that separated him from Jessie.

At first, he never seemed to get closer. But then suddenly he was there, and with a final yell he dove for her. Grabbing Jessie around the middle, he took them both to the ground, covering her with his body to protect her from the bullets he knew were going to rip into them both.

"Neil! *Neil!*"

He flinched at the touch on his shoulder, barely hearing his name called next to his ear over the yelling Jessie was doing from under him. Bitching at him for ruining her dress, calling him crazy, that she was going to have him arrested for assault.

Typical Jessie. Some thanks for saving her damn life.

"Neil, please, let her up!"

He froze.

Alex?

What was she doing in the middle of a firefight? She shouldn't be here. It was too dangerous. She should be back in—

Shelby. He was in Shelby.

Turning his head slowly, he saw Alex's colorless face. Her eyes wide, staring at him from where she knelt beside him, looking at him like she'd never seen him before, and he knew. Knew the woman he had pinned to the grass wasn't Jessie. Knew they weren't in that hellhole of a village in Afghanistan. Knew that whatever had just happened, it hadn't been an attack, that no one had been in any danger.

Except from him.

Knew that whatever pipe dream he'd constructed for himself about a life with Alex, he'd just destroyed it for good.

Chapter 15

She wasn't going away.

Neil came to that conclusion as he sat on the floor of his bedroom, back wedged into the corner. The steady pounding on his front door had been going on for the past twenty minutes, reverberating in his head like a kettledrum. Before that, it had been phone calls, and then text messages. Now Alex was at his door, determined not to be ignored any longer.

But it was exactly what he intended to do.

She'd heeded his wishes the night before and not followed him when he bolted from the fiasco he'd made of Colin's party. Though she'd called and texted several times, begging to come over, he'd answered all the requests with the same short response.

No.

Finally, somewhere after midnight, she'd given up.

He'd been relieved, but a small, stupid part of him had mourned.

Now, this morning, she was back at it. Only this time, he wasn't replying, wasn't engaging. He just wanted to block the entire fucking world out, and that included Alex. She'd want to tell him it was okay, that things weren't as bad as he thought, but the truth was they fucking were.

She just didn't want to admit it.

He hadn't simply embarrassed himself last night. He'd destroyed every freaking drop of normalcy he'd achieved by moving to the other side of the state from anyone who knew him. To start over with a fresh slate.

Bailey pressed against his leg and whined softly.

Neil gave her ears a half-hearted scratch. The dog had glued herself to him since the second they'd gotten home. She'd even refused to leave him alone long enough to go outside to pee alone. Forcing him from the safe cocoon of his home to accompany her for a quick squat, followed by a fast dash right back to his side. As though afraid he might take off running and leave her behind again.

Like he had last night.

He groaned and banged his head back against the wall as the broken pieces of that mad dash flashed through his brain, wishing he could bang the memory right out. But unless he knocked himself unconscious, he was stuck with it.

He didn't remember everything about what he'd done. Just a hazy impression of shoving people aside as he'd torn through the crowd, maybe even knocking some of them down.

But he had a crystal clear memory of taking Vanessa to the ground in the spectacular finale of his career-ending meltdown.

Way to go, Crawford. A personal and professional destroying twofer.

The pounding stopped for a second, then started again. Louder, as though Alex was using something heavier than her fist to batter the door. Maybe her foot. He closed his eyes and cursed. The woman just could not take a hint.

"Neil, I know you're in there. Open this door and talk to me, damn it."

Alex had to be really shouting for him to hear her all the way in the back bedroom through two closed doors. Fine. Let her yell. It wasn't like he had any neighbors close enough to call the cops on them for disturbing the peace.

"I am not going away, Neil. Not until you look me in the eye and I know you're okay." More pounding. "Swear to God, Neil, if you don't open up in the next two minutes, I'm calling nine-one-one and telling them I think you've hurt yourself and have them come out here and knock this damn door down to check!"

Hell, shit, fuck, and damn.

She'd do it, too. He knew that tone of voice.

His muscles protested as he got to his feet, cramped and rubbery and barely able to get him where he needed to go as he stumbled out of his room. Turning the lock on the front door, he leaned one hand against the wall as he pulled it open with the other, making a cage with his body to block entry.

The relief on Alex's face was so raw it cut into his gut like a dull bayonet. It took everything he had not to weaken.

"Go home, Alex." His voice came out rusty, his throat painfully dry.

"No." She hefted the decorative rock with his house number on it she'd evidently been banging on his door with. "And if you close that door again, the next thing I use this on is a window."

They stared at each other a long moment as he considered his options. He wasn't sure she'd actually do it.

Then again, he wasn't sure she wouldn't.

Surrendering to the inevitable, he turned and walked back into the house, leaving the door open for her to follow or not as she chose. Like there was any doubt. Alex wouldn't leave until she'd had her say.

Fine. He'd let her talk, and they'd be done. Then he could start trying to figure out how to move forward through the wreckage he'd created of his life.

Again.

Eyes gritty from lack of sleep, his body propelled him to the kitchen in search of caffeine. As he scooped grounds into the basket, Alex made a small sound of distress from somewhere behind him. His hand faltered, then finished the last scoop, started the brewing process, and he turned to look at what he knew provoked her reaction.

The bottle of cheap whiskey sat open on the table where he'd left it. Liquor barely one step above paint thinner glistened in the drinking glass beside it, filled almost to the brim, the quantity guaranteed to knock him on his ass.

If his stomach could tolerate the rot-gut quality and keep it down.

"I picked it up on the way home last night." His voice stayed flat despite the horror that flared in Alex's eyes. "I cracked it open, poured a glass, and had every intention of polishing off the entire bottle. Or passing out, whichever came first."

He paused, remembering the tantalizing familiar aroma as he first removed the cap. How it had made his mouth literally water with want.

"But you didn't," she said softly. Hopefully.

"I wanted to. *God*, how I wanted to." He stalked to the table and pressed his hands to it, staring across the wooden expanse at the thing he wanted most in the world.

And at that moment, it wasn't Alex.

"I stared at that glass for half the night before I finally got up and left the room. Can't even count how many times I came back in here to look at it and think, what the hell, why not?" His laugh was bitter and hard. "I mean, what do I really have left to lose, right?"

"Everything."

With a grunt, he pushed himself up from the table and crossed his arms over his chest. Partly to hide the shaking of his hands.

"Alex, I'm really not in the mood for your fucking Pollyana 'everything will be fine if we just believe it is' crap."

She looked like he'd slapped her, which had been his intent. She needed to have her eyes opened to the harsh reality that was his life.

Some things—some people—were just too fucked up to be made okay again.

Ever.

Drawing in a deep breath, Alex said shakily, "Yes, the flashback and what happened were bad—"

Another harsh laugh escaped. "Bad? Try a fucking disaster."

"But," she soldiered on, "it wasn't your fault. You had no way of knowing there were going to be fireworks. Nobody knew except Vanessa. She swore she didn't realize it might adversely affect your PTSD."

Adversely affect sounded so much tidier than *trigger the fucking flashback from hell.*

Too bad it didn't make the end result any neater.

"She's full of shit," he said, stalking over to the coffeepot as it started to spit and hiss, signaling the end of the brew cycle. "That bitch knew exactly what she was doing. She just didn't expect the result she got."

Like having two hundred pounds of crazy body-slam her to the ground in front of a hundred witnesses.

"It doesn't matter if she did or not," Alex said grimly. "She's been strongly encouraged to take one of the offers from the other networks, whether it's a good one or not. Her time at WMKN is over."

Ding-dong, the bitch was gone.

A spiteful part of him wanted to celebrate, but the rest of him couldn't work up enough effort to truly care. It didn't really matter to him, anyway, since he wouldn't be at the network anymore, either.

Taking his coffee and sitting at the table while pointedly not offering Alex any was supposed to make a point. But in true Alex fashion, she chose to ignore it. After pulling one of the mismatched mugs from the cabinet and filling it, she sat down across from him.

Both of them ignored the bottle and glass that sat at the opposite end of the table like an unwelcome guest.

"Who's Jessie?"

Hot coffee scalded his hand as he jerked in surprise, but he barely noticed. Pulse pounding in his throat, he stared, her words echoing over and over again in his head.

"You were calling her name," she said without him needing to ask. "Last night. When you..."

When he was taking Vanessa to the ground.

Only it hadn't been Vanessa he was seeing. It was Jessica.

The remembered bits and pieces of last night were overlaid with chunks of older memory, so it was like watching a poorly edited film playing in his brain, jumping every few seconds from Vanessa to Jessica. Vanessa, Jessica. Vanessa. Jessica.

Fuck.

"Is she the one you dream about?"

Another jerk, and this time he hissed at the pain that cut through his quickly spiraling thoughts. Shoving his chair back with a screech, he sidestepped a concerned Bailey to stalk to the sink and run his hand under cold water. Using the time to try and pull himself together.

How the fuck did she know that?

He'd never told her about Jessie. Never brought up that hot, horrible day or the endless chain of what-ifs he tortured himself with about it. How if he'd moved sooner, yelled louder, done something, anything differently, Jessie might not have gone back to her family in a body bag.

He flinched when Alex touched his shoulder. Refusing to turn and look at her, he kept his attention focused on his hand under the numbing stream of water.

"How do you know that?" he ground out.

"You've yelled the name a few times. In your sleep."

Which was exactly why he hadn't wanted her spending the night, even in a different room. Mere walls and doors couldn't contain his nightmares.

Turning off the water, he turned. Alex was standing there with the towel that usually hung on the oven handle in her hands. He briefly considered ignoring it and grabbing some paper towels instead, just to really make his point.

But he wasn't entirely sure what his point was anymore.

He took it and dried his hand, avoiding any eye contact. Once he mopped up the mess on the table, he slung the soiled towel into the sink, where it landed with a soggy plop.

Through it all, Alex just stood silently. Watching. Waiting.

His temper kindled at her quiet determination to insert herself into his blown-up life and try to make it better.

Why didn't she understand *nothing* would ever make this better?

"She was the reporter on the documentary crew I was a part of my last time over there," he finally said, facing the sink and gripping the edge with all his might. To keep from turning and letting Alex wrap her arms around him in comfort, or to keep from bolting out of the room and hiding.

He wasn't sure which.

"We'd stopped in a little shithole of a village. Jessie—Jessica Lynch—was standing with Lieutenant Henderson. She wanted to interview some of the women, get their perspective on how the war had affected their lives, their families, but we needed permission from the village elders first. We were standing around, waiting to meet with them when..."

The badly edited film in his head was back, stutter-stopping as Henderson's face exploded in a vivid spray of crimson. Jessica's horrified confusion about what had just happened. The life leeching from her eyes as the bullet entered her brain, her hand still stretched out toward him in a silent plea he didn't answer.

Bailey pressed her nose into the back of his knee, hard enough to throw him off balance and bring his focus back to the present.

He had to force out the next words.

"We came under fire. Both the LT and Jessie were out in the open, standing by the village well. They were the first ones killed. I saw it. I was looking at them. Right at them. At her. And I couldn't do a damn thing to stop it. I was *too damn slow to stop it*," he repeated, slamming his hands onto the sink edge.

"Oh, Neil." Alex touched his arm. "Sweetie, it wasn't your fault. You weren't even a soldier then. You were her cameraman. It wasn't your job to keep her safe."

"Don't you think I know that?" he shouted as he swung around, knocking her hand from him with a wild motion that had her taking a step back, eyes wide. "It doesn't change the fucking fact I see them die, over and over in my head, and I can't change a fucking thing."

"And last night, it seemed like you could," Alex said softly as she put the pieces together. "God, the fireworks, the wishing well... Does Vanessa look anything like Jessie?"

"She could be her sister."

"So, your mind took you back to that day, to the horrible moment that's your worst memory, and this time, you were able to change the outcome. You got to save Jessie."

"Are you fucking kidding me? I ran through the crowd like a deranged maniac and threw a woman to the ground in front of all of your family and my coworkers. I didn't save anyone. There wasn't anyone to save. Jessie's dead, and nothing changes that fact. All I did was lose my shit in front of an audience."

"I...I didn't mean you actually..." For the first time, Alex seemed a little uncertain.

It was about damn time. She needed to stop making excuses for him. God knew he'd stopped making them for himself a while ago.

"I just meant that you didn't attack Vanessa. You were trying to save her. Well, Jessie, I mean."

"I was seeing things that weren't there. *People* who weren't there. It doesn't matter what I *thought* I was doing. What I was *actually* doing affected *actual* people. I could have hurt someone and not even realized it until it was too late."

I could have hurt you.

The possibility was oh, so real, and it scared him more than anything else that had happened. If he'd done something to Alex, intentional or not, he'd never be able to live with it. The guilt he felt over Jessie would pale by comparison.

Which was why he needed to open her eyes, once and for all, and get her the hell away from him. No matter what it took.

"When are you going to accept the fact I'm just too damn dangerous to be around?"

Damned if that little chin of hers didn't come up. "When are you going to stop trying to convince me that you are?"

"Jesus." Running a hand through his hair, wanting to tear it out in frustration, he stalked away across the kitchen. "You just don't give up, do you?"

"On you?" She shook her head slowly. "Never."

"I knocked Vanessa to the ground. I nearly choked out my ex-fiancée. How can you not understand what that means?"

"You didn't hurt either of them," she protested stubbornly. "Not really."

"Jesus, Alex, I nearly killed my niece and nephew!" He stared at her, wild-eyed, hating that he'd had to make the admission but knowing nothing else was going to do the trick. His stomach knotted at the first flicker of doubt in her eyes.

"No." She shook her head again, refusing to believe. Damn her.

"I was babysitting. My sister wanted a date night with her husband, and she convinced Aaron it would be okay to leave the kids alone with me for a couple of hours. He'd never liked me all that much to begin with, but after I started drinking to try and numb the memories..." He grimaced. "He saw more than Joanna did. But he gave in, because he loves my sister, and he was willing to trust her judgement and give me a chance to prove myself."

"Neil..."

"I was in the living room with Kristin and Bryce, watching some stupid kids show on TV after dinner. They were sitting on the sofa, one on either side of me. I remember thinking how good that felt. And about how much I really, really wanted a drink. But Jojo was counting on me, so I held off, even though I had a bottle out in the trunk of my car, because I didn't want to disappoint her. I had those kids to take care of, and I was going to get the job done, no matter what."

"What happened?"

"An electrical transformer exploded on the block. Practically right next door." He swallowed, the remembered tang of metallic fear sharp on his tongue.

"Christ, it was like a bomb went off. The windows rattled, the lights went out, and I could feel the shock wave vibrate the damn house right underneath us. And that was it. One second, we're in the living room watching SpongeBob, the next I'm right back in the desert getting shelled by the fucking bad guys."

He hated that.

Hated how his own mind could make him so fucking helpless, so lost to his imagination and memories that he didn't know where they ended and reality began.

"I reacted on instinct. I grabbed the kids and ran to what I thought was safety. In my head, the basement was a bunker, I guess, and I had to get us down there in case there were any more explosions. The kids were scared of the loud noise and the lights going out, and they were crying and hanging on to me at first. But then after they calmed down a little, I guess they started to get more scared of me keeping them down in the dark basement, and they wanted to leave. I wouldn't let them."

His mood grew grimmer as he spoke, reliving that cluster-fuck of a night.

"When Jojo and Aaron got home, I was yelling at the kids that they had to stay where I put them or they were going to die." Shame washed over him, like it always did. "Fuck, Alex, they were just babies. Four and six. And I was *screaming* at them in the dark like some monster. They were terrified of me. Not that I blame them in the least."

"Oh, sweetie, you didn't—"

"Do *not* say I didn't mean to scare them," he snapped, shame morphing into anger. "It doesn't matter what I meant to do. Bottom line, I was responsible for those kids, and I failed them. My sister had every right to cut me out of their lives."

We just can't risk having you around the children being the way you are.

The words still sliced hard and sharp almost three years later, but he had no one to blame but himself. He'd endangered his sister's babies. He was lucky Aaron hadn't ended his existence right then and there.

"Okay, yes, you scared them," Alex conceded. "But you didn't hurt them."

"I could have. I wasn't in my right mind when I carried them down those stairs in the dark. Damn it, I could have tripped. Could have dropped them. And who knows what might have happened if they didn't listen to me and had actually tried to leave? How far would I have gone to stop them?" Bile rose in his throat every time he thought about it.

How far *would* he have gone?

"No. You were trying to protect them. Neil, everything you've ever done has been to protect someone."

"I'm sure Laura would disagree with that assessment," he replied with a harsh laugh.

Alex scowled. "I still think there's more to that incident than what she told you happened, so let's exclude her from this for now."

"You just don't want to accept the truth."

In typical Alex fashion, she ignored him and continued making her point. "Every other time—the kids, Vanessa, even when the smoke detector went off at my place and you grabbed me. You weren't trying to hurt me. You curled yourself over me, protected me with your own body from whatever danger you thought I was in."

"*But there wasn't any danger.*" Why couldn't she grasp that fact? "It was all in my head. I wasn't protecting anybody from anything but my own fucked-up imagination."

"But your instinct was to protect. Not attack. There's a difference."

"How is it any less dangerous for everyone just because the danger is actually coming from me? No." He cut off the protest he saw coming.

She needed to accept what he was telling her, once and for all.

"You saw me last night, Alex. Full blown, hardcore flashback mode, in all its horrifying glory. I didn't see who I was pushing out of my way. Didn't care. What if it had been your mother I knocked to the ground? Or your grandfather? I could have *hurt* him, Alex. Broken bones, or worse. I could have hurt *anybody* who got in my way. Just because I didn't doesn't mean it couldn't happen. That it *won't* happen. Because I'm telling you, it will. And there's no fucking way you'll ever forgive me when it does."

"Of course, I would." When he didn't say anything, Alex said, "I can help you, Neil, if you'd just—"

"*I don't want your help.*"

The small kitchen practically vibrated with the shouted words. In the silence that followed, he and Alex stared at each other from opposite ends of the room, like gunslingers facing down at high noon.

"I don't want your help," he repeated. "What I do want is for you to listen to me, *really listen* to me, just for once."

Eyes wide, she gave an uncertain nod. "Okay."

He drew in a shuddery breath. He had to do this, but fuck, it hurt.

"I'm broken, Alex. Therapy, Bailey, AA...they're all just patches on the cracks. But when there are too many cracks, it doesn't matter how much patching you do. There just isn't enough to hold the pieces together anymore." He had thought he could. That *she* could.

He'd been so fucking wrong.

"You're not freaking Humpty Dumpty, damn it."

"No, I'm worse. I'm a trained killer who isn't in control of his actions from one minute to the next. Stop thinking of me as this harmless guy with a camera. You *know* what I am."

"You're Neil."

"I'm a soldier. I did five combat tours in eight years. It changes you. Gets into your blood, your bones. Your head. It's not something that just goes away once you come home and take off the uniform. And it's definitely not something your brain forgets when you suddenly think you're back in country and your ass is in danger. You keep insisting I would never hurt anyone. Well, I'm telling you, it's only a matter of time until I do."

And there's no way in hell I'm going to let that someone be you.

"You have Bailey," Alex said, sounding a little desperate. "You have *me*. God, Neil, don't do this to yourself."

"That's the problem, Alex. It's not just me I have to worry about."

"So...what? What are you saying here?"

"That I need you to leave me alone."

She swallowed, hard, like she was trying not to cry.

Damn it!

"Okay," she said, sounding like she meant anything but. "For how long?" When he didn't answer right away, her voice turned strident. "For how long, Neil?"

For good.

But try as he might, he couldn't make himself say the words. Not with her looking at him with all the love and confusion and desperation she was feeling right there on her so-expressive face for him to see.

He'd done that to her.

Hurting her was the last thing he'd ever wanted to do, but he had anyway. It was like his fucking superpower. Hurting the ones he loved.

"Just...for a while," he managed to say, the words harsh coming from his tight throat. "Give me some time, some space, okay? I just...I can't be around anyone right now. Not even you."

Especially you.

"Are you sure you don't want me to—"

"Fuck, Alex!" He scrubbed his hands over his face, biting back harsher words. "Just...can you please just do what I ask? *Please*?"

"Okay." She swallowed again. "I'll take care of things at work so you can have the week off. Will...will that be enough time?"

To do what he needed to get done? Probably.

He nodded.

"Okay, then." She tried to smile, but it was so weak she gave up the effort. "I guess...I guess I should go."

She looked so miserable and lost. There was nothing he wanted more than to wrap her in his arms and breathe in the soft, warm scent of her, to lose himself in her. He forced himself to stay where he was, even though he had to lock every muscle in his body to do it.

When she took a step towards him, he actually flinched back. No way could he let her touch him. He was hanging on to his resolve by his fucking fingertips.

Pain flashed through her eyes, but being Alex, she recovered her composure and went to squat down next to Bailey, as though that had been her intent all along. Who knows, he acknowledged bleakly. Maybe it had.

"Be a good girl," Alex murmured to the dog, giving her ears a rub, "and take care of our guy while I'm gone." Standing briskly, she looked at him wearing her office face, her chin notched into fighting position. "I'll give you the space you want. For now. But don't for a second think this means I'm giving up on you. You can try to scare me off as much as you like, but we McKennas are made of sterner stuff than that."

As if he didn't fucking know that already. She'd stuck with him this far, hadn't she? But as he listened to the front door thump shut behind her, he knew it was only a matter of time before everything truly sank in for her.

No matter how stern their stuff, the Mckennas wouldn't tolerate someone like him disrupting their lives. Especially not the life of the family princess. He'd just been deluding himself about that all these weeks.

And when Alex got to work tomorrow and listened as everyone told and retold the story about what had happened to those who'd missed the show. When she had to endure the titillated whispers and pitying glances...then she'd understand.

There were a lot of ways he could hurt her, and not all of them were physical.

"Damn it!" He threw his head back and shouted the words. "Damn it, damn it, *damn it* to fucking *hell!*"

There was already an empty, aching chasm echoing inside his chest, and he'd only just let her go. How the hell was he supposed to handle this? How?

Without thinking, he spun and drove his fist into the kitchen wall. Sheetrock buckled as he pounded it again and again and again while a primal scream of rage and anguish erupted from his throat.

Finally, throat raw, knuckles torn and bloody, he turned and pressed his back to the ruined wall, breath coming in hard painful gasps. The feel of the wall giving way was satisfying, but not nearly enough to quench the fire burning inside of him, brighter than it had for a very long time.

The monster inside him, so long dormant, still needed to be fed. He went to the table and grabbed his half-empty coffee mug and threw it as hard as he could against the wall. The ceramic shattered into a hundred colorful pieces.

The familiar feeling of destruction was so satisfying that he grabbed the mug Alex had used and did it again. Adrenaline sang through his veins. This was good. Anger was good.

Much better than the loneliness and despair.

Caught up in the frenzy of the moment, he grabbed the next thing on the table and prepared to throw it.

And hesitated.

Lowering the bottle, he gazed at the amber liquid, inhaling the sharp promise of oblivion that rose from it as it sloshed lazily against the glass.

His pulse drummed in his ears, filling his world with a desperate beat. Reminding him he'd been here before, in this very position, caught between the angry beast that clawed at his temper and the one whispering sweet promises in his ear. Promises to numb the anger, the pain, *everything*. The answer to all of his problems was literally in the palm of his hand.

And at this point, he really didn't have anything left to lose.

Chapter 16

Five days.

That's how long it had been since she'd forced herself to walk out of Neil's house. Five long, miserable, lonely days since she'd gone against every instinct she possessed and given in to the plea in his eyes. The desperation that had turned his voice rough with emotion.

Leaving Neil when he'd been so obviously hurting had been the single most painful thing in her entire life.

But what else could she have done? He'd all but begged her. And it had made sense, after everything that happened, to give him some space to gather himself and regroup.

She hadn't expected it to take this long, though.

Not that she had left him entirely alone, of course. There was no way she could do that. She texted him several times a day. So he wouldn't think she'd given up on him. And, if she was honest, because she needed some way of knowing he was okay.

She had basically blackmailed him into replying the first time, telling him if he didn't, she'd be back at his front door, rock in hand. After that, he'd responded to every text. One-word answers, mostly, but it was enough for her to be able to keep from staying up all night long worrying. Wondering.

Like she had that first night.

She hadn't been bluffing about calling the police to check on him. After doing all the research and interviews for the special on

PTSD, which was finally going to air the following night, she had a much better understanding of just how strong the lure of suicide could be to those in such unrelenting pain.

Not physical pain, although that sometimes played a part. But the psychological torment that plagued these returning warriors every waking minute of every single day.

Not all of them had as specific a reason they could point to as Gus and his boy with the basket of bread. For some, it was a cumulative effect of all the various horrors war could bring. For others, it was coming home and finding they no longer fit into the lives they'd had before. That they couldn't feel things the same way, interact with people the same, even love their families like before.

They were strangers in their own skin, living a lie with every single breath they drew.

But for so many, that pain, that inner turmoil, led them day by day down the deadly path toward oblivion. Along that path might be drugs, or alcohol, or any number of self-destructive methods to try and numb themselves. But at the end of the road was always the lure of finally quieting the demons in their brains and finding some kind of peace.

She'd never even considered Neil might contemplate suicide.

Not until that first morning when she couldn't get ahold of him.

Standing on his front step, pounding on the door and getting nothing but icy silence in response, she'd had an awful image of him lying somewhere inside, dead or maybe dying. Because he'd finally been pushed that last dangerous inch over the cliff's edge, and she hadn't been there to yank him back to safety.

Pulling into her parking spot at the studio, she shook that horrible image out of her head. She just had to get through to-day. Then she'd have the entire weekend to tackle the problem of Neil and his stubborn refusal to see reason.

It wasn't that she didn't understand what he was worried about. She absolutely did. It was that she thought—no, she *knew* he was worth whatever issues he came with.

Several people stopped her on the way to her office to ask about how Neil was doing. She kept her answers vague but upbeat. It had been that way all week. Everyone checking up on him. Asking when he was coming back. Wanting to know if there was something, anything, they could do for him.

It had made her heart happy, having Neil's coworkers rally around him even though he wasn't there to see it. The man had a lot more friends than he was willing to admit.

Which was a good thing, because he was going to need every one of them in order to move forward.

After dropping her purse in her desk drawer, she grabbed the oversized mug Neil had given her that read *Life Happens, Coffee Helps*, trying to ignore the irony. With sleep being so hit-or-miss the past several nights, her brain refusing to shut itself off, coffee was no longer a luxury. It was a necessity.

She'd already inhaled her travel mug on the ride in, with little effect.

Time for infusion number two.

As she stepped into the hallway, her assistant popped out of her office across the way. "Alex, good morning. I thought I heard you come in."

"Good morning, Joy. Be right back, then we can get started." She kept walking, intent on her quest.

"Mr. McKenna wants to see you," Joy blurted, hurrying along at her heels like a frantic Chihuahua.

"Coffee first."

"He said as soon as you got in."

She bit back a whimper. The break room was just a few more feet down the hall. So close she could smell the tantalizing aroma of freshly brewed salvation. But if Colin had said as soon as she got in, then he was probably already wondering where she was.

Dang it.

"Did he say why?"

Joy shook her head, sending her sleekly bobbed dark hair swinging.

Her sigh of resignation came from somewhere down around her toes. No coffee for her. "Okay, thanks."

She turned to backtrack, but Joy held out her hand, palm up. With a grateful smile, Alex relinquished the mug with a heartfelt, "*Thank you.*" At least she could count on her caffeine fix being on her desk when she got back.

There was an unexpected jolt of melancholy as she entered the stairwell for the climb to the top floor and there was no Neil lurking there to kiss her senseless. Those stolen moments with him had never failed to put a smile on her lips and a rosy tint in her cheeks for the rest of the day.

She missed that.

God, she missed *him*.

She definitely needed to go see him after work and get things straightened out, once and for all. She couldn't stand this separation much longer.

With a smile she said good morning to Colin's PA, who returned the greeting and indicated she could go right in. She gave a quick knock and pushed open the slightly oversized wooden door she'd always secretly likened to the entryway of some ancient throne room in a Scottish Highlands castle. Colin McKenna had no qualms about using small touches like that to remind everyone around him who was in charge.

It was good to be the king.

"You wanted to see me, sir?"

Colin stood by the wall of windows looking out over the valley extending southeast from Shelby toward the Smokey Mountains.

Hands clasped behind his broad back, he looked every inch the laird of the manor surveying his kingdom, totally reinforcing the image the door had conjured.

"Alexandra, come in." He stayed where he was, so she walked across the room to join him. "Beautiful, isn't it?"

She nodded, taking in the breathtaking view. "It is."

"I promised Rose if she married me and came to America, I'd find her a place almost as lovely as Scotland to live."

"Only 'almost'?" she teased, knowing the story well. The brash young farmer's son who'd wooed the banker's daughter into marrying him instead of the man her father had handpicked to groom as his own successor. Then taking her all the way across 'the pond' to start their new life with barely two pounds in his pocket but a big dream in his heart.

Colin had long since surpassed his father-in-law's wealth. But that hadn't slowed him down one bit in his quest to prove to someone long dead that his daughter had chosen the better man.

"Ah, lass, you know there'll never be a place in all the world as sweet as the Highlands." Colin pushed more of a burr into his voice than usual.

"That I do," she agreed, trying for a burr herself. And failing, if Colin's pained expression was any indication. "But Shelby is the next best thing."

He nodded, still looking out at the mountains in the distance, before visibly changing mental gears and becoming the focused, driven CEO. It was the same 'office face' she used to deal with things she'd rather not, only more effective because Colin didn't just mask his personal feelings. He could ignore them completely.

Which was why his next words made her stomach do a flip.

"Have you been in contact with Crawford?"

Colin the grandfather had been sympathetic and understanding about Neil's PTS issues and the unexpected, awful finale to his birthday party.

Colin the boss would only see the bottom line. And that line was an employee who hadn't been showing up to work for a full week now.

"I've been texting him every day, just to check in. I did put him down for sick leave for the week." She really hoped he wouldn't push the issue of Neil returning to work before he was ready. "He just needed some time before he'll feel comfortable coming back."

And facing everyone who saw him with his inner demons exposed.

"But you haven't actually spoken with him?"

"No. Not since Sunday." She didn't tell him about the voicemails she'd been leaving, since that didn't actually constitute speaking *with* Neil. She'd just been speaking *to* him.

Every night after she crawled into bed, she called and talked about her day. What was going on at work, how much she missed him. Everything and anything, just to help him stay feeling connected to some part of his regular life.

To her.

She didn't even know if he listened to them or not. But at least those one-sided conversations gave her some sense she was actually *doing* something, since there was nothing else Neil would allow her to do.

"I'm planning to go over and see him after work today." If Colin felt she was staying on top of things, he might leave it in her hands.

He merely grunted and went over to sit behind his desk. She took a chair facing it, unable to tell if that answer had been the right one or not.

Colin's expression was still unreadable as he picked up an envelope, tapping it against the blotter.

"You can't fire him," she blurted, then cursed her wayward mouth. Telling Colin he couldn't do something was worse than waving a red flag at an angry bull.

Noting his cocked eyebrow, the one that dared her to continue, she chose her next words with extreme care.

"What I mean is, he hasn't done anything that would constitute a fireable offense. If you let him go because of what happened Saturday night, or because he needed to take some time off when he has it on the books, then you're opening the network up to a possible lawsuit."

Colin tapped the envelope a few more times before he let it drop to the desk. She released a shaky breath at the sensation of having just dodged the proverbial bullet.

"What if I had some other reason to let him go?"

And the gun was cocked and loaded again.

"First, I'd say that you don't. You can't. Neil's work has been exemplary since the day he started with the network. And second, I'd say if you somehow found something that gave you the excuse to let him slip through your fingers, then you aren't as savvy a businessman as I thought you were. Neil Crawford has a rare talent with a camera, and we're lucky to have him on our team. Letting him go would be a huge mistake."

She was pleased to get through her little speech with a perfectly even tone. But inside, she was quaking hard enough to feel nauseous. What had happened she didn't know about that would cause Colin to suddenly consider firing Neil? And how could she stop him?

"Is that a future CEO talking," Colin asked, eyes narrowing, "or a soft-hearted woman?"

She didn't care for the way he said 'soft-hearted woman,' but chose to address the first part of the accusation instead.

"It was definitely a future CEO talking. You don't just let go of talent when you have it in your hand. You hang onto it."

"You can't run a business using emotion. Haven't I taught you that?"

"You taught me to use every advantage I could find. And believe it or not, sir, emotion can be an enormous asset. And being a woman has nothing to do with it," she felt compelled to add, feeling oddly hurt. "Haven't I done everything exactly the way you've wanted? Have I ever given you any cause to question my dedication to the job? To the network? To *you*?"

"No. Which is why you're the only one of my blood who's ever had a serious shot at sitting in this chair."

"I'm the only one in line for that chair because no one else wanted it." Which stung, but was still the truth. "I know you would have much rather had Dad or Uncle Roderick take over. Or Lyle." Anyone who possessed the last name McKenna and a penis.

Missing one half of the desired equation was part of the reason she'd worked her butt off all these years. To prove she was just as good despite it.

Or maybe because of it.

Colin made a derisive sound. "Didn't have the drive. None of them. But you, my girl, *you* have it in spades. You've got what it takes to make it in this business. You're like me. Eye on the prize, no matter what. That's what's important."

A month or two ago, hearing Colin compare her to himself like that would have put her on cloud nine. Now, she was slightly unnerved.

Was she really that much like him? Driven, to the exclusion of everything else?

Of everyone else?

Maybe she had been. Before. But being with Neil had shown her there was more to life than just the job. She'd been filling the empty spots with the wrong things, thinking that working fifty, sixty-hour weeks was a sign of dedication.

It wasn't. It was just sad, because it meant she'd had nothing else important in her life *but* work. But now she did.

She stilled.

Was *that* what this was all about? Had Colin gotten it in his head her involvement with Neil was taking her focus off of her job? Was he looking for a way to get Neil out of the picture, out of her life, out of her *way*, by firing him?

She didn't want to think her grandfather could be that much of a coldhearted bastard. But she knew without a sliver of doubt Colin the CEO wouldn't even blink over that kind of ruthless manipulation.

"You're right," she said finally, sitting up straighter in her chair and giving Colin full eye contact.

Show no weakness.

"I am driven, and I do have my eye on the prize. Do I think I'd make a good CEO? You bet. I know this network better than anybody else, top to bottom and inside out. And I know I could not only keep it running as efficiently and profitably as it is now, but that I could take it to the next level."

A smile started to bloom on Colin's face at her words.

She took a deep breath, knowing she was about to wipe it right back off again.

"But you're also wrong, sir, because I'm *not* like you. I used to think I was. I thought the job, the network, was the most important thing in my life. That it had to come before everything else. Even before me. But then I found Neil, and...I realized that living for the job isn't living. It's existing. And I want more out of life than that. I want love, and happiness, and laughter, and..."

She shrugged. "I guess I want it all. Maybe I can't have it, but I'm going to try and grab as much as I can. You might not think I can still do the job as well if I'm not giving one hundred percent of myself to it. I can promise that when I'm working, I *am* giving a hundred percent. Of the work me. But there needs to be the private me, too. And work doesn't get any part of that me. Not anymore."

The smile didn't just disappear. It dragged down into a scowl. "I still have your cousin Richard, you know."

She just looked at him.

The expression on Colin's face acknowledged the weakness of his bluff.

"Nothing says I have to turn the company over to family. I can hire someone else who's qualified to take my place."

A ball of anxiety clogged her throat at the threat.

She swallowed it down. "I think that would be a mistake, sir. But that's your prerogative. As you say, it's your company." One she'd dedicated her entire adult life to.

But unlike the neurotic, need-to-please Alex of the past, there wasn't a carrot enticing enough to make her back down from her position on this. If she was going to stay with the network, it would be on her own terms, or not at all.

God, she wanted to throw up.

Instead, she kept looking at Colin, waiting for his next move in this little power play they were enacting.

"Damn right it's my company," Colin growled, getting to his feet and prowling around the desk back to the windows. "I built it from nothing, using my brains and my determination. It's been my whole life." He pressed his thick, working man's hands to the glass as he peered outside. "And that was my biggest mistake."

"Sir?" Had she heard him right? Had Colin just admitted to a *mistake*?

The mind boggled.

"When I married your grandmother, I was determined to make sure she never regretted it. I took her away from her comfortable life, with her pretty clothes and fancy house, and dragged her to America to live in a one-room tenement that only had hot water on a good day. I was a selfish bastard about it, but I swore, *swore*, I was going to give her back the life she'd given up for me, no matter what it took."

"And you did," she said quietly.

"Aye, I did. But it just never seemed enough. I wanted to shower her with jewels and clothes and everything I could to make up for those lean years we had. I built her that mansion so she could show everyone she was a lady of means again."

More like he could show them he was a man of means.

She remembered her grandmother as a slightly plump white-haired woman who didn't mind getting her pretty clothes dirty playing in the yard with her grandchildren. And the only jewelry she wore was her wedding band and a simple gold locket around her neck with pictures of her two children in it.

As if reading her mind, Colin said, "It took me a while to figure out she didn't want them. The expensive presents. Oh, she'd thank me pretty as you please for them, and mean it, because that's the kind of woman my Rosie was. But they didn't make her happy. So, I asked her finally, what *she* wanted. With all of my wealth, I should have been able to give her whatever her heart desired."

Her own heart pinched. "What did she ask you for?"

"The one thing I didn't seem able to give. More of my time, my attention. That was all eaten up by my work, y'see, and try as I might, I just couldn't seem to change it. To change myself. When Rose suggested a place out by the lake, I built the house, but hardly ever spent time with her there enjoying it.

"And when she said she was homesick for Scotland, I should have brought her there to see what was left of her family. But I was always too busy to take the time off to go with her, and too selfish to be so far apart from her to send her off by herself.

"So instead I had that bloody wishing well shipped over from her family's estate, stone by stone, and told myself it was just as good as her going there to visit. Better, even, because it was a piece of home she could touch every day. And, God love her, my sweet Rosie never said a cross word about any of it. She just accepted me for who I was and made do with what I could give her."

Colin shook his head, sadness deepening the lines on his face. "She shouldn't have had to make do. Not about that. And neither should you, Alexandra. There's more to life than just work, no matter what I've made you believe otherwise."

She could only stare at her grandfather in confused amazement. Who was this man?

"Are you dying?" Because that kind of introspective talk sounded like something a person making peace before meeting his maker would say. And curmudgeonly as Colin was, she wasn't close to being ready to let him go yet.

The question seemed to tickle his sense of humor. He laughed and crossed back over to his desk, this time sitting in the chair beside Alex in front of it rather than in his throne-like seat behind it.

"No quicker than I was yesterday," he assured her, patting her hand where it was gripping the arm of her chair. "I just wanted to make sure you meant what you said, about giving a hundred percent of your effort, but not a hundred percent of your life to your work. Promise me you won't make the same mistakes I did. Don't get so caught up in the work that you let life pass you by until suddenly you're left with nothing but regrets for what might have been, and no time left to fix the things you screwed up."

She had to blink a few times to push back the silly moisture trying to leak out and embarrass her. She nodded and cleared her throat.

"I promise. I know I can balance running the company with having a personal life. I won't let either one of them suffer."

"Good." Colin picked up the envelope from his desk and held it out to her. "Prove it."

Chapter 17

This time, Alex didn't bother with knocking.

She went right to pounding.

Her hand was probably going to end up bruised, but at that moment, she couldn't have cared less. She was *furious*.

After what seemed like an eternity, but was more likely less than a minute, the door jerked open, causing her last swing to nearly clip the chin of the man who stood there. Not that she would have minded all that much if it had.

Actually, it might have been very satisfying to hit him, just once, unladylike behavior be damned.

Recollecting herself to why she was there, she held up the white envelope crumpled in her other hand, practically shoving it in Neil's face. "What the hell is this?"

His expression gave nothing away as his gaze flicked to the envelope and back. "I thought it was pretty self-explanatory."

"Self-explanatory?" Her laugh sounded a little wild, even to her, but she couldn't help it. It was that or scream. "No, it doesn't explain a damn thing. You can't just quit."

Neil nodded at the envelope. "I believe I already did."

"Well, I don't accept your resignation."

"I didn't give it to you. I gave it to Colin."

"Who gave it to me as your immediate supervisor. And I don't accept it." She ripped the envelope and the wretched sheet of paper it held in half. It was a ridiculously melodramatic gesture, but satisfying all the same.

"That doesn't change anything. I still quit."

Stupid, stubborn man!

"*Why?* Why would you throw your career away like this?"

"I'm not throwing it away. I'm just making a change."

"By running away?" She looked pointedly over her shoulder at the "For Sale" sign newly staked into the front yard. As upset as she'd been by Neil's resignation letter, it wasn't until she saw that sign as she pulled into the driveway she'd truly started to panic. If he'd already contacted a real estate agent to list his home, he was dead serious about leaving Shelby.

About leaving her.

And, damn him, she wasn't about to let him go without one *hell* of a fight.

Something passed through Neil's eyes before he shrugged. "There's no reason for me to stay."

A knife couldn't have made a more direct wound to her heart.

Still, she didn't let it show. Calling on years of experience, she molded her expression into one of mild scorn. "Please. That was a little juvenile, don't you think? If you really want to make me mad, then at least come right out and say you don't love me."

Neil's face turned to stone, and the seconds ticked by in desperate silence as she waited for him to say something. Anything.

Finally, he did. "I never lied to you."

Never lied, because he'd never actually told her he did.

Less than a week ago, she'd been so sure the words didn't matter. Neil had shown his love in other ways. With every touch, every gesture. With his trust. A man who didn't love could never have opened himself up the way Neil had bared his heart and soul to her.

Oh, yes, there was love there between them, of that she had no doubts.

But Neil was running just as scared now as he had been when she'd come to see him on Sunday. Trying to push her away in some misguided attempt to protect her. Maybe even more scared, if the For Sale sign was anything to go by.

If he felt the need to put actual distance between them, that meant there was still hope, because he knew he wouldn't be able to resist changing his mind if he stayed.

Unless, of course, he had another reason to leave.

Dreading the answer, she asked. "What's the rush? Do you already have a new job lined up somewhere?"

She saw the instant he considered lying to her. It was there in his eyes, in the way his lips pressed together and he swallowed as his gaze darted away from hers evasively. Then the impulse seemed to pass, and he shrugged.

"Actually, I was thinking about doing some freelance work for a while. Hit the road, see what inspires me. Get back to the simplicity of just me and my camera."

And nobody else. Especially her.

The thought brought a spurt of temper.

"Stop trying to protect me," she snapped.

He just looked at her.

"Oh, come on!" She threw her hands up in frustration. "That's what this is all about, isn't it? Quitting your job, leaving town? You've still got it stuck in your head you might end up hurting me by accident, possibly, *maybe*, someday. And you're running scared. Admit it."

"Not everything is about you, Alex."

Nothing could have punctured her bubble of certainty as quickly as those words, spoken with a depressing air of quiet reason.

Weary resignation shone in his washed-denim eyes, but so too did a sense of steely determination. He'd made up his mind about this, and nothing she said was going to change it.

Panic thrilled through her at the realization she might really lose him. That he might actually refuse to see reason, and stick to his plan to leave Shelby.

To leave *her*.

No. She couldn't let that happen.

"No, you're right," she said slowly. "It's not about me. And it's not about you. It's about *us*, and that means you don't get to choose for us both. We figure it out *together*."

"Alex..."

"No." She jabbed her finger into his face. "I do not give up on the people I love, Neil Crawford, no matter how stubbornly wrong-headed and stupid they can act sometimes."

She wasn't sure which of them was more surprised when the "L" word popped out of her mouth. Probably Neil, judging by the way he paled and took half a step back as though to distance himself from both her and her declaration.

But as terrified as she'd once been of them, the words no longer had the power to keep her from saying exactly what she felt.

"That's right, I said it." She tossed her head and stuck out her chin. "And nothing you say can make me take it back."

Neil closed his eyes as though it hurt to look at her. "Alex, don't embarrass yourself like this."

"Nope, not even that." But oh, the reminder of her soul-searing humiliation in college hovered right at the edge of her resolve, just waiting for an opening to sneak in and suck all the bravado right out of her. Before that happened, she needed to make a strategic retreat.

Fast.

But first, she needed a plan.

Fixing him with her best boss-face to hide her nerves, she said, "I want you to promise me two things."

"Alex..."

"Two. Things. You owe me that much."

He stared at her as though debating whether or not to shut the door on her. Then he sighed. "What?"

"Don't do anything rash this weekend. Don't sell your house, don't take another job, don't..." She swallowed but soldiered on. "Don't hurt yourself."

"I don't have any plans to hurt myself."

His words were almost gentle, but she knew they were a lie.

"Really? And how much of that bottle did you drink?"

His stony silence was answer enough. Her heart wept.

"Please, Neil. Just promise me you won't make any life-changing decisions for the next few days."

"Fine. I promise."

"Thank you." She wanted to be relieved, but knew it was hardly more than a Band-Aid on a much larger problem. At least she'd bought herself a little time.

"Is that all?" he asked, his hand going to the door to close it.

"No. *Two* things, remember?"

With a long-suffering sigh, he waited.

"Promise me you'll watch the show tomorrow night."

He flinched. "No."

"Please, Neil."

"I live it every damn day, Alex. I don't need to hear myself talking about it."

"Maybe you do. And maybe you need to hear what the other men and women had to say, too." Because after listening to Gus, she'd realized there were probably a lot more veterans out there dealing with the debilitating aftereffects of war, even just in their small corner of the world, whose stories needed to be told.

She'd ended up interviewing three more vets for the special, which had ballooned up to a full hour. Including Big Tom and his wife, who had spoken candidly about their son's brush with suicide.

"Stop trying to fix me," Neil gritted out. His hand tightened on the edge of the door until it turned white with the effort, making the scabs on his knuckles stand out.

And causing her to wonder how he'd gotten them.

"I'm not trying to fix you. I'm not the one who thinks you're broken."

They glared at each other for a long moment. Alex's heart ached. The urge to reach out to him, to wrap him in her embrace, was so strong she had to cross her arms to restrain herself from doing just that.

"Please, Neil."

"Fine."

"Promise."

"I fucking promise, all right? Are we done now?"

They were nowhere close to done. But sometimes a strategic retreat was the smartest move to make. Especially when you were ahead.

"For now."

Her eyes tracked over his face, which had grown so dear to her in such a short time, noting the dark tint below his eyes, the brackets that seemed to have carved themselves deeper beside his mouth since she last saw him. Was he having the same trouble sleeping as she was? Had his nightmares come back?

"I'll be talking to you, Neil." She just hoped he'd be listening.

It was the hardest thing she'd ever done, but she turned and walked down the driveway, arms still hugged tight around herself. She didn't hear him shut the door, but when she got into her car, it was closed.

Backing out into the street, it was hard to resist the urge to veer a little to the left and take out the damned For Sale sign.

Not. Going. To. Happen.

No way was running the answer to their problems.

And if she had to, she'd beat him over the head with that sign until he realized it.

At least she'd bought herself a little time. Now she just had to decide the best way to use it in order to reach him. If Neil was going to give up on them, it wouldn't be before she used every single weapon at her disposal to change his mind.

"You're a fucking jackass."

"Thanks, Gus." Neil rolled his eyes as he flipped two burgers onto waiting buns and closed the grill's cover. "Always nice to know you've got my six." He brought the food over to the table where his friend was sitting on the back patio.

"I do," Gus argued, accepting the paper plate Neil slid in front of him with a grunt of satisfaction. He reached for the ketchup. "Why else would I be telling you something like that?"

"Because you're a crusty old fart with a mean streak a mile wide?"

Gus cackled. "That too, that too. But you know I'm right. Just like you know you need someone to kick your ass and talk you out of this cockamamie idea of going out on the road like you're Jack fucking Kerouac or something."

"Kerouac was a writer, not a photographer," he pointed out before biting into his burger.

"Who the fuck cares? The point is, you've got a good thing going here in Shelby. Nice house, good job, pretty girl. Why in the hell would you want to screw with that?"

Because I'm a damaged freak, and Alex deserves so much better.

"I told you what happened at the party. Why do you think?"

"Oh, boo hoo, poor fucking you. Alex saw you having a flashback. Get over it. It was going to happen sooner or later."

"And look what happened when it did."

"Yeah, look what happened. She stuck. Didn't get all bent out of shape, didn't raise a fuss, didn't try to make you feel bad. That girl did everything she could to show you she loves your stupid ass, warts and all. And you're just throwing all that right back in her face like it ain't worth the shit on the bottom of your shoes."

Neil pushed the uneaten half of his burger away, appetite gone.

"Don't you think I know Alex is the best thing that's ever happened to me in my entire life?" he ground out, his hand fisting on his thigh. "That she's willing to accept me and stand by me, no matter what? That's exactly *why* I'm doing this."

Gus shook his head. "Like I said. Fucking jackass."

"What if I hurt her, Gus? What if I have a nightmare, or a flashback, and I fucking *hurt her*?"

"And what if you don't?" Wiping his mouth, Gus balled up his napkin and tossed it onto his plate. "You can't live your life constantly worrying about what bad things *might* happen, son. If we did that, nobody'd ever leave their damn house. You gotta go after the things you want while you can, because let me tell you, there's nothing worse than looking back after it's too late and regretting the things you didn't do."

He leaned forward in his seat and caught Neil's eye with his own rheumy gaze. "Boy, you keep pushing that girl away, and eventually she's going to stop pushing back."

"That's the plan." He ignored the look of disgust Gus gave him. Instead, he drained the last of his Coke, also ignoring the whisper that said a beer would taste better. He may have jumped off the wagon with self-destructive glee, but he was five days sober again, with a meeting to show for every one of them.

His hand touched the pocket where his new white chip resided. No way was that particular demon getting the upper hand again.

Although tonight might put that resolve to the test.

He bounced up from his chair and started clearing away the remains of their meal. "Look, are you sure you want to watch this stupid show? We could play some chess. Or watch a movie." Or anything other than sitting through an hour of pure masochistic torture.

Gus pushed himself to his feet with a grunt of effort. "Thought you promised your girl you'd watch."

He'd already given up pointing out that Alex wasn't his girl anymore.

"So what?"

"So, you might be a jackass, but don't make it worse by being a *lying* jackass." Gus grabbed his cane from where it hung off the edge of the table and stepped towards the kitchen door, careful to avoid Bailey's paws.

He knew Gus was right, damn it. Just like he knew that half the reason he'd invited him over to watch the special at his house was because Gus would keep him from chickening out and make him watch.

Even thinking about it made his gut squirm like a nest of angry scorpions.

As he settled onto the end of the sofa a short while later, he tried to focus on getting through the next sixty minutes, one minute at a time. Bailey, sensing his edginess, jumped up between him and Gus and settled her chin on Neil's leg with a soft snuffle. His hand went to her head, grateful for the contact.

He didn't know what to expect. Alex had told him about the different segments she'd added as the special had grown beyond its original concept, but he hadn't been involved in filming any of the other interviews.

It had been hard enough doing his own.

But he'd gotten through it. And afterward, after he stopped feeling like he'd just scraped himself hollow like a damned Halloween pumpkin, he'd been able to admit it had been slightly cathartic.

Not as good as talking to his therapist, but still, he'd felt just a little...lighter.

A little less invisible.

Alex's voice from the TV as she did the introduction jolted through him like an electric current. Reawakening all the feelings he'd been so ruthlessly trying to bury under his long list of why leaving was for the best.

She gave the blunt statistics of how hard Post Traumatic Stress Disorder was hitting the troops returning from combat. Ones he already knew all too well. How the military was losing more of its people to suicide every year than were lost in the last ten years of the wars they'd been traumatized fighting.

But as laid out by Alex, all he could hear was how much she cared about what she was saying. How much those numbers meant to her, personally, as a human being. People were suffering, dying, and nobody was noticing. Nobody cared.

But she did.

He'd known it when she'd done his interview. And as he watched her gently lead Gus through a talk about his time in Vietnam and the hostile atmosphere he'd returned to back home after serving three combat tours there, it was obvious this wasn't just a story to her. It was a cause. And Alex was its champion.

Their champion.

"It was a different time then," Gus was saying from the screen. *"Nothing about that war was popular, and nobody wanted to talk about it once we got home. We just wanted to forget. But, well, just because you want to doesn't mean you can."*

Neil looked out of the corner of his eye toward his friend, not surprised to see him hunched down as he watched himself speak. One gnarled hand crept over to rest on Bailey's hip, fingers twitching against her golden fur.

He understood, and Gus was welcome to whatever comfort he could take.

"How did your family handle the changes in you when you came home?" Alex asked.

TV Gus gave a rusty chuckle. *"How do you think? I wasn't the fresh-faced kid who'd gotten on a plane and left four years before. I was harder. Meaner. I had nights where I couldn't sleep, and days I couldn't stay awake. I was angry, all the time, at everyone, including myself. Got married, but that didn't help. My wife tried for a lot longer than I did to make it work, but in the end, she did the right thing, taking our daughter and leaving."*

Neil listened as Alex led Gus through the next few years. His dependence on alcohol, the homeless year he'd spent on the streets of New Orleans eating in soup kitchens and sleeping in the bayou.

"Out in the swamp like that, it was almost familiar, you know? It was strange, but when I was out there, I could finally sleep."

"That bayou was a nice place," Gus sighed wistfully. "I sure do miss it sometimes."

Neil wondered if it was the open skies that had appealed to Gus most, or the isolation. Staying away from people was one of the easiest—and hardest—ways to deal with PTS.

He'd tried to straddle the middle line. Having a job that put him in contact with people but didn't require him to interact all that much from behind the camera. Then retreating to the seclusion of his house, with no neighbors to bother him. And it had worked.

Until Alex had dragged him kicking and screaming back into the world.

And he'd liked it.

Knowing dangerous ground when he saw it, he forced his attention back to the screen, where Gus was still talking.

"It's too late now to wonder how things might have been different if the Army understood better about how bad war can mess with a man's mind when I got out. But it's never too late to get some help for it. I've screwed up a lot over the years, believe you me, but I'm five years sober now. And I got me a therapist I talk to who's helped me

figure some stuff out. I used to think needing to talk to a shrink made you a wuss, but that Isaac, he's a pretty okay guy. Damn smart, too, even if he is a kid."

Neil snorted. Isaac was easily in his forties, but he supposed to Gus that still qualified as a kid.

"I never did thank you for putting me together with him," Gus said to Neil, his voice a little rough. "Saved my fucking life."

"Gus..."

"No, I mean that. Talking to him saved my life. I...I was saving up my pills. The pain meds. I just...I was so fucking tired of it all. You saved me, man. Thank you."

Chapter 18

He wasn't sure what to say.

Wasn't sure what he *could* say. Gus had planned to kill himself? *How the hell did I miss that?*

Or maybe he hadn't. Maybe his subconscious had picked up on it, and that had been the reason he'd pushed so hard for Gus to go see Isaac right when he'd evidently needed it most. Or maybe it had been pure dumb luck.

Either way, the knowledge chilled something deep inside him.

For his part, Gus let the matter drop, seeming to relax now that his segment on the program was over. But he continued to stroke gnarled fingers over Bailey's soft fur as he stared at the TV, so maybe not all that relaxed, after all.

The next person up was a young woman who had served with the Air Force and done several tours overseas. Who admitted her PTSD had gotten so bad she had actually attacked her boyfriend one night while they were sleeping after she'd returned to civilian life.

Neil stiffened as he listened to her story, which so closely echoed his own worst fears he had to wonder if Alex had chosen this particular veteran for exactly that reason.

"Sure, you get checked out before you separate from service, but sometimes the symptoms don't start to show until months later, so they don't catch it. And even then, you don't want to admit anything's wrong. There's such a stigma out there about PTSD, that

it makes you crazy or that you're damaged goods if you have it. Weak, somehow. None of that is true, but it sure feels that way sometimes. And it makes people try to deny what's wrong with them until something makes them finally sit up and realize they just can't ignore the facts any longer."

For her, it had been the night she'd fought back against what she'd thought was an enemy soldier, but had actually been her boyfriend of two years trying to wake her from a nightmare. She went on to describe the painful decision to seek treatment, and the long, unhappy road of being prescribed a shopping list of drugs. Prozac for depression, Klonopin for anxiety, and various other combinations of pharmaceuticals that had really only served to mask the symptoms rather than treat the problem.

And then someone had told her about the service dog program.

"It was like I'd been given a second chance. Here was this wonderful animal that could help me get my life back. I'd be able to get off of the drugs and start feeling human again, maybe finally start a family. People I talked to who had them said it was the closest thing to normal they'd felt in a long, long time. So, I contacted the VA to try and get one. Only I found out that PTSD service dogs aren't supplied by the VA, because they haven't deemed them a proven, effective treatment for the disorder."

The woman shook her head. Neil understood her bafflement. He'd had the same reaction when he first went in search of a service dog on Isaac's recommendation. The doctors would prescribe all the meds he wanted, but no one was willing to admit the dogs could do the same job just as well. Or better.

"There are lots of organizations out there that train service dogs to help with PTSD and other disabilities, and they're all wonderful, terrific places. But they run on donations, and it can cost upwards of fifty thousand dollars to raise and train a single dog. That means there are never going to be enough dogs to cover the demand. Which means soldiers who could be helped won't be, because they're stuck on

a waiting list a year, maybe two or three years, long. Just like me. I waited over a year and a half before I finally got the call that they had a dog for me."

The camera pulled back slightly to show the gray and white greyhound lying patiently beside her chair. *"Teddy is the best thing that ever happened to me. Aside from my husband, of course,"* she added with a grin aimed off camera.

Something hit Neil's chest like a mallet at the realization she was married. How could she put someone she loved at that kind of risk? She'd already been physical once. Just like he'd been with Laura.

Why would she take the risk of it happening again? Even with the dog, there were no guarantees. It was a foolish chance to take. Selfish, even.

But clearly her husband didn't feel that way. He joined her for the second part of the interview, and he was very clear about that.

"Of course, there's always the chance it could happen again, even with all the therapy and with Teddy," he admitted. *"But when you love someone, you're willing to take that chance, just to be with them."*

No. Wrong.

The rest of the interview faded to white noise as Neil fought a battle within himself, furious that these people could make such a huge danger sound so insignificant.

Willing to take the chance? Maybe for them it was okay, since the one who might lash out in violence was a woman. It was different if it was a man. Neil could inflict so much more damage on Alex than she could on him if their roles were reversed.

It was a weak defense, and he knew it.

So weak, in fact, that Alex would probably kick his ass herself if she ever heard him say anything of the kind. But he needed something to grasp onto and hold up as a bulwark against the holes each of the people being interviewed were slicing in his armor of excuses to keep Alex away.

Because if he let himself dare to hope, even just a little, his conviction would crumble under the weight of his own selfish desires.

Finally, the moment he'd dreaded most came.

As uncomfortable as he'd been doing the interview, watching it was worse.

And it wasn't only because he preferred being behind the camera. Alex had somehow gotten him to talk about things that had only ever seen the light of day during his therapy sessions, either the official ones with Isaac or the more impromptu ones with Gus.

It had felt important at the time to talk about them. To help people like Tommy Coulter, whose parents had just finished speaking about how they hadn't understood how depressed their son had become before he'd tried to take his own life to escape the pain. How they'd missed the warning signs, because they hadn't known to look for them.

Now, though, as he watched himself, stiff as a hunk of wood as he sat in the interview chair, it felt like he'd agreed to witness the flesh being flayed from his bones, one question at a time.

The first ones were simple, starting with his alcohol addiction, his difficulty in maintaining his temper, and finally losing his job because of both. Being in and out of the VA seeking treatment. The night he'd scared his family so badly with his actions, they'd decided it would be safer for them if he were to keep his distance.

"I don't blame my sister. I was out of control back then, I realize that now. I hadn't been diagnosed with PTSD yet, so I didn't understand what was going on inside my head wasn't something that would just get better and go away with time. I thought I could handle it, if I only tried hard enough.

"But it was after that incident, after I almost drank myself to death from fear and disgust over it, I finally accepted I needed help. Real help. And the next time I went to the VA I met Isaac, and he knew pretty much right away what we were dealing with. You wouldn't think it, but it was such a relief just to have a reason. To be

able to point at it and say, see, that's what's wrong, and now we're going to fix it."

"But it wasn't that simple," TV Alex said, gently leading him to the next layer of skin being removed.

"No, nothing's ever that simple. But the first step is knowing what's wrong, and I finally did. Second is wanting help. For sure I did. I wanted to get better. And I have. Don't get me wrong, there's no miracle cure. But I've learned what most of my triggers are, and I work hard to avoid the ones I can, and others we've done different types of therapy to help lessen their impact. But there are always going to be times when something surprises me, that I can't or don't have time to avoid, and that's where Bailey comes in."

Onscreen, Bailey reacted to her name, tongue lolling out as she looked up at TV Neil as he reached over to scratch behind her ear.

"She's my lifeline. If I start to have a panic attack, she can either break my focus on whatever's causing it, or she can lead me away from it altogether. Or if I have a flashback, she knows to react and do what she needs to in order to bring my focus back to her, and to where I really am. If I have a nightmare, she's there to wake me up. She's even trained to turn on a light in the bedroom, so I can see where I am, and not where my nightmare says I am."

"So, she's with you twenty-four, seven?"

"Yes."

"That must become an issue for you sometimes."

"Yeah," TV Neil sighed, stroking his hand down Bailey's neck as she laid her chin on his lap. It looked like she was just enjoying the attention, but she'd really been keying in on his unease during the entire interview process, performing a low-key version of deep pressure therapy.

"Service dogs—all service dogs—are supposed to be allowed into public places. But a lot of people either don't know the law, or they think they can police who they believe is really disabled and who isn't.

I don't have a visible injury like a missing arm or leg, so some people assume I'm faking it. I've had people accuse me of that to my face.

"And honestly, I can't really blame them all that much. Because there are people out there who just buy a vest off the internet for the family pet and call it a service dog so they can take them into stores or on planes or wherever with them. It's not right, but there's no way to stop them, either. Unfortunately, that means people with an actual need for their service dog are sometimes put in a very awkward position of having to justify themselves in order to get into a restaurant or a store."

"Or a movie theater," TV Alex added.

Neil couldn't stop a snort. "She just can't let that one go," he murmured, remembering the fire in Alex's eyes when she'd gone all hell and brimstone on the theater manager in Knoxville.

"The Americans with Disabilities Act classifies service dogs as medical equipment," TV Alex said. *"But it's easy to see there's a lot more to your relationship with Bailey than just using her like a wheelchair or a crutch."*

"The law may classify her that way, but I sure don't," TV Neil stated firmly. *"Bailey is my friend, my companion, my nurse, my confidante...I don't know what I'd do without her."*

"Some people might voice concern that service animals have to work all the time, and aren't allowed to enjoy just being dogs."

"Untrue. We play ball, fetch, tug, she begs for belly rubs, all the things any other family dog might do. Bailey's not just well cared for. She's loved."

"With everything you've been through, everything you've had to overcome, what do you see for yourself going forward? Can you have a happy, normal life?"

TV Neil paused, while Neil caught his breath. He hadn't remembered this question until just now.

"You know, I didn't use to think so, but a very special woman has been pretty persistent in changing my mind about things like that.

'Baby steps,' she's always telling me. Well, I think with baby steps, I can finally find my way to a relationship, to a family, that I never thought I'd be able to have. I used to think the PTSD diagnosis was like being sentenced to being alone for the rest of my life. She's made me realize that with the right person, anything is possible."

"Smart woman," Gus commented.

"It's bullshit," Neil snarled, practically throwing himself to his feet. He stalked across the room, needing to hit something, throw something, fuck, *drink* something. Anything to drown out his own stupidly optimistic words echoing in his head. "Wanting doesn't make it real."

Not even if you wanted it with every last inch of your soul.

"No, what *you're* spouting is bullshit," Gus snapped back. "You're running scared, and you're throwing up whatever roadblocks you can come up with, no matter how stupid."

"Damn right I'm scared. I'm trying to protect her, damn it!"

"No, you're trying to protect your own dumbass self. That girl is willing to take whatever risk comes with loving you. You're the one who's decided *you* can't live with it."

"Well, one of us needs to be reasonable."

"Reasonable?" Gus repeated, his lip curling back in a sneer. "What's reasonable about running away? Whatever happened to fighting for what you want?"

"I'm fighting to keep Alex safe. That's the only thing that matters." Even if it meant tearing his own heart out to accomplish it. "I'll leave, her life will go back to normal, she'll be safe, and that'll be enough."

It would never be enough.

Not for him.

He'd carry the pain of walking away from the best thing in his life with him for the rest of his sorry, solitary existence.

Alex's voice spilled from the television as she did the wrap-up for the end of the show, giving the names and numbers for several organizations that trained service dogs and the contact info for the VA and the Veterans Crisis Line. Neil grabbed the remote to shut it off. He'd kept his word, watched the damn thing despite how much it hurt.

That didn't mean he had to give up the last layer of skin he still had remaining by listening to the voice that would haunt his dreams for years to come.

"Leave it on."

The snap in Gus's voice had his thumb hesitating over the power button. "Why? It's over."

A mulish expression came over the old vet's face. "I promised her I'd make sure you watched to the end. It's not the end yet."

"You promised..." Why was he surprised? "Why?"

"Didn't ask. Figured she had her reasons."

His thumb twitched, but in the end, curiosity got the better of him. He threw himself back onto the sofa, arms crossed tight across his chest as he steeled himself for whatever final blow was about to come.

The screen changed from the graphics with the names and phone numbers to a shot of Alex. What immediately caught his attention was the fact she was wearing the same white dress with tiny pink apple blossoms on it she'd had on the day before when she'd nearly battered down his front door.

Either it was a massive coincidence, or she'd taped this segment yesterday. Long after the rest of the special was already completed.

"The program you've just watched is one that resonates on a very personal level for me. There were dozens more stories that could have been told, each of them important and unique in their own way. Each one is the story of someone who has suffered for their service to this great country, and every one of them deserves to be told. Hopefully, they will be. I wish it could be me that got to tell them. But I have another undertaking which will occupy most of my time for a

while, so I'll have to leave it to someone else to keep fighting the good fight."

Almost against his will, Neil leaned forward as her words sank in. A cold knot started to tighten in his chest. "What the fuck does that mean?"

"Shut the fuck up and listen."

"The reason this issue is personal for me is because the man I love is one of the people you just heard from. And despite the optimistic answer he gave about how with the right person anything is possible, we still have an uphill battle ahead of us before he's totally convinced that's actually true. So, I've taken a page out of his book and handed in my resignation so I can—"

"What?" Neil roared. "She can't—"

"Be quiet, goddamn it!" Gus snatched up the remote and raised the volume.

"I'm not sure where our road will lead us, but I know wherever it is, I'm going to be at his side every step of the way. If he stays, I'll stay. If he goes, I'll go. There's absolutely nothing I won't do to prove to him he's worth everything we might have to go through to be together."

TV Alex smiled, but it was sad. *"He worries being with him could hurt me. What he needs to understand is that being without him will hurt me so much worse."*

"She's lost her fucking mind," he muttered, unable to tear his eyes from the screen and Alex's very determined expression.

"I apologize for this personal and unprofessional message, but I knew I'd only get one shot at really grabbing his full attention. Public declarations are something I tend to avoid, for reasons he knows all too well. But in this case, it was the only way to prove to him I mean what I've been saying all along." TV Alex looked so directly into the camera lens that it was like she could actually see him through the television screen. *"Neil Crawford, I love you, you incredibly annoying, complicated man. Whatever happens, like it or not, I'm going to be by your side. Count on it."*

As the image on the screen went black and shifted to a commercial, he sagged back. Had anyone else listening heard the underlying threat in those words?

Alex may have sounded all sweet and loving, but there had been pure, unbendable steel in what she was telling him. She wouldn't let him just leave and disappear from her life. She was going to follow him, whether he let her go with him or not. There was a small part of him that warmed at her persistence.

The rest of him, though, was horrified by what she'd just done.

"Well, now." Gus sounded thoughtful as he clicked off the television. "Didn't see that coming."

"She...she...she can't do that."

"Sounds to me like she just did."

"Fuck, Gus, this isn't funny!"

"Didn't think it was."

No, he clearly didn't. Far from smiling, the old bastard was eyeing him with what Neil was pretty sure was a smug sense of eager challenge.

He bolted to his feet, ignoring the way Bailey went on alert as she slid off the sofa and sat, carefully watching him as he paced. "That job is her life. She can't quit on a whim like this. She'll come to her senses in a few days and regret throwing away everything she's worked so damn hard for."

He knew she would.

He'd spent the past year watching her bend over backwards to gain the approval of her grandfather. To earn her place in the top office. Walking away from that would be like cutting off a limb.

Worse. It would be like cutting out a piece of her heart, since quitting the network meant giving up her family legacy. She couldn't do that.

He couldn't let her.

Chapter 19

"HAVE YOU LOST YOUR ever-loving *mind*?"

Standing at her front door, Alex felt a sense of reverse déjà vu as she stared out at a thoroughly agitated Neil planted on her doorstep. Her heart, which had started to pound the minute he zoomed into her driveway like a NASCAR racer, was now running jackhammer fast in her chest.

She wasn't sure what she'd expected his reaction to be after seeing her hastily taped declaration. But the fact it brought him out of hiding and to her door was a good sign.

At least, she hoped it was.

"I guess this means you watched the show." She sent a silent thank you to Gus.

"Goddamn it, Alex, you can't fucking quit!"

Dropping two major curses in her presence meant he was nearing the edge of his control. Good. She wanted him out of control. Not to make him mad, but so he'd stop letting that overly protective nature of his dictate every action and just go with his emotions for a change.

It was a gamble. Neil didn't do emotion very well. But it was the only way she could come up with to break through that stubborn wall of his.

She shrugged. "It's just a job."

"But you love that job!"

"Not as much as I love you."

They stared at each other for a long moment as the words sat in the air between them. The most incredible thing for her was the fact they were absolutely true.

She'd done a lot of soul searching over the past twenty-four hours, and finally come to that inescapable conclusion. There wasn't anything else in her life as important to her as Neil was.

Not even her dignity.

When he said nothing, she gave an inward sigh and walked back into the house, leaving the door open. She hadn't really expected him to say the words back, not when he was trying so desperately to convince the both of them he didn't actually love her.

But it still stung.

She was almost to the sofa before the door closed. It was a few seconds more before his footsteps and Bailey's tippy-tap of nails followed after her. The breath she'd been unconsciously holding let out in a not-so-silent whoosh.

Thank God.

There had been a brief second when she worried he'd been on the wrong side of that door when it shut. If he had been, she was fairly certain she would have abandoned the last few shreds of her self-esteem to chase after him.

And if she had to hold him down and beat some sense into his stubborn hide, well then, she'd do that, too.

"I can't believe Colin would ever accept your resignation." Rather than take a seat, he stood several feet in front of her, body rigid, hands clenched at his side. Bailey sat almost as rigidly at his left knee, gazing up at him intently.

"He wasn't exactly happy about it." It was hard not to wince at that colossal understatement. "But he didn't really have a choice."

"Alex..." He shoved a hand through his hair. "Be reasonable."

"I tried being reasonable. You didn't want to listen. So, now, I'm going to be as *un*reasonable as it takes."

"As it takes for what? To ruin your life?"

"To get you to realize running away won't work the way you wanted it to if I follow you, for starters. And I will. Wherever you go, no matter how hard you try to ditch me, I *will* find you."

She brushed aside how very creepy that sounded. She was in the right here. If she had to go to some stalkerish extremes, then by God, she would.

"You're *insane*!" Neil spun and stomped a few steps away, turned, stomped back. He looked torn between bolting and wanting to shake some sense into her. "Alex, you have to stop this."

The tone of his voice, the one that said she was acting irrationally, struck a spark against her already tinder-dry temper. "I *have to*?"

Clearly not sensing his imminent danger, Neil said in the same tone, "Yes! God, Alex, be reasonable."

"You already said that," she snapped back.

"Well, maybe it's worth repeating, since you clearly aren't listening to a word I'm saying! Damn it, this is your *life* we're talking about."

She jumped to her feet, tired of him towering over her as he lectured.

"That's right. *My* life. *Mine.* And if I want to waste it chasing after a...a snarly, stubborn, impossible man who can't get out of his own way long enough to see his own worth, then that's exactly what I'm going to do."

She stepped forward and poked a finger into his chest. "I love you, Neil Crawford, so you'd just better get used to it."

Body so tightly held that he looked like he might shatter at any moment, Neil sucked in a ragged breath, but he didn't step away. He just stared down at her, his eyes so filled with conflict it was almost painful to see.

But she refused to back down. Not when she was so close.

"God, Alex." The raw whisper sounded dragged from somewhere deep within his soul. "You have to let me go."

"And you have to stop telling me what I have to do."

"If I stay, I'll only hurt you."

"What do you think leaving me would do?"

"At least you can't die from a broken heart."

She wasn't so sure about that.

"So, the answer is what? To keep running away every time you get too close to someone? Like you did with Laura? With your sister? Live the rest of your life alone?"

"If it will keep you safe, then yes, damn it!"

"Keep *you* safe, you mean."

Grabbing her shoulders, Neil gave her a small shake. "Stop acting as if I'm taking the easy way out by leaving. Like it's not a big fucking deal for me. Leaving you is ripping my goddamn heart out, Alex. You've turned my entire life upside down. You just started making me live again, and now I have to give that up. I have to give *you* up, or I'll destroy you just like I've destroyed every other decent thing in my life. I would rather slit my throat than have that happen."

He shook her again, his voice turning more ragged. "Don't you understand? You mean more to me than anything in this world, and that includes my own happiness. If I have to walk away to ensure you're safe, then I'll do it, no matter how much it kills me."

She heard the words, but more, she heard the strength of emotion running beneath them. Fear, despair, anger, but most of all...

"You love me." It was impossible to keep the words from slipping out as she stared up into his dear face in wonder. She smiled at the flare of acknowledgment in his eyes that he just as quickly doused. "You love me," she said again, this time smugly.

Slowly, Neil drew an uneven breath. "Enough to walk away."

Because his hands were still on her shoulders, it was a simple matter of taking a step closer to put her own hands on his chest, where his heart was hammering away.

"Love me enough to stay instead."

A shudder ran through his body as his hands convulsed tightly on her shoulders.

"God, Alex…"

Before she knew he'd even moved, Neil crushed her to him, his mouth descending on hers with a sense of absolute desperation. Her lips met his with the same urgency, both of them pouring all of the love, the fear, the loneliness of the last week into the kiss. Teeth nipped in punishment, lips and tongues soothed the sting in apology.

Hands clenching at his shirt, she pulled him even closer, reveling in the wild insanity of the moment. She had him now, and she wasn't letting go.

In fact, if she didn't get a whole lot closer to him in the next few minutes, she was going to go up in flames right where she stood.

All it took was for her to slip the first button on his shirt free.

Clothes flew in all directions. Skin met skin, and like the kiss, it was a wild conflagration of desire and desperate yearning. Her nerve endings were on fire.

Every place Neil touched, she burned.

When his fingers slipped between her thighs and inside of her, she exploded.

It was too much, and not enough, and just right, all at the same time.

They tumbled to the sofa with her on top, though she had few illusions she'd stay there once Neil decided he'd had enough of her torture. But until that happened, she planned to make the most of it.

With a nip on his chin, warning him to stay still, she kissed and licked her way down his beautiful chest, forgoing the pleasure of tormenting his already rock-hard nipples or finding the spots along his hipbones that were oh-so slightly ticklish.

Her focus was on one goal, and one goal only.

When she reached it, she gave one quick, teasing swipe along the sensitive crown before sliding the hot length of his erection between her lips, giving his testicles a gentle squeeze.

It was enough for him to almost buck her off as his body convulsed at the sensation. When she sucked him all the way to the back of her throat, he let out a shout and bucked again, which forced him deeper for a brief second where she couldn't breathe.

Then he was gone from her mouth and their positions were reversed, and he was sliding into her, and it was so good she nearly wept with it.

It was like coming home.

He was so hot and hard she didn't think she could stand it if he went slow. Luckily, he obliged her. Neil's body moved with the strength and speed she'd come to expect from him, but none of the finesse. This was wild, desperate need being fulfilled.

A statement. A promise.

She saw it in his eyes, and she couldn't have looked away if the house started burning down around them.

She was still locked in his gaze when her climax suddenly leapt up and brought her crashing back down with its intensity, nearly shattering her. Then she did shatter, watching the joy and desire and absolute love in Neil's expression as he watched her go over.

A second later, he threw his head back and his body stiffened as his own climax overtook him, the muscles in his neck drawn taught and his jaw clenched as he continued to stroke into her. Striving as he always did to give them each every last drop of pleasure.

Finally, both of them wrung dry, Neil lowered his head so he could meet her gaze again. His face was naked with emotion, and his voice ragged but sure when he rasped out, "God, I love you, Alex. So much it's killing me."

She knew what the words had cost him. The tiny piece of her heart she'd been holding back, just in case he went ahead and broke the rest of it, slipped free into his care.

Reaching a hand up to stroke along his dear, dear face, fingers feathering over the tiny scars that would forever mark the day his life changed, she knew a moment of both triumph and sorrow.

Triumph she'd finally broken through his usually unbendable resolve.

Sorrow that no matter how hard she tried, she could never fully take his demons away.

But she *could* love him enough to help him live with them.

"You're going to stay," she whispered, more a command than a question.

It was obvious he heard the difference as well by the small quirk of his lips despite his very serious expression. "I'm going to stay," he agreed. "I'm still not sure it's the right thing to do, but I can't let you throw away what you've worked for all your life by chasing after me to who knows where."

"I would," she said. "I still would. If you decide staying here in Shelby isn't what's best for you, then—" Neil's lips on hers blocked the rest of her words, and after a few seconds she didn't care. All she could think about was kissing him back.

"We'll stay," he said when the kiss finally ended. "I like it here. The town, the people, my job..." His eyes widened slightly.

"I told you, I never accepted your resignation."

He huffed out a laugh. "Stubborn woman."

"You better believe it."

"Speaking of resignations..."

"Mmm?"

"You don't think Colin will give you a hard time when you try to rescind yours, do you? I know he's your grandfather and all, but he can be..."

"A spiteful bastard who holds a grudge?" She giggled at Neil's comical expression of agreement. "Yeah, he can be, but in this case, he actually understood why I was doing what I did. He wasn't happy about it, but he understood it."

Well, after a lot of yelling and threats on both their parts, he did.

"We'd had a talk earlier in the day about not letting the job get in the way of everything else. Colin wanted to make sure I didn't make the same mistakes he did."

"*Colin* said that?"

She grinned. "I know, right? Shocked the heck out of me, too, when he said it."

"Huh. Well, somehow I doubt you handing in your resignation was the result he expected from telling you that."

"You're probably right."

Now that the heat of passion was gone, the air conditioning felt a little cool on all that exposed skin. She shivered, just slightly, but it was enough for Neil to notice, because he reached over and dragged the light throw from the back of the sofa, covering them both.

Laying her head on his chest with a contented sigh, it was hard not to pinch herself to make sure she wasn't dreaming. She had Neil, he loved her, and he was going to stay and fight for them.

Things weren't that simple, of course. She wasn't naïve enough to think they were.

But if they were both dedicated to making it work, then they'd find a way.

After a few minutes of comfortable silence while Neil's thumb rubbed small circles on her ribs where his hand was resting, he said quietly, "I'd like to introduce you to Isaac. My therapist. He...he's a great guy, and I think, no, I *know* he'll be able to suggest some things that might make things easier. And safer."

"Of course. I'd like to meet him." She turned her head slightly so she could press a kiss to his chest. "Thank you." Neil hummed his reply, which rumbled beneath her ear and made her smile.

"No." Neil shifted so he could look at her. "Thank you. For turning my world upside down and shaking it hard enough to force me to face life again. Thank you for being willing to take a chance on me. On us. For loving me." His large hand cupped her jaw tenderly. "You're a gift I never expected and definitely don't deserve, but I'm not giving you back. Ever. You're mine now."

"Well, that's good, then, because you're definitely mine, too." She kissed the palm that had cradled her face before snuggling back down into his embrace. "No returns, no exchanges, mister. You're stuck with me. Live with it."

His arms tightened around her. "That's exactly what I plan to do."

Epilogue

5 Months Later

Everything was going incredibly right.

As he adjusted his tie in the mirror, Neil couldn't help still being baffled and a bit humbled by that amazing fact. And to worry just a little, as he always did, that something was going to come along and wreck it all.

The months since his decision to stick things out in Shelby and try to make a life with Alex, despite all his fears and reservations, had been sometimes rocky, sometimes smooth. But always filled with love.

And with love, he knew now he could get through anything.

Two arms slid around him from behind. The feel of Alex pressed against his back as she hugged him was familiar and yet still never failed to amaze him. That he had this wonderful, caring woman in his life. A year ago, he'd been all alone except for Bailey and his camera. Now, his world was fuller than he could have ever hoped.

Well, not entirely true. He was hoping for it to get a little bit fuller before the night was through.

Alex slid to his side and grinned into the mirror at him. "Looking good there, Mister Crawford. You sure do clean up nice."

"And you're as gorgeous as always, Miss McKenna." In the red wool dress wrapped around her like a glove, she was a stunning present just begging to be opened.

"Aww." She dropped a quick kiss on his cheek. "But you know you didn't need to get this dressed up. It's just my family."

Which was exactly why he'd chosen to go the suit-and-tie route.

Alex might think of her relatives as "just" her family, but for him they were the people he had to prove he was good enough for Alex to. Colin liked him well enough. Her father was warming up to him. Lyle and Brax had both stopped threatening to do him bodily harm, so he guessed they were, too.

Helen McKenna, though, was a tougher nut to crack. She was no longer openly insulting, at least to his face, but she'd yet to so much as crack a smile in his direction. It didn't really bother him, but for Alex's sake he'd like to attend a family function without feeling like he had to armor up for battle.

As if reading his mind, she rolled her eyes at him. "Stop worrying about my mother. She'll come around."

"If she does, it'll be a Christmas miracle," he replied wryly, grinning when a laughing Alex smacked his arm. "What?"

She just shook her head and turned to grab her purse from the bed.

"Come on. If we don't leave now to pick up Gus, we're going to be late for dinner. And I can promise you, that is *not* going to help you with Mom."

Gus and Colin had met not long after the special had aired. Surprisingly, the two old codgers had hit it off and struck up an unlikely friendship. One more thing Helen McKenna could blame him for.

But he was still glad the men had found each other. Even if they did sometimes sound like an old married couple the way they bitched at each other.

He followed Alex out of the bedroom, enjoying the view. That dress really did amazing things for her body.

"Actually, Gus's daughter is going to drop him off at Colin's on their way home, so we have a few extra minutes."

One of the best things to come from the special had been when Gus's daughter saw it and decided to reach out and reconnect with her father. It was early days yet, but Lily had driven over with her husband and one of their adult children—Gus's grandson—to spend part of Christmas Eve with him before they headed back to Charlotte, so things looked promising.

So did the Christmas card he'd gotten out of the blue from his sister. He still wasn't sure what to make of it, but it was a puzzle for another day.

Gifting him with a sultry smile, Alex stopped and turned to slide her arms around his neck. "Well, then, whatever should we do with all this extra time we suddenly have?"

His body had some very definite ideas about that, but he ruthlessly squashed them. Getting sexy with Alex right before he had to go face her entire extended family wasn't a smart move, even if he hadn't had something else already in mind.

"Not that," he said, biting back a grin at the flash of disappointment on her face.

"Party pooper."

"Sex maniac." He nipped her pouting lip before soothing it with a quick kiss. He stepped back when she tried to deepen the kiss. If he didn't, they weren't just going to be late. They most likely wouldn't make it to dinner at all.

And then Lyle and Brax probably *would* break his legs.

"So, I know we agreed to exchange gifts in the morning. But when my sister and I were little, we used to pester our parents so hard about what was under the tree that they'd always let us open one present on Christmas Eve, to kind of take the edge off. So, um, I thought maybe it would be nice if, um, we could do that, too. Maybe make it a tradition or something. Our tradition. If you wanted to." Recognizing he was rambling, he snapped his mouth shut.

Smooth, Crawford. Real smooth.

As usual, Alex didn't seem put off in the least by his less than eloquent speech. Just one more thing that made him love her.

"I think I would love to start our own Christmas tradition," she said softly. Her eyes glistened a dewy green.

With a jolt, he realized why. Starting a tradition meant expecting many more Christmases to come.

Planning for a future.

Taking a deep breath, he walked to the huge tree that took up one entire corner of Alex's soaring great room. He plucked a small, gaily wrapped box from under it and brought it back to her. She smiled as she accepted it, but he didn't miss the tiniest hint of disappointment in her eyes when it wasn't the right size or shape to be a ring box.

The tightness that had bound his chest all day eased a bit.

"Oh, Neil, it's our lighthouse!"

This time there were actual tears after she opened the oblong velvet box to reveal a silver necklace with a delicate lighthouse pendant, striped black and white like the one they'd climbed on their trip to Cape Hatteras in the fall.

That long weekend away had been a gigantic step for him. For them. A strange hotel room on a huge stretch of beach, and only one bed. But he'd had Alex, and Bailey, and the soothing sounds of the ocean to help him through. Alex had spent every night in his arms, with not a nightmare in evidence.

It had been the best three days of his life. So, it had only seemed right to commemorate it with something equally special.

"You like it?"

"I love it! It's beautiful."

He reached out and ran his finger over the pendant the same way she had, stopping at the small but brilliantly hued diamond anchored at the very top where the light would be.

He swallowed the emotions that threatened to make him as weepy as Alex.

"This is you, you know. You brought the light back into my world. You chased away the shadows I was living in and gave me hope, kept me from crashing onto the rocks and drowning. Thank you for being *my* lighthouse. My light in the darkness."

"Oh!" Alex's trembling hand went to her mouth as the tears began falling in earnest. Then she threw herself at him, holding him tight as she sniffled against his chest.

Fighting his own roiling sea of emotion, he just held her and rubbed her back until the sniffles abated and she pulled away to grab a tissue. Her eyes were damp and the tip of her nose was bright pink when she turned back to him, but her smile was all that mattered.

"Thank you. I absolutely adore it, and everything it means. I am so happy to be your lighthouse, Neil." She sniffled again and held the box out. "Can you put it on me, please?"

After he unhooked the necklace she'd been wearing and latched the new one on in its place, he couldn't resist the temptation of her bare nape as she held her hair out of the way. She squirmed and giggled under the kiss, then turned and kissed him back, ending it with a happy sigh.

"My turn. Although compared to this, all of my presents to you are going to suck," she added with a fake pout.

"Actually, I think Bailey's next."

"Bailey?" With an amused smile, Alex looked over at the dog, who got to her feet at Neil's command and went to the tree to retrieve a small gift bag the way they'd practiced. Carrying it over by its sturdy handles, she presented it to Alex with a swish of her tail.

Alex laughed as she took it. "Why, thank you, Bailey, you shouldn't have."

Bailey sat and gave a doggy grin, clearly proud of herself.

Patting her head, his eyes stayed on Alex as she pushed her hand through the endless layers of tissue paper he'd stuffed the bag with. Okay, he might have gotten a little overzealous there.

He knew the exact moment her hand closed around what was at the bottom of the bag.

The exact second she guessed what it was.

She froze, her eyes going wide as they sought out his.

It was hard, but he managed what he thought was a smile of encouragement, even though his face seemed both frozen and on fire at the same time.

Swallowing, Alex withdrew her hand and the small black velvet box she held. "Neil," she whispered. She looked at him again, hope and doubt and wonder chasing across her beautiful face.

Taking the box from her, he cracked it open and went to one knee in front of her. He'd practiced this a hundred times in his head, but now that the time had come, all the fancy words he'd so painstakingly memorized deserted him.

So, he spoke from the heart instead.

"You already know you're my light. But you're also my heart, and I can't imagine going through the rest of my life without you by my side. You're my everything, Alexandra Aileen McKenna. You're my love, my safe harbor, my home. Please say you'll also be my wife."

His heart galloped as he waited, every second that ticked by like a tiny slice of doubt to that vulnerable organ. Thankfully, Alex recovered quickly to put him out of his misery.

She dropped to her knees in front of him, her hands closing over his and the ring box.

"I don't think that's the way this is supposed to go," he said, trying not to laugh.

"I don't care." Alex bit her lip, looked at their joined hands, then back to him. "You're my everything, too, you know. My heart, my soul, my world. Being loved by you is the best thing that ever happened to me. So yes, Neil Patrick Crawford, I will most definitely be your wife, because that means I get to keep you forever."

"Thank God." He slipped the ring onto her finger and kissed her, oh-so sweetly, with just a hint of promise for later. Then he pulled her into a hug, awed and amazed that his life, which had been so dark and lonely, was suddenly so filled with light and love and hope.

There might always be shadows and darkness that haunted him, but with Alex by his side, he'd never lose his way in them again.

A Note From the Author

I hope you enjoyed Neil and Alex's (and Bailey's) story!

This series holds a special place in my heart. The inspiration for these books sprang from seeing guide dogs being trained all around my home town when I was growing up. And later, meeting a family who fostered guide dogs-in-training during their first year, teaching them basic social skills and commands. With all of that marinating in my brain, it was only a matter of time before the Wounded Warrior Legacy books were born.

I'd like to thank everyone who helped me with this book (and there were many!).

First, my husband, whose understanding when I lock myself in the office to hit my deadlines is boundless. Thanks to the folks at America's Vet Dogs, who graciously answered my one million questions when I was still fleshing out the idea for this series. And a huge shout-out to my sensitivity reader, Shelby Kessler, who helped make sure I didn't muck things up about Neil and Bailey too badly. (And it's just one of those strange convergences of the universe that she shares a name with my fictional town!)

Any inaccuracies that remain are mine alone, and were sometimes necessary for the story.

We still have one more service dog with a story to tell, so keep an eye out for the next Legacy book coming out early next year. Judd Aiken has lost a lot in a short time. His marriage. His career with the SEALs. His leg. But he's not about to lose his kids, no matter how hard he has to fight for them. And what he might have to give up.

If you want to know more about the other books in this series or my other ones, scan the QR code below to visit my website (nikarhone.com). While you're there, claim your FREE book just by signing up for my newsletter. You can also stay up-to-date on all future releases by following my author page on any of the major book retailer websites.

And finally, if you enjoyed this book, please take a moment to leave a review with your favorite book retailer. They're what feeds an author's creative soul. Thank you!

Claim Your FREE book here:

Resources

If you or someone you know is in crisis, please reach out:

Suicide & Crisis Hotline: (toll-free 24/7) call 988 and press 1
Suicide & Crisis Website: 988lifeline.org
National Call Center for Homeless Veterans: 1-877-424-3838(4AID-VET)

Americans With Disabilities Act: ada.gov

Please consider volunteering at or donating to your local service dog organization. If you don't have one, here are a few that I know of:

America's VetDogs: vetdogs.org
Guide Dog Foundation for the Blind: guidedog.org
Guiding Eyes for the Blind: guidingeyes.org
Guide Dogs of America: guidedogsofamerica.org
International Guide Dog Federation: igdf.org.uk
National Federation of the Blind: nfb.org
Paws of War: pawsofwar.org

Also By Nika Rhone

<u>Boulder Bodyguards series</u>
What the Lady Wants
Finding Forever
Can't Help Loving You

<u>Boulder Beaumonts series</u>
Worth Any Price
Never Let Me Go
All I Need Is You

<u>Wounded Warrior Legacy series</u>
Just the Way You Are
A Light in the Darkness

About the Author

Nika Rhone spent her childhood wearing out library cards as she read her way through the extraordinary worlds far beyond her small hometown on Long Island, NY. By her teens, her imagination was taking her places all on its own, forcing her to learn how to type (badly) so she could get all the stories down on paper. After a long love affair with science fiction and fantasy, she finally discovered romance, fell head-over-heels, and now spends her days crafting happily-ever-afters for the characters who still tell their stories faster (and better) than she can type them. She's currently the author of the Boulder Bodyguards, Boulder Beaumonts, and Wounded Warrior Legacy series, with more to come.

You can keep up with all the latest book news, events, and giveaways by visiting her website www.nikarhone.com and joining her newsletter. She'd love to hear from you.